For Josephine, completely

For Josephine, of course.

S. WILLIAMS

Tuesday Falling

KILLER
READS

Killer Reads
An imprint of HarperCollins*Publishers*
1 London Bridge Street
London SE1 9GF

www.harpercollins.co.uk

This paperback edition 2015
1

First published in Great Britain by
HarperCollins*Publishers* 2015

A catalogue record for this book is
available from the British Library

ISBN: 978-0-00-813275-0

Set in Sabon LT Std by Palimpsest Book Production Limited,
Falkirk, Stirlingshire

Acknowledgements

I first discussed writing a thriller whilst living in a halfway house for ex-cons and drip release psychiatric patients with my friends Jonathon and David, so my first thanks goes to them; had they ridiculed the idea, Tuesday may not have happened.

I'd like to thank Stickgirl, Thaddeus, Hester, Cassian and Magdalene for putting up with me, and giving me meaning.

Next to my readers, who helped shape the novel into something resembling a story: Archie, Christine, Frances, Guy, Josephine, Loretta, Martin, Michael, Michelle, Oliver, Philip and Wai. A special thanks to David, Dominique and Leonie; you know why.

Also to Asha, for helping me over many years with the swearing; there is none finer.

Thanks to Gog, whose flat I just completely stole and put into my book.

Thank you to Kate and the team at Killer Reads who have made the whole process a pleasure.

Finally, I'd like to thank my agent, Anne-Marie, who believed in me and, more importantly, believed in Tuesday. Thank you Anne-Marie; thank you for the phone calls and the support. For the advice and the staying power. This book would be lying in a drawer if it weren't for you. Words cannot express. I'll try and write one with less cussing in next time.

And, of course, thank you to all those who read this.

S. Williams

Sometimes, I like to just sit on the tube, travelling from station to station. The station, then the tunnel, then the station. Over and over.

The white. The black.

I never look directly at anyone; I always look at them in the windows. See them reflected in the dark of the machine.

Sometimes, when the noise in my head threatens to make me snowbound, I just travel the tube, tuning everything out. Leaning my head against the connecting door. Feeling the vibration. Feeling the ghosts move through me. Waiting for it all to stop.

1

The boys pile onto the tube, all drop-crotch trousers, and Jafaican whine. Their eyes are hard and shiny from too much speed laced with too little mephedrone. Their clothes scream *outsider* whilst looking desperate to fit in. They want to be seen separate, but together. Little boys in grown-up bodies, confused and broken by a society they can't keep up with, and try to laugh at instead. It's pathetic really. If they weren't so dangerous I might try to take them home and mother them.

But me, a mother? I don't think so. The last time I was a mother I was fourteen, and it worked out just fine for about fifteen minutes.

There are six of them, these boys. The youngest is maybe thirteen, and the oldest about sixteen. If you added up their IQs the total wouldn't even equal my shoe size, and yet they think they're so clever.

I love messing with boys like them. They see me sat in the corner of the carriage, a little Gothette. A tiny emo. They look at my army satchel and they think, 'poetry book'. They don't think, Columbine.

Actually, I'm giving them too much credit. They don't

think at all. They function on crowd-brain. Follow the leader. Seek out the weak.

The weak. That's me. Five foot fuck-all and dressed in black, like I've got nothing better to do with my time than watch *The Matrix*, and make pretty pictures on my arm with a blade. A pretty girl, pretty fucked-up.

Ripe for the plucking.

Come on then, boys.

Pluck me.

2

'Who is she?' DI Loss is looking at the CCTV from the tube train. Even though it's a recording, not a live link, the tension in the room is a physical presence. The air seems razor-thin, and there is a whine at the back of the DI's thoughts like a broken light-filament. The image on the screen is in black and white and the pixilation is terrible. There's grey-out everywhere, and the faces are smudgy, as if they've been partially rubbed out.

It doesn't, however, disguise the blood.

'Dunno, sir. We're checking the cameras from the entrance now.'

His DS is not looking at what her boss is looking at. She's already seen it and is still, several minutes later, having to swallow the copious amounts of saliva her body is producing. It's either that or throw up on her lap-top.

On-screen there's blood everywhere. All over the bodies of the young men lying motionless on the floor of the tube carriage. Splashed on the seats and the windows and in long splatter streaks on the tube walls. Even though the image is black and white and the pixilation is terrible the inspector can tell it's blood. And he knows it's not the girl's blood because he just watched her walk out of the tube without a scratch on her. The DI sighs deeply and reaches for his e-cigarette.

'Roll it again,' he says.

The screen goes blank for a moment, and then the carriage is back to a time before the carnage. No blood. No bodies. Just a small teenage girl in the corner and six junked-up predators piling in through the sliding door. They mess about for a bit, hitting each other and mouthing off in silent comedy violence, and then they spot the girl. Even with the white-out. Even with the pixels more spaced out than a SkunkMonk, DI Loss can see that the boys think it's Christmas. Two of them low-five each other, and the pack begin to move down the carriage towards the girl, unstoppable in their gang-power. Completely in control of their environment. Top of the food chain.

Loss stares at the screen. Stares at the animal hunger visible on their smudged-out faces.

'I wouldn't count on it, boys' he whispers.

3

Well whoopy-doo, here they come.

The one in the hoodie spots me first. What am I talking about – they're all in hoodies. Of course they are. They want to look the same, as if they're American gangstas. Don't they realize it's all shit? That those people they idolize have the life expectancy of a sparrow? Honestly, if you think it through, what I'm about to do is a mercy. These brothers aren't really living, they're simply decomposing in slow motion.

Time to speed up the film.

What I *meant* to say was, the one at the front in the slightly more *hoodie-ish* hoodie than the other Marys, spots me first. I'm thinking he's what passes for the brains of this crew. He can almost walk upright, for a start. He low-fives his drone-clone and starts edging towards me, the others following as if they're connected by puppet wire.

Did I tell you I love these guys? All tough stances and thousand-yard stares when they're in a group. I reckon if I met one of these boys by themselves outside a church on Sunday and gave him a leaflet he'd say thank you very much.

I don't want you to think I'm part of the God-squad, by

the way. Fuck that. I'd rather have my teeth pulled out than get down on my knees in front of a priesty-prick.

No, what I'm saying is without his crew, his structure, he's nothing but some brain-dead mother's son with the processing power of a leaking punch-bag.

Doesn't excuse him, of course.

I observe their approach through the reflection in the carriage window. When they're a couple of feet away they come to a smug stop, almost in time with each other. Well done, boys.

Here we go. Mega-hoodie grins at me and speaks, his voice dagger-friendly.

'Hey, Weirdo, how about you come with us, yeah? Do some stuff?'

It's brilliant. Mega-hoodie is like the Shakespeare of the gang. He's the Romeo. He's managed to reduce thousands of years of linguistic evolution to the verbal equivalent of showing me his cock and saying 'How about it?'.

Really, I've got to leave him till last, if I can. He's just so much fun! I pull my knees up to my chest and carry on staring out of the window. Into the dark tunnel flashing by at a million miles an hour.

They start to smile and jitter up. They think they've scored a hot one here. They think I'm scared and ready to pop.

'Hey, Emo! I'm talking to you. Nothing to look at out there, girl. Plenty to look at in here, though.' He starts to laugh, one elbow banging into his mate while he stuffs his right hand down the front of his pre-ripped Diesel combat trousers.

Two things here:

One. There's *plenty* to look at because we're in a tunnel with the lights of the carriage bright and sparkly. That makes the window a mirror. I can see everything they're doing.

Two. Mr Ape has just stuffed his right hand down his

trousers to have a good old jiggle in front of his mates, and so I'm guessing he's right-handed, and has just about made it impossible for him to attack me.

I mean, you couldn't make it up, could you? Intimidate the stranger in front of you by handicapping yourself! It's like being threatened by the Teletubbies.

I can't be fucked anymore. I turn back round to face them, pull the knife out of my bag, and stab Trouser-boy in the throat.

4

The DI watches the girl on the tube do her thing. Even in the washed-out colour he can tell she's smiling. Even with the time-stutter visuals and the horror film lighting that starts halfway through, when she pulls the emergency cord, he can tell she's happy. There is a beauty and fluidity to her movements as she walks back down the carriage that sings of her satisfaction with her work. It is like witnessing a human tsunami as she flows down the carriage. Loss takes a drag from his e-cigarette and continues to watch, the vape obscuring not one grisly moment.

5

It's not hard to stab someone in the throat. You just pull the knife out of your army satchel and shove it in his neck, cutting into his carotid artery, just a few centimetres to the side of his trachea. Of course it's not hard; he was going to rape you, and then watch as you were cluster-fucked by his clones. Completely self-defence.

No, the hard thing is not freezing up and stopping there, staring at the boy dying in front of you as he spasms around on the floor. That's where most people go wrong. You have to stab him in the throat, then immediately pull out the knife, turning his body with your scuffed oxblood DM so that none of the blood hits you. Marks you. Then you've got to not freeze as the blood pumps out of Dying-boy in great gushes of red, spraying over his mates and the walls as his body spins away from you.

But you're not looking as the body falls. No you're not. You're already slashing the eyes of drone number two as you run along the length of the bench-seating to the other end of the carriage. Between the blood fountain and the screaming you've gained yourself three or four seconds of shock before the adrenalin kicks in and they come for you as a pack. Of course, if they do that, you're fucked. Beyond fucked. But by the time they've got it together you've already got your back pressed against the wall and big loony smile on your face.

It's important *which* wall you're pressed against. The tube train is travelling at 56 mph and when the emergency cord is pulled, which is what is about to happen, the momentum placed on the standing body of a drugged-up rape-junkie will be enough to make him face-dive the floor. It would also be enough to make a little Gothette sail through the air and crumple herself against a window, so it's important that *she* is against the wall that will immediately arrest her momentum, and *they* are at the end that will give them the furthest to travel, thereby – one can only hope – breaking every bone in their rape-mongering bodies.

Smile. Pull. The scream of the brakes barely registers in my head, cos it's full of snow and ice, but the boys in front of me are looking a little bit not so fucking clever now.

Oh, and rather helpfully, once the cord is pulled, the overhead lights go out, leaving the carriage lit by the stutter of the emergency fluorescent trace bulbs in the walls and floor.

Have a nice day, boys. I open up the satchel and pull out two curved scythes. I stand up and walk towards them.

Swish swash.

It doesn't take long. It never takes long. If it takes long you're in trouble. If it takes long you're dead. The carriage is silent. I walk back up the train and put the scythes away. I won't use them again but I don't want to leave them for the police, either.

I mean, I don't want it to be too easy, do I? Where's the fun in that? There is, however, something I do want to leave for the police, and I take it out of my vintage American army shirt pocket and place it on Trouser-boy. Not surprisingly, he doesn't object.

12

Then I look up at the camera so the boys and girls in blue get a good shot of me.

Then I leave.

Job done.

6

The DS taps at her keyboard and the scene backs up a few frames, and then freezes at the place where the girl is smiling up at the camera. DI Loss can feel a pressure building in his stomach and quietly belches; his hand in front of his mouth. The room fills with the smell of bacon fat. It makes him feel nauseous. More nauseous.

'The cameras outside the station?' he asks, reaching inside his jacket for some antacid tablets. His DS indicates the split-screen on her laptop, showing the CCTV views of the entrance to Embankment tube station, where all the passengers had to disembark after the emergency cord was pulled on the train.

'Nothing, sir. According to the cameras she never left the station. She walked through those boys as if she was some sort of ghost ninja and then . . .', she makes a throwing away gesture with her hands, '*puff*, disappeared.'

The DI continues looking at the girl on the screen. She couldn't be more than seventeen. 'And how many of those fine young men did she kill?'

'Amazingly, only one. The leader.' The DS taps a few keys. 'One Jason Dunne from Sparrow Close, Crossquays.'

14

'Lovely.' Sparrow Close was well known to DI Loss. If one took a sink estate, an estate so deprived of government investment, but so rich in monies from drugs and stolen goods, and then dumped a load of stone-cold bastards in it, you'd have Sparrow Close.

'Although none of the others will walk again,' continues his DS. 'She sliced their Achilles tendons and cut through the hamstrings behind the knee.'

The DS stops looking at her laptop and turns to face him. 'Actually, she did more than that but I don't want to think about it.'

Loss doesn't blame her. All the blood in front of him on the screen is starting to make him light-headed. Even though on the monitor it's not in colour, it's in colour in his head, and it's turned up to full-tilt. 'And what was it she put on his body?' he asks

She turns back to her laptop and starts tapping, her fingers hammering at the keys, and the screen is filled with a close-up of the body of Jason Dunne. Lying on his jeans, stuck onto them with blood, is a piece of white card, like a business card. Typed in Ariel font is one word: *Tuesday*. The DI sighs heavily.

'And is it?'

'Is it what, sir?'

'Tuesday.'

Stone smiles tightly, staring at the image on the screen. 'No, sir. It's Friday.'

7

It's all over the news, screaming out on every media platform going.

One murdered and five crippled for life!

Jason Dunne, 16, and five other teenagers, all excluded pupils of Sparrow Secondary School, were brutally attacked in a Tube train late last night. Mr Dunne died at the scene. At present the police are asking for witnesses of the crime to come forward, and say they will shortly be giving a statement. They are particularly keen to speak to a young woman whom they believe to be at the centre of the incident.

When Lily sees the report she feels faint; she thinks she's the young woman the police want to question. After a moment reality slams back in, and she breathes a shaky sigh of relief.

Of course it isn't. It can't possibly be her.

She was in all night.

Just as she'd been instructed.

Lily kills the image on her laptop and climbs out of bed. Without the noise of the news report filling the room, the rain can be heard plainly, tip-tapping at the window, behind the curtains. Lily is dressed in her favourite M&S brushed-cotton blue PJs. She has to roll the top of the pyjama bottoms

16

over a few times to stop them falling off her. Lily has lost weight fast, and now weighs just under five and a half stone. Her bones hold up her skin in the same way a hanger does a hand-me-down dress. They look like they've borrowed a smaller girl's body. Putting on her dressing-gown, she goes slowly to her bedroom door and presses her head against the wood, listening for sounds that shouldn't be there. All she can hear is the noise of the radio in the kitchen, and her mother systematically beating breakfast into submission.

No sounds of doors being smashed. And people stumbling in.

No reek of drugs, and booze, and hate.

No jackal laughter. No violence and ripping and body greed.

Well, there wouldn't be, would there?

Lily pulls back the bolt on the lock that she had fitted three weeks ago and walks through the flat into the kitchen. She doesn't walk much these days, and she is slightly unsteady on her painfully thin legs. Her mother is standing over the cooker, a look of complete incomprehension on her face. Lily smiles. It feels good. Lily doesn't smile much anymore.

Before it all, her mother rarely cooked for her; too busy working three jobs just to make sure there was food in the fridge and credit on her phone. Lily had repaid her by working hard at school and trying not to get in too much trouble. On Lily's estate that wasn't easy, but she had tried really hard. Now her mother doesn't leave Lily alone in the flat. Lily no longer goes to school and rarely leaves her room. There is no longer any need for the cooker.

You don't eat when you want your body to die.

Lily's mum looks up from the cooker and stares at her daughter. Lily sees her own eyes in her mother's face. Bruised from too much crying. Dry from too little tears.

'Have you heard?'

Lily nods and stares back at her. Outside, the rain speaks a language all of its own as it lashes at the window. Lily's mum looks at the radio; the quiet, measured radio-voice is talking about the attack on the six boys on the tube train. Lily's mum nods her head sharply. Just once.

'Bastards deserved everything they got.'

Lily smiles again. Hearing her mother swear, however mildly, makes her feel grounded. Not like she is walking through a cotton-wool dream world in her head where nothing matters and everything's all right.

Lily goes over and gives her mum a hug, but only gently so that she doesn't feel how sharply her bones are pushing at her thin skin. Lily knows her mum blames herself for what happened to her. When she was at work.

'I tell you what, Mum. You mix me a Complan while I check my messages, and then we'll swear at the radio together.'

It isn't much, but it's the best she can do. Interaction is a skill that has become lost to her. Weaving words to make a shield used to be part of her structure. Now words are a maze that confounds her. Lily leaves her mum crying in the kitchen, staring after her as she walks back to her bedroom. The last time she saw her daughter eating was two days ago, and that was a carrot sliced so thinly it looked as if it had been shaved.

8

There are over forty abandoned tube stations in London, some of them only a short distance from the ones that are still used, but only a few of them fit my needs.

They need to have more than one way in or out, for a start. It's no use making a crib with no escape tunnel. When I first started living underground I holed up in an old tunnel just off Green Park: near enough to the platform to feel safe, but far enough away so as not to attract attention. There are hundreds of these tunnels in the system. Some of them are for storage, or work stations. Some connect to lines that are now redundant. Some, well some I haven't got a scooby what they're for. I thought the one I was bundled up in was perfect. The walls and ceiling were made up of all these little white porcelain bricks as if someone had used toy bricks to make a full-size thing. Like I felt all the time. It had an old camp bed in there and a lamp and stuff.

Compared to where I'd been living before I thought it was the Ritz.

Never occurred to me that it might still be used. I thought it was a remainder from the War or something.

Third night in and I get woken up by a workman, skimming

a few hours off a ghost-shift. I don't know who was more freaked: him or me. Anyhow, there was no back door to the tunnel, so I ended up having to bite him just to get past. Living as I was then, he must have thought I was an animal.

That was then, this is now.

After I leave the boys on the train, I walk through a service tunnel to Charing Cross, taking off my wig and stuffing it in my satchel, and putting on a baseball cap. I reverse my army shirt so it shows green rather than black, then wait until a train pulls into the station. I have a skeleton key for the emergency tail-door, which is always still in the tunnel when the train stops, so all I have to do is slip out of my alcove, climb on board, and bump it one stop to Leicester Square. Change to the Piccadilly line and ride it up to Holborn.

Little-known fact about Holborn Station is that it's a replacement station. There's another station almost opposite it, on the other side of Oxford Street, that closed in 1933; the British Museum Station.

You can probably guess, can't you?

I get off the train with the other passengers, keeping my hat low and my satchel slung round my back like a haversack, its leather straps over my head but under my arms. I follow the crowd so far, then ghost through a maintenance door and slip along the running tunnel that takes me to the abandoned station. I light the way with the halogen torch I take from my satchel, and then shade through the winding chambers and connecting corridors that bring me to the air-raid shelter that was used in the Second World War.

Home sweet home.

9

Lily turns on her computer, directs the arrow to the *Google* icon, and clicks. As she waits for the machine to connect to the Internet she goes to her window and snitches back the curtain, looking through snakes of rain crawling down the pane at the estate outside.

Lily lives on the first floor of a three-floor block. On each of the floors there are ten flats, all identical to hers. Across the battle-ground below her that passes as a play area is a block of flats that exactly mirrors hers. To her left and right are precisely the same again: four blocks of identi-flats; lives wrapped in concrete.

Everybody knows each other to look at, but not to confide in: living in a war zone. There are at least a dozen languages spoken on Lily's estate, but only two that are understood by everybody: fear and power. Below her Lily can see teenagers on children's bikes. Peddling from block to block with drugs, phones, iPads, whatever. Above the blocks, in the distance, she can make out the neon lights and shiny bank-towers of Canary Wharf: an untouchable future from another world.

Behind her the computer makes a quiet, muted noise, indicating it's connected to the Interweb, and Lily turns away from the window, and sits down gingerly. One month on and the bruising has gone, but the stitches still hurt. She opens up the *Facebook* page specially created for her, and is unsurprised to find it completely empty. There is no photo tag, no likes or dislikes, no friends.

Of course, no friends.

Lily types, ARE YOU THERE?

A computer pause; the cursor flashing like fingers tapping on a desk, then:

YES.

The reply font is electric blue.

Lily is unconsciously biting her lip, causing petals of blood to flower as she stares at the screen. There is so much she wants to ask, but knows she can't. That isn't how it works.

She types, HAVE YOU HEARD THE NEWS?

Pause

YES. WHERE WERE YOU?

Pause

AT HOME WITH MY MUM ALL NIGHT WATCH-ING TV

Pause

GOOD. ARE WE DONE?

Lily turns to look at the raindrops sliding down her window, then back at the words on the screen. They are so simple. *Are we done?* So simple, but impossible for her to fathom. Lily sucks at the cut on her lip and uses her sleeve to drag the tears away from her eyes.

ARE WE DONE, LILY-ROSE?

Pause

YES. WE'RE DONE. THANK YOU.

OK. FOLLOW THESE INSTRUCTIONS, AND THEN HAVE A NICE LIFE. YOUR BODY IS YOURS. MEND IT.

Lily is given directions for her to manipulate her laptop settings, allowing her computer to be accessed remotely. Once done, she watches the ghost hands systematically remove all traces of their correspondence from her laptop. All references of the Pro-Anna forum where they first made contact. All the conversations they have had in the cyber-basements of the Interworld. *Omecle*. *Whisper*. All of them. The *Facebook* account specially set up for their meetings ceases to exist. Everything. Every connection between Lily-Rose and the person remotely-controlling her keyboard. The last thing written on the screen before the computer shuts itself down is:

GOODBYE, LILY-ROSE

Lily-Rose sits in front of her blank laptop, its dead screen, and the *future-girl* stickers with which she'd personalized it in another life, and wonders what is going to happen next. She feels as if there is a door between her and the rest of the world, and the handle has been removed. Even though she has never met the person on the other end of her computer there was a connection: a way of understanding the pain and self-loathing inside. Lily-Rose does not know whether she will ever be able to take the advice and stop being frightened. Whether she'll be able to take control of her life enough to live it. She wraps her arms around herself and stares past the curtain of rain at the grey world outside, seeing nothing. There is a knock on her bedroom door. She turns round to see her mum standing in the doorway to her bedroom, a mug of Complan in her hand, and her face set in an expression Lily-Rose is unable to read.

'Mum? Are you all right?'

Lily-Rose sees past her to a tired-looking man in a zero-style suit and a weary-looking woman in an even worse one staring back at her.

'It's the police,' her mother says, her voice tight-leashed. 'They want to ask us some questions.'

10

It's not hard to hack a computer. Anyone who says differently is a liar. It's like lock-picking, or face-reading: all you need is the right teacher, and the correct motivation. All these films showing nerdy kids sitting around watching *Star Trek*, and *Quantum Geek*, and hacking into NASA or whatever, it's just bollocks. Just another way to bully the weirdies. Box them in. Make them this. Make them that. Make them sit alone in the dark.

Mind you, I like sitting alone in the dark. It means nobody else is there.

Most of the tube stations have Wi-Fi now, including Holborn, so all I had to do to get a signal was set up a booster along the running tunnel between there and the British Museum Station. It's not hard. There are so many redundant cables and junction boxes down here that finding a power source was easy, and disguising it unnecessary. The walls look like something out of *Alien*, all rubber-coated armoured cable and danger signs. No one can tell what belongs to what, down here. That's why they never remove anything. Pull the wrong thing out and a train stops moving. Or all the lights go out. Something awful might happen, so leave it alone; that's the thought process.

Works for me.

I've made my crib in the part of the station that was used as an air-raid shelter, the deepest part of the structure. It's still got the 'Dig for Britain' posters on the walls. I've got fairy lights hanging from the ceiling, a camp bed, a laptop with remote speakers, and a rail for my clothes. There's still a working toilet in the main part of the station, although I have to fill it with water from a stand-pipe in the running tunnel. Really, It's more home-y than home ever was.

I've got other cribs in other stations for other things, scattered all across London . . . I don't like to have all my eggs in one basket in case one of them breaks.

There are three ways out of this crib, so I feel OK. Any less and I get jittery. I set the alarms, tune the laptop to the *World Service,* and lie down in my cot. I stare at the fairy lights sparkling above me, their little twinklings reflected in the millions of tiny dust particles that are no doubt poisoning my lungs. The computer is all news speak. Fucked-up country this. Fucked-up climate that. All happening in a world I'm so separate from, it might as well be made up. I tune out and lie here, looking at the tiny porcelain tiles that make up the ceiling. Honestly, it must have taken them years to fit all those bricks in. Why did they do it? Why did they make the bricks so small? And where did they make them? I can't think of an answer so I stop thinking about it, and just lie here, breathing in and out.

Like I'm alive.

That's about it really.

Lights out. Night-night.

11

Even from the doorway where he and DS Stone are standing, DI Loss can tell the girl has been messed over good and proper. She's got that gaunt look of someone who's lost weight suddenly: skin too tight and eyes too big. Like a cancer victim, or someone who's undergone extreme circumstances. War. Famine. Or, he thinks sadly, someone who's been repeatedly raped and beaten and no longer sees her body as an ally.

They are shown into the living room. It is a rectangular box identical in structure to thousands of other rectangular boxes the DI has been shown into over the years. The mother has tried to personalize it with pictures and paint, furniture and rugs, but to Loss's mind it's still a rabbit hutch on a sink estate that might as well be a prison.

The mother is staring hard at them, her hand on her daughter's shoulder. Protecting her. Pouring strength into her. Neither of them wants him here. Or his DS. He can tell that from their faces. He can see that from their posture. Have to be blind not to. What he can't tell is why. It could be that, after the attack, the police were brutish and unsympathetic. They often are where rape is concerned. In some police circles,

26

rape is just another word for 'changed her mind'. Not in all. Much better than it used to be, but some. It could be that, mother and daughter have simply had enough, and want to shut themselves away and heal, or try to heal, and they, the police, are a reminder of past horrors. It could be all these things and more besides. Loss had noticed a strange expression on the daughter's face when she'd first caught sight of him. Almost guilt. And that furtive look at her laptop? The DI doesn't know what to make of it, so decides to make nothing of it and get on with why he is here. He leans forward in his chair.

'I'm sorry to disturb you this morning, Mrs Lorne, Lily, but I've got some information possibly relating to your, er . . .' He is at a loss what to say. Sitting here in this tidy small flat with its touches of humanity, even using the word 'rape' seems to invite an evil that doesn't belong in this place. He can see the mother's hand whiten as she squeezes the daughter's shoulder.

'We heard it on the radio, Inspector . . . ?' The mother wants his name again. Even though he's told her. Wants to keep control. He doesn't blame her.

'Loss.'

'Inspector Loss, all I can say is those animals got everything they deserve.' The mother's face is flushed high with anger, and the daughter is staring at her hands. Loss notices she has bitten her nails down to such an extent that the skin has been chewed and the end of each finger is raw and bloody.

'I'm sorry to have to ask, Mrs Lorne, but because of the nature of the attack on the young men . . .'

'Animals!' Mrs Lorne interjects vehemently. 'They raped my daughter, beat her up, and then raped her again. Everything that happened to those vermin, it wasn't enough.'

'And because it was those *specific* young men,' Loss continues, lowering his voice, 'well, I'm afraid I have to ask.'

27

The seconds tick by, and mother and daughter just stare at him. Finally Mrs Lorne understands what he is saying. Asking. She looks at him with loathing and says, 'We were in all night. That's what you want to know, isn't it?'

'The CCTV shows a young woman at the scene of the crime . . .' Loss stops speaking as Mrs Lorne makes a cutting motion with her hand.

'Enough. We were here *all night*. People called round. Unlike those animals who attacked my daughter, we have witnesses apart from ourselves.' Mrs Lorne curls her lip in disgust. For a second Loss thinks she's going to spit on her own floor. '*They* just back each other up. Cover each other's tracks and sneer at us as if we're nothing.' Loss can see that Mrs Lorne is only just holding her rage in check. 'Not that we'd need witnesses if those bastards had been locked up. The last month I've not been able to leave the flat without one of them hanging around, laughing into their phones. Even when I go to the shop downstairs I have to get a neighbour to sit in or else Lily starts screaming, or worse.' Both Mrs Lorne and Lily-Rose seem to be falling apart in front of him, and Loss experiences a deep sense of self-loathing. All these people want to do is heal, and here he is twisting a screwdriver into the wound, opening it up for inspection. Making things worse. So he twists it again.

'Does the word "Tuesday" have any special meaning to either of you?'

'Get out.' The mother is striding to the door, barging past the DS. 'I'd like you to leave now. My daughter needs to rest.'

'Yes, of course.' Loss stands up and follows her to the front door. As he passes Lily-Rose he has an urge to touch her shoulder, seeing his own daughter in her, but resists. 'Even with the incident on the tube we'll continue trying to corroborate your statement. The officers who were assigned to your case have handed over transcripts of all the interviews. It might be that given the new, ah, circumstances they have something more to add.'

Lily-Rose looks up at him, staring. And then she smiles, and it's like the last rays of the sun before it sinks into the sea.

'They'll have difficulty raping anyone else from a wheelchair, yeah?' And then she turns away from him and stares at the floor, leaving him cold and empty.

Outside on the concrete walkway in front of the closed flat, the detectives look out at the rain-soaked estate. Although the rain is coming down in sheets, they can still see the boys on their bikes with their rucksacks full of consumables. Commerce doesn't stop because of the weather. Loss takes his e-cigarette out of his pocket, taps it a few times to charge the atomizer, and pulls a breath of nicotine down into his lungs. The DS sniffs, places her hands on the walkway balustrade, and looks down at the concrete playground beneath them.

'Definite reaction when you said "Tuesday", sir.'

12

After I've finished wiping everything from Lily-Rose's computer I pull the hard-drive out of mine and put it and the console in my satchel for throwing in the sewer later. It's not so much that I'm worried about getting caught, I couldn't give a fuck about that, it's more that I don't want my clients to have to deal with any shit. No hard-drive, no record.

New client, new laptop.

I keep the speakers, though.

Clients. That's what I call them. Girls and boys who have no one else to turn to when everything gets fucked up and they end up in the nowhere world of self harm and suicide . . .

Anyway, I won't be getting any more clients, will I?

Before I get rid of the hardware I have a Red Bull and write down the names of the boys from the train on my wall. Later on, once I've hacked the CCTV footage from the underground, I'll attach a QR code next to their names. I've already pre-linked the code to the site where they've put up video footage of Lily-Rose. If anybody tries to watch 'the Lily-Rose rape show' they'll find themselves watching 'the tube train gang boys getting completely outclassed and fucked up show' instead.

I grab the hardware and my MagLite and enter the stair-well. The stairs aren't in as good nick as the main areas, so I have to do a little scrambling. I go up a couple of levels to where there's a tunnel that connects to the sewer system. The walls are made up of the same Victorian brickwork as in some of the stations. Really, what is it about Victorians and tiny bricks? The whole of the sewer network is full of them too. I know a lot of the sewers and the early tube tunnels were built at the same time, but were all the bricks being made by midgets, or something? Was it some sort of work-house orphanage scheme?

I dump the laptop in the slow-moving effluence. There's a kind of walkway by the side of the channel and I go along there for about half a mile and then dump the hard-drive. You've got to be alert in the sewers. There's a lot of noise, and workmen are often down here, doing something work-y . . .

I read in one of the free newspapers that litter the stations that London is going to get a new super-sewer tunnel, and that a lot of the old tunnels that stitch lower London together will be demolished. Good luck with that. There's so much secret stuff down here that anyone trying to do a full recce will blow their mind. In my wanderings I've found hash farms, secret garages full of stolen super cars, and factories for making crystal meth. Half of the London underworld keeps its stuff underground. Once I even found a tank. A tank!

After I've got rid of the computer stuff I go back to the British Museum Station, and begin slowly checking all my alarms, working my way up to the 'loot-chute': a tunnel dug in the Second World War between the tube station and the basement of the British Museum. The thinking was that if the Nazis started bombing the crap out of London, then the most valuable artefacts could be brought down here and kept safe.

The ones, that is, that the government hadn't already hidden in mines in Wales, or sold off to the Americans as a bribe. It's amazing what you can learn from documents people forget they even have. There's a tunnel under MI6 as well. That's the old MI6, not the swanky new one. It's like the Death Star under the new one; I stay well away from there.

Anyway, I put an ABUS disc-cylinder padlock on the connecting door between the tunnel and the station to make sure no one who found the entrance accidentally would get very far, and a trip alarm to let me know if they did. Not that I think anyone ever would, but it would give me time to run.

I undo the padlock and make my way up to the door that leads to the basement of the museum. I say basement, but there're hundreds of rooms. The place has been going since 1753; that's a lot of stuff, with more added year after year. I'm willing to bet that most of the stuff they've got they don't even *know* they've got anymore. Old artefacts from around the world. Maps and clothing. Instruments and weapons.

They've got weapons from all over the empire, and beyond.

Like these Burmese hand-scythes, for instance.

13

DI Loss stares at the whiteboard covering the back wall of his office, and wishes he still smoked. In the two weeks since the attack on the tube by the unknown girl, he has been slowly placing tiny bits of information on the board. Filling it up with snippets of facts and conjecture that he hopes will add up to some defining whole. There is a grainy still from the CCTV showing the girl staring out at him, a look that has begun to haunt odd moments of his day. Underneath the picture, using a bold black marker-pen, he has written:

HOW DID SHE LEAVE THE STATION?

DISGUISE?

The names of all six of the boys she attacked – *defended herself against* – a small voice inside him says, and their addresses, underneath he has written:

SPARROW ESTATE

DRUGS?

SEXUAL ASSAULT?

There is a picture of Lily-Rose, taken at the hospital, less than an hour after her mother found her. Loss can't look at it without a little piece of his heart being sliced away and swallowed by despair. The bits of body that should be inside, but were outside. The swelling. The blood. The sheer brutal animalism that it must have taken to do that to another human being. It makes him think of his daughter, but he can't think of his daughter because it will make him cry, and he'll never be able to stop. Underneath he has written:

REVENGE?

LAPTOP? INTERNET RECORDS?

ALIBI?

That Lily-Rose is hiding something he has no doubt, but he can't for the life of him work out what it is. They'd checked out her internet history, but, apart from some pro-anorexia sites and extreme self-help forums, found nothing unusual.

Apart, that is, from the lack of social networking. Girls her age normally had a Facebook account, or Google+. Something. Lily-Rose had nothing. Her presence in the Interzone barely skimmed the surface. There is something odd about it, but Loss can't quite get to grips with what it is.

At the top of the board, in bold stark letters, he has written:

TUESDAY MEANS WHAT?

And at the bottom of the board, next to the picture of the white card stuck to the dead boy's jeans, the card with 'Tuesday' scrawled on it, he has written:

WHAT DOES SHE WANT TO TELL US?

In the middle of the board is a still of the strange knives she used to cripple the youths. Loss has sent the image out to all the weapons dealers in the city, but so far has had no luck in identifying them. Underneath the still he has written:

ANTIQUES?

As Loss is staring at the board, trying to make sense of the disparate pieces of information, his laptop chimes an alert: denoting a message. He looks at it, his mind still on the words and images on the whiteboard, and then suddenly

34

his attention is fully on the incoming mailbox; there is no sender address, just two words in the subject line, along with an emoticon of a smiling face.

GUESS WHO?

DI Loss feels the hairs rise on his arm, as his skin contracts. There is no text when he opens up the email, just an MPEG attachment: a photo, or a video. He feels the tension in his body notch up as he stares at the screen, then presses the buttons that will access the file. He looks at it for a moment, eyes soaking up the image in front of him, and then he says one word:

'Fuck.'

14

The boys fall out of the back door of the club and into the alley, the skanked-up bass music spilling out with them and bouncing off the walls. It's completely beyond them to just walk out. They have to shove each other, and swagger and attempt to live up to some image in their video-drone heads. It's pathetic. Who are they posing for? Certainly not me. They haven't seen me yet. I'm sat by the bins, and they'd have to look beyond their own little-boy world to notice me.

Like that's ever going to happen.

They take out glass pipes and small rocks of crystal meth wrapped in cellophane, and fire up. I hate watching people take drugs. It's like watching someone stab themselves repeatedly in slow motion. If they weren't such horrible bastards I'd feel sorry for them. But they are, so I don't. I stand up and switch on the camera I've placed on the metal step of the fire escape next to the bins. Why the bottom of the fire escape is surrounded by bins is beyond me. What would happen if there was a fire? The boys are leaning against the club wall, laughing and sucking down their drugs. Each time they inhale, their faces are lit up, floating in the dark caves of their hoodies.

They look *so* cool – I'm surprised none of them are wearing sunglasses.

The alley is a dead end, with the opening to the main street at the front of the club, past the drug-boys, and me and the bins at the back, smack against the office wall. I take out a soft-pack of cigarettes from the top pocket of my Chinese army shirt. I can't stand here all night waiting for one of them to notice me. I shake the pack, spilling a single smoke into my fingers.

'Hey, boys! Got a light?'

All three of them stop what they're doing and look up, squinting through the smoke to where I am.

Now they've noticed me.

15

Loss stares at the images unfolding on the screen. Without taking his eyes off the laptop, he reaches over and buzzes Stone to come in. The footage has no sound. It has been filmed on an expensive camera with night vision. The colours are various shades of green. When one of the boys lights the girl's cigarette, it looks as if he's using a roman candle. *Some sort of thermal imaging*, he thinks, reaching into his pocket for his e-cigarette. In the corner of the screen is a frame counter, chronicling the seconds as they tick by; cutting time into slices of violence and pain. There's a knock on the door and Stone comes into the room.

'Sir?' she says.

Loss can't drag his eyes away from the screen. He beckons the DS over. Raising her eyebrows, she comes around the desk and stands next to him. After a moment she registers what she is looking at on the computer.

'Fuck.'

16

I walk up to the boys, letting them drink me in. I've got on a pair of black pilot trousers over black leggings, ripped at the knees, and my green Chinese Red Army shirt with the collar torn off. I can see them watching me come towards them, slightly addled by their drugs, but not so far gone that I'm freaking them out. One of them pulls back his hood and stares at me. His skin is speed-tight, with crack-burns around his nostrils. And he's got cold eyes; eyes like weighing scales. He's not judging me; he's just trying to work out the odds. He's a z-channel hurt-merchant with no future past this alley, but he's trying to work out the chances of doing me. He cups his hands and sparks up his Zippo. Of course it's a Zippo. With them it's always a fucking Zippo. I lean in and light my cigarette.

'Cheers,' I say, and walk back towards the fire escape. Towards my satchel. Well, I've got to give them a chance to do the right thing, haven't I?

I can feel their eyes on my back, working out the risk. Little Goth-girl like me, long night ahead, no witnesses. Really, for them, it's a no-brainer. There's a pause as the rusted cogs in what passes for their brains kicks in, then:

'Hey, *Nirvana*, where d'you think you're going? Why don't you come back here and have a little fun, yeah?'

Nirvana. Jesus, they can't even get their sub-cultures right.

I smile and reach into my bag.

Fun. Why not?

17

DI Loss and DS Stone watch as the girl walks towards the camera. Even in the strange green light of the thermal imaging they can tell it's her: the girl from the tube. She's not wearing the same clothes, but the hair is the same, and the face, and the smile. The detectives know that something awful is going to happen, but they can't look away. The timer continues to count the scene. The smallest numbers, the hundredths of a second, are a blur. The girl stops in front of the camera, looks right at them, and throws the cigarette to her left. Even though Loss knows that the image isn't live, he can't help feeling that she is looking directly at him.

The boys behind her grin at each other and begin to walk forward: leopards approaching a deer. The one with the hood down is saying something to her. Loss can guess what it is. *Stay with us. Play a while. Don't make any long-term plans.* The girl bends down out of shot, and then straightens. The detectives can see that there's something in her hand, but she's too close to the camera for them to identify what it is. She turns round to face the boys slinking toward her, and Loss whispers:

'Here we go.'

18

I shoot Mr Hood-down through the right eye. His right, not mine. There's no sound because I'm using a crossbow pistol. The bolt leaves the mechanism at a million miles an hour then buries itself in Hood-down's brain. Or what passed as his brain.

Night-night, on the ground. Sleepy-time now.

I turn away while his friends are still trying to work out what the fuck is going on, and put the weapon back in my bag.

'Danny? Hey Danny! What the fuck are you doing, man?'

Danny's not doing a whole lot right now, except maybe twitching a bit. I take out the flare gun and shoot the other two in the face.

19

When the flare gun detonates its charge, the entire screen goes white, then black; the super-sensitive setting on the camera overloading.

'What the hell was that?' DS Stone asks. DI Loss doesn't answer her, nor does he take his eyes off the screen. Swirls of green light, and black and white heat flowers are blooming all over the screen, then dying and fading in front of him. When the image returns, the two boys are on the floor, clawing at their faces, white hot blobs thrashing left and right on the screen as the super-heated metal filaments embedded in their skin sputter and die. The girl is walking away from the camera towards the three figures on the ground. Loss instinctively clenches his jaw, expecting to see some new slice of violence, but instead the girl steps over them as though they're litter and walks to the club wall.

'What the hell is she doing?' breathes Stone. Loss shakes his head, his eyes never leaving the screen. The girl is shaking something in her right hand, the image blurring. She stops by the door to the club. The detectives watch her as she starts to graffiti the wall with spray paint. After the first two letters, Loss grabs the phone on his desk and dials the crime-processing division, requesting all information on a triple assault involving a flare gun in the past two weeks. He hangs up when he has the information he wants. On the screen in front of him the girl has finished writing on the wall. In letters three feet high she has sprayed:

TUESDAY

in Gothic bold print.

'Bloody hell, sir.' Stone is shaken by the brutality of the last few minutes. On screen, the girl walks back to the camera, looks directly through the lens, then reaches forward and turns it off. The screen goes blank, and both detectives stare at it, as if expecting something else to happen. Something to make it make sense. And then Loss taps some buttons and makes it start all over again in a pop-up window in the top right-hand corner of the monitor. The rest of the screen is taken up as he utilizes the information given to him on the phone.

'Candy's. It's a pop-up drug club, last in residence,' he says, his fingers working the keyboard, 'just off London Bridge. St. Clements Court. Incident reported at 12.45 this morning; one dead, two blinded, probably permanently. No witnesses.'

He runs his fingers through his hair, trying to scrape his brain into top gear. Any gear.

'I want you find any CCTV that shows the entrance to this alley. Interview the FOS officers, find out if anybody saw this girl, saw *anything*, and fingerprint the fire escape, just in case.'

He stops the scene on his laptop and swipes his fingers over the touchpad, re-winding a few seconds. The girl in front of him pulls the cigarette out of her mouth and throws it away. He rewinds again, pausing it just as she is pulling the cigarette out of her mouth. He can't tell in the weird green light, but he's pretty sure she's smiling.

'And find that fag . . .'

44

20

It was all over the news. Again.

The youths, all of whom are known by the police to be associated with the Sparrow Estate drug gangs, were found mutilated in the early hours of this morning in an alley near London Bridge. The police will not confirm that one of the youths, a Mr Simon Garth, was found dead at the scene . . .

Lily-Rose sips her tea and nibbles a Ryvita, tuning out the voice on the radio. Since the murder of one of the boys who raped and brutalized her, she has gained a shadow of weight to her frame. She does not think of what happened to the boy as murder. She thinks of it as redemption. Redemption for her, for her mother, and for many other girls on the estate. After the attack, the whole block went into lockdown. All the drug boys on their bikes disappeared, their handlers holding onto their gear until the trouble had settled. Lock-ups remained locked. There were no tattooed men sitting outside pubs, smoking countless contraband cigarettes and talking on cloned mobiles, their muzzled status dogs at their feet. Lily-Rose even saw a young mother pushing her child on a swing in the playground courtyard.

Lily-Rose smiles and sips her tea. Of course, the mother

was young. Round here, any woman over thirty was more likely to be a grandmother than a mother. Seeing Lily-Rose smile is like seeing a flower growing in a smashed-out window. She knows that the person who attacked the boys outside Candy's is the same person who attacked the youths who raped her. And she doesn't have to be signed up to any of the social networks to know what is going on. It's all over the Interweb, all over the street. She only has to look out of her window.

Down in the war zone between the concrete blocks that make up her estate is a new tag: a whitewashed wall with a name graffitied across it in paint the colour of dried blood.

TUESDAY

No one on the estate knows whether it refers to an event in the past that sparked off the spree of retribution, which occurred on a Tuesday, or whether it refers to an event yet to happen, on a future Tuesday. Everyone is holding their breath, waiting for more details.

A date. A target. A name.

Lily-Rose smiles and frosts the glass with her breath, obscuring the world outside. On the misted pane she draws three little Xs with her finger, making a small squeaking sound.

Then Lily-Rose goes back to bed.

21

Well I think I've probably got everybody's attention now.

After my little bit of business at London Bridge I pack my gear away. Stuff my wig in my bag, reverse my shirt, and ghost through the underground. I use my pre-loaded Oyster card, topped up with cash. I used to clone it, but now, with the new high-resolution cameras focused on the turnstiles, you're more likely to be spotted.

I head down the escalator for the city branch of the Northern line. I love going down the escalators: the little push of pressure you get from below; the sub-rumble of machinery beneath your feet; and the feeling of above-ground time slipping away. This late at night it's beginning to close down. The only people about are the drunks and the hustlers, each of them trying to get to somewhere that doesn't exist. I love the feel of the underground when it's almost empty: it's like sneaking inside a machine. Gusts of warm air come at you unexpectedly, and if you put your hand to the walls you can feel a quiet throbbing. For such a massive structure to be so empty, it's as if all the people have been stolen.

Which of course they have. They just don't know it.

Sometimes my brain slows down and ticks gently, nothing

going in, nothing going out. Just ticking. The Mayor is talking about opening some stations twenty-four hours. Non-stop progress to nowhere. Skeleton crews on a shadow train.

I make sure that the cameras spot me in London Bridge, and then again at Bank. But after that, I'm a ghost in the machine.

I've got stuff to do.

I hobo from Bank to Oxford Circus on the Central line. The train is one of the old ones, pre S-class, so I can crank down the window at the end of the carriage, filling my head with noise. From the connecting tunnel off the platform, I go through the maintenance door that joins the network to one of the tunnels under Oxford Street. Under the big stores.

I'm sure you must've wondered, when you've been in these massive department stores there, with their floors and floors of stuff. Where does it all come from? I mean, this is central London, not some robot dormitory town with mega aircraft hangars of retail space. All these shops, with thousands of people buying shit every day, where does it all get stored?

You've probably guessed, haven't you?

All these stores, with their five or six floors of stuff, also have three or four floors below street level: a mirror store underground. For every object on display there are at least two or three stored in one of the basements. And coming off the basements are dozens of tunnels. And this isn't just in one store. This is *all* the stores. It's a wonder Oxford Street hasn't collapsed in on itself. There's practically nothing left under there. It's like an ants' nest.

I first heard about these tunnels when I was still living above, on the street. One of the people I hung out with was signed up to a shadow agency; a rip-off shop for immigrants and street rats, and was trying to get me to join. It was coming up to Christmas, and he had got some work in the basements of whatever the shop was called – *Miss Selfish,*

Marks and Render, CockShop, who cares? – cataloguing the clothes and hanging them on racks

'You wouldn't believe it!' he said to me in the café one night. 'They've got racks a mile long! They've got whole tunnels full of racks!'

And it's not just clothes. It's hardware, too. They have to have air conditioning down there, so that stuff doesn't rot or rust.

He's dead now, the person who told me this stuff. I didn't kill him. He shoved a bullet up his nose in the shape of cheap brown skag.

Never mind. Lie down.

The only lock on the maintenance door is the one I put there, but I check the traps just in case. I've got a camera set to detect any movement made by something bigger than a rat, and a pulse 'disorientator', which emits a 400-lumen strobe of light that'll make your eyes bleed, should I need a quick getaway with no follow. I've got low-tack adhesive sprayed on both sides of the door with a layer of calcium-dust that'll show a hand print if someone has touched it, and I've got a scary bio-hazard sign proclaiming 'contaminated waste', because sometimes a sign is all you need for a security guard who gets paid fuck-all on a zero-hour contract.

Once I'm in the tunnels I head for the one that contains the stuff I need. The tunnels are lit by low-watt festoon lighting and there are large pools of darkness between each light. Unlike the underground, these tunnels are red brick instead of white tiles, but they're still teeny-tiny. Seriously, if I weren't who I am, this thing with the tiny bricks would begin to seriously creep me out.

Finally, I come to the tunnel I want, and begin packing up the necessary supplies.

22

DI Loss hasn't had a lot of sleep. His suit is crumpled, and worn continuously for so many hours it has begun to smell of the cigarette brand he used to smoke. His hair is greasy and his skin has a lived-in look as though it needs to be cleaned. Possibly replaced. Rain is slithering down his window as if it wants to be somewhere else. DI Loss doesn't blame it. *He'd* be somewhere else if he could. The overhead fluorescent light in his office is making his eyes hurt, and that whine in his brain from too little sleep is making it hard for him to concentrate.

He misses his computer; it has been taken away to be analysed. The computer has pictures of his daughter on it. Their absence is a physical pain; he has so few pictures of her. He has no pictures of his wife.

Loss leans back in his chair and sighs heavily. DS Stone, sitting opposite, wonders if her boss will make it through the day.

'OK,' Loss stares at the window, but not out of it. 'Tell me what we *do* know.'

'Well, the good news is that Candy's has been under

surveillance by the Drugs Unit for some time; first in Docklands, and then later at London Bridge, and we have clear video footage of the entrance to St Clements Court right through the night in question.'

Loss is staring at the rain leaking past his office. He wishes he could close his eyes, but every time he does he thinks he's going to fall over.

'And the bad news?'

'At 12.45 on Sunday morning, the officers on duty in the van witnessed two youths staggering out of St Clements Court, clutching their faces. The officers ran to assist, and upon discovering what appeared to be foul play, reported the incident and called for back-up.'

Loss looks at his DS and raises his eyebrows.

'Foul play? You're going with "foul play"?'

'Absolutely.'

He feels unutterably weary. He misses smoking and sleeping and sunshine, but most of all, he misses his daughter. He waves his hand in the general direction of his DS, urging her to continue.

'Still waiting for the bad news,' he says.

'Once another unit had arrived, the officers carried out a search. They found one youth, dead, who had been shot through the eye at close range with an antique crossbow bolt, and a large piece of graffiti, still wet, proclaiming one word: "Tuesday". There were no other persons found in the alley, which is a dead end. The only exit was under all-night video surveillance. The officers took photos of the deceased, and the graffiti.'

Stone spins her laptop round for him to see. It's the report from the surveillance officers, including pictures of the dead boy. Images of the video sent to his computer slices through his vision.

'The club door?' he asks.

'Could only be opened from the inside. Apparently there was some form of knocking code.'

'Very *Scarface*. Any other doors? Windows? An office, perhaps?'

'Nothing. And the fire escape only went up two floors, once again ending in a door that could only be opened from the inside.'

Loss rubs his hands over his eyes, wondering how much worse he can possibly feel. 'And I suppose our boys were on the ball enough to check the bins?'

'And girls. Full of paper from the offices, and bottles and cans from the club. It's all in the report, sir. The Drugs Unit were staking out that club front all night, and as far as the video shows, the only people who went into the alley were our three crack friends, and only two came out. The girl, who we clearly saw on the video sent to your computer, appears to be a spirit who can walk through walls.'

Loss contemplates the incident board. He is pretty certain that very soon it's going to need to be much, much bigger.

'However, there's one other bit of news,' Stone adds.

'Yes?'

'The back-room boys and girls taking apart your computer, were able to use the video to determine where we might find the cigarette butt our ghost-girl threw away. This was reported to the forensics team who were nit-combing the alley, and the said butt has been recovered and sent off for DNA analysis. With any luck in the next day or so our girl will have a name.'

The phone rings, its single loud trill making DI Loss's ears hurt. He knows that he is becoming unwrapped, and badly needs some sleep. He looks intently at the DS as she speaks to the person on the phone. He can tell she is excited about something. She frantically taps notes into her iPad, thanks the caller and hangs up.

'Let me guess. That was our MurderGoth, asking where we want her to appear next?' he says, trying for grim humour and missing by a country mile.

'No,' she says. 'That was Mr Brooks, of Brooks Military Antiquities, saying he can tell us all about the scythes that were used in the tube train assault, and who he sold them to.'

23

It's not the hardware, it's the operating system

I avoid the systems most people use. They're always updating, always prying. It's like sticking a tiny plaster over a great big cut: loads of crap just keeps oozing out. And the more they try to fix it, the longer it takes to run, and the more they know about you. I always go free source. You're still on the grid, but at least you've got a bit more control.

When I was living on the street there was this boy called Diston, but everybody called him Deadman. He was rib-puncture thin with stinking dreads and had a unique approach when it came to panhandling for money. He used to go up to a person and ask them if they could give him some cash for his coffin. He would stare at them, hair down in front of his eyes, like some fucking zombie, and ask them for money. The poor sods used to be so freaked out they'd hand over whole wads of cash just to make him stop staring at them.

The thing is Diston truly believed he was dead. He was just trying to raise enough cash so he could lie down and go to sleep forever. He had borderline personality disorder, or at least that's what he told us.

Me, I always thought he was a fucking liar. Anyhow, one of Diston's things, one of the things that sparked up his plugs, was computers. He used to say he could leave his soul scattered across the Interweb. Diston knew all about computers.

How to build them. How to link them up through the ether.

And, most importantly for me, how to program them.

We used to sit in the underpass by Tottenham Court Road, surrounded by hobos, blinded by anti-freeze-strength white sui-cider, and sludge-blooded, old-school clock junkies, one needle away from being compost. Diston had this Asus tablet that ran open-source: completely adaptable. Fuck knows where he charged it up. I know he used to steal the Wi-Fi codes from local offices. He said it was easy. I never knew how easy until he taught me.

Really, just changing your password every week isn't enough. You need to change your keypad too. Once Diston was into a computer, he had programs that could tell how frequently a key was pressed and then work out the passwords that allowed access to whatever the system was linked to. He blacked out whole swathes of information for fun, and then gently wiped his electronic feet, and left.

And then there was the Internet. Once he was in the Interzone he was away. A spider ghost in the World Wide Web. The way he described it, when people cruised the Web, they thought they were in their own little virtual bubble, their own private cyber car. That, he said, was bollocks. It was more like they were in a taxi, a black cab. You'd type in your web address and click, and then get in the cyber taxi and it would take you to your destination.

Recording all your information on the way.

Who ordered the cab.

Who got in the cab.

Where it picked you up. Where it dropped you off.

Diston used to tell stories, his face mad and rippled in the flames from a tramp fire. Stories of governments and corporations. Of cyber-tracking and data surveillance. He used to tell ghost stories too. About people who built clone cabs, cabs that navigate the Interzone without detection. About people who became the taxi driver rather than the passenger.

He was a scary boy, Diston. I didn't trust him, and I didn't like him, but he knew what he was talking about when it came to computers. He taught me all about C codes, and UNIX, and open-source hacking. He taught me how to spirit-slide behind legit apps and about mirror protocols, and mimic programs. Really, it's quite simple once you're into the groove, so to speak. It's like anything else; it's just a matter of application.

It's not fucking art, is it?

Anyhow, that was then, when I wasn't what I am now.

Branching off the main tunnels are little alcoves, *cul de tunnels*. They're twelve metres long and kitted out with polymer racking systems to allow maximum storage. There are big, square, silver condensers bolted to the alcove roof with concertinaed tubing snaking away to remove the moisture and prevent corrosion.

I walk in, open up my satchel, and grab a couple of high-end laptops with solid-state delivery, and a bunch of mid-level phones. Most smart phones these days have a GPS chip soldered directly onto the board so the phone can be tracked, but you can still find units that only have it as an add-on, but are still ok for Wi-Fi hot-spotting. I also pick up some external drives and some Bluetooth headsets.

All the stuff down here in the tunnels isn't registered yet, cos half the staff are on the steal. It doesn't actually get on any books until it goes front-of-house. Perfect for me. I take a couple of prestige pieces to sell and then shadow-walk my way out of there, through the system and back to my crib.

For a while I toyed with buying stuff off the Silk Road before it got shut down. And then off BMR. I kept one laptop solely for subbing through the Dark Web: the web hidden under the Web, used by criminals and hackers, and art-terrorists and, for that matter, real terrorists. The BMR is a kind of eBay for Dark-webbers. I thought I could get my hardware there. Maybe some guns.

Well I could have, but the whole system was so full of spooks from all the covert security agencies that it was like scuba-diving through police sea, so I sacked it.

When I get back to my crib I do the rounds, making sure everything's safe and secure, and then I hook up my new gear to my speakers and cue up the *World Service*. It's late and there's a programme on about the formation of matter. I tune out my head, and wash myself down, and do my business.

Then I drink down a protein shake and go night night.

Nothing to see here.

24

Brooks Military Antiquities is the kind of shop in the kind of alley that demands dark skies and even darker conspiracies. From the moment they come out of the tube station at Leicester Square and walk down St Martin's Lane, DI Loss is filling up with foreboding. The sky is a seething mass of grey, and black, and blue, and as low as if London had a ceiling over it. His phone vibrates in his pocket: a text. He pulls out the phone and opens it up.

'Jesus!'

'What, sir?'

'The footage of Lily-Rose's rape, which kept on being posted on all those revenge-porn sites that we failed to shut down cos they never show faces and are not controlled in this country, and God knows what else . . . it's been replaced with footage of the mayhem on the tube.'

'Good.'

'What?'

'I don't mean good as in it was good what happened to those boys. I just mean good as in I'm glad the Lily-Rose images aren't there anymore. Just because no one was identifiable, well, it's still going to be understood by all those kids on the estate, isn't it? And now they're seeing those boys who did it.'

'Allegedly.'

'Whatever. Now they're going to see them get fucked over. So "good".'

Loss replaces his phone, feeling as if control is not so much slipping away from him, as running full-pelt. The air of the capital is hot and humid, and the bombardment of smells coming from all the street vendors makes him both nauseous and light-headed. The noise is incredible: tourists armed to the teeth with electronic gadgetry, clicking, and whirring, and flashing, all shouting at each other. The locals no better; many speaking a language he can't understand, either because he's too old and can't decode the intonation, or they aren't speaking in English. Almost half have strange contraptions in their ears and are shouting at the air in front of them. Amazingly, his DS seems to be enjoying herself. She even stopped and bought them each an ice-cream from a vendor working out of a rickshaw with a cooler-box attached to the back.

As they stroll down the lane towards the Coliseum Theatre, a deep throb of thunder pulses across the sky, as if it's being fracked. Loss is having difficulty walking. He isn't sure whether it's because he is so tired, or because the pavement has begun to melt in the heat. The entire city is becoming surreal to him as though he's a few seconds out of sync. A permanent shudder in reality. Stone stops suddenly, and grabs his arm.

'What?' he asks. Stone smiles at him and points. Loss looks at what she's pointing at.

'You've got to be kidding.'

Between the theatre and a music shop is an alley, no more than fifty centimetres wide. Spanning the gap, attached to both sides of the narrow street, is a lamp, making an arched entrance-way.

'Brydges Place, sir. I believe this is us.'

The day is now so dark that the lamp marking the entrance sputters into life. As they walk single-file under it and into the alley, Loss briefly wonders if he has gone back in time. Steam seeps out of the walls in front of him through cracks in the mortar, and he feels as if the walls are barely staying upright that, at any moment, they might close up and crush him. He is dizzy with hunger, sleep deprivation, and claustrophobia. If it weren't for the narrowness of the lane he might very well fall down.

After ten metres the alley opens up into a tiny courtyard, and Loss feels the constriction in his chest ease slightly, although his sense of displacement increases. The courtyard has a scattering of tables and chairs; an outside extension of the Marquis of Granby pub. In one corner sits a ragged dust-coated scarecrow of a figure, playing a violin, with an upturned bowler hat at his feet. Loss doesn't recognize the tune, but it sounds vaguely eastern European. The only other occupant is a pavement artist, chalking a winged figure falling from the skies. From his perspective Loss can't make out much of the picture, but he suspects that it's Icarus, who flew too close to the sun. From where he is standing Loss can only see the back of the artist and he can't tell if they are male or female.

'Over here, sir.' Stone nods her head at a dark blue door to their left. Above it is a painting of two antique duelling pistols, and a brass plaque next to it:

K BROOKS
MILITARY ANTIQUES AND EPHEMERA
BY APPOINTMENT ONLY

Next to the plaque is a brass bell-pull. The DS gives it a firm tug. After a moment a cultured voice enquires after their

60

business. Once the DS has given the required information there is a click as the door is remotely unlocked, and then they walk inside.

'Hello? I'm up here!' The same cultured voice rings out from above them, and urges them up a steep staircase. The stairs are old and the bare wooden treads are not flat, making them difficult to climb. The narrowness of the staircase, coupled with its seemingly random twists and turns increases Loss's claustrophobia. By the time they reach the glass-walled garret at the top of the building Loss is so out of breath he thinks his heart is going to explode. His vision is just colours with no pattern or meaning to them. He feels himself falling.

'Oh my poor chap!' A tall scruffy man, his appearance at total odds with his voice, is quickly at his side, a firm hand on his elbow. He studies the DI, concern printed on his tight-skinned face. 'Do sit down.' He ushers Loss into an over-stuffed armchair.

After a few moments his vision settles and he is able to take in his surroundings. He blinks several times and wonders if perhaps he is drunk. Pointing directly at him is a cannon. Next to the cannon is a pirate brandishing a flint pistol at his DS. It's only after some moments that DI Loss realizes it is a waxwork model.

Following his gaze, the scruffy man beams brightly. 'I got him from Madame Tussaud's. I think he's supposed to be Calico Jack.' The gaunt man is standing by the armchair holding a glass of iced water. He hands it to Loss, who drinks it down gratefully, and gazes around the room.

The walls are covered with weaponry of all kinds; from pistols to blow-pipes. There are esoteric potted plants every-where, and the dry smell of them, mixed with the shadows they create from the enormous amount of light streaming into the room through the glass roof and walls, gives the feeling of a tropical forest. Loss wouldn't be surprised if a

61

Pigmy reached up and grabbed the blowpipe off the wall. The room is divided by glass exhibit tables. Loss stands up and peers into the one nearest him. The proprietor comes to stand beside him and looks into the case. Resting on red felt, and neatly labelled, are two wicked looking axes, about thirty centimetres long.

'Those are Egyptian quarter axes, popular around 1500 BC,' the man beside him says. 'The first ones were made out of bronze, of course, but they were so useful in combat that they lasted right up to the Iron Age. I'm Kavenagh Brooks, by the way,' he grabs Loss's hand and gives it a single, dry pump. 'I understand you've been looking for information concerning these.'

From out of another case the antiquarian produces a slim box and places it on the display glass in front of the detectives. When he opens it Loss feels a slick of saliva flood his mouth. Inside are two scythes, identical to the ones he'd last seen separating flesh from bone on a tube train, not very far from here. Beside him his DS gives a sharp intake of breath. Loss sways slightly.

'Steady on, old chap.' Mr Brooks places a concerned hand on the DI's arm.

'Where did you get them?'

'These are one of two sets I brought back with me from Burma. Actually, it's quite remarkable to find one pair in such good condition, let alone two.'

Loss can't take his eyes off the knives, at the wicked curve of them, and the way they seem to sliver the light into flat silver snakes.

'And who did you sell the other set to?'

Mr Brooks strokes the knives gently, as if he is putting them to sleep.

'Why, the British Museum.'

25

Lily-Rose is getting dressed. Her clothes are too big for her now, and when she wears them, the impact of her recent experiences comes into sharp relief. She is a ghost inside her own skin. She puts on a pair of scuzzy old jeans, and uses a dressing gown cord threaded through the belt loops to keep them up. She doesn't need a bra beneath her ripped black Joy Division tee shirt – since she stopped eating her breasts have almost completely disappeared. This is one of the reasons she still eats so little. She does not want her breasts to return. She does not want to be a sexual being. Over the tee shirt she wears a Russian army jacket with the collar cut off, and on her feet, a pair of Doc Martins. She does not look at herself in the mirror. She has broken all the mirrors.

When the police returned Lily-Rose's computer she did not touch it. She was not sure if, when she started it up, knowing that everything on it had been examined, she would feel violated again. She wasn't worried about them finding anything incriminating; the girl she met in the Pollyanna chat room was obviously very good at covering her tracks. But just the fact that strangers had electronically thumbed through her hard-drive. Her photos. Her texts. Her life.

Herself.

She wasn't sure she could cope with it all.

In the end, she decided she couldn't and, instead, used her iPad to re-connect to the Interzone. She created a new email address, which she gave to no one. Of course she didn't. There was no one to give it to. Since her assault she has systematically shut down all her contacts with the school and the estate. It wasn't hard. Most of her friends have abandoned her, seeing her as broken: damaged goods. Or worse, blaming her for bringing down trouble onto the estate. Her rape was in some way a difficulty that reflected badly on them. An inconvenience; rocking the boat, and allowing the corpse of fear to surface.

She collected all the information on the web concerning the girl the media were now calling Tuesday. She re-entered the anorexia/ self-harm forums, the scar-bars she haunted after she was raped, searching for her.

This morning she received an email. It had no IP address and seemed to originate from nowhere. She opens it up and reads it.

The words make her break out in a shivering sweat but she reads it to the end.

Once Lily-Rose has finished dressing, covering her hands with a pair of fingerless grey mittens and wrapping a black keffiyeh round her throat, she leaves the house for the first time since her attack, and heads into town.

26

When Loss and Stone leave Mr Brooks' premises, the sky is a ribbon of boiling black above them, and the busker and street painter have disappeared. Seeing the scythes at close quarters has brought home to the detectives just how much pain and fear must have been in the carriage on the night they were used.

'I need to sit down.' Loss lowers himself into a chair at one of the tables opposite the door from which he has just emerged. Stone walks through into the Marquis of Granby, and returns a few minutes later with two Cokes. Loss can feel the moisture in the air, as though the rain has already arrived and is just waiting for somebody to notice. There are glass beads of condensation on the outside of the glass. He takes a sip of the Coke. It is not real Coke, but some glucose-rich variant from a soda-stream.

'So whoever she is, she probably nicked them from the British Museum – unless she had access to similar weapons elsewhere.' Stone sits down next to him and sips her drink. Flashes of lightning cross the narrow strip of sky above them. 'But what I don't get is why? Why use such a bizarre weapon, one that's going to be quickly identified? And why leave a calling card, look at the camera, and then go to such extremes as to disappear by walking through walls. It just doesn't make sense.'

Loss can't disagree. The whole case is making him feel stupid. He can't seem to be able to grasp a bigger picture. He knows there must be one. He feels it deep inside him. He just doesn't know what it could be. He drinks his Coke, examining the pavement in front of him. It takes him a few minutes to register what he is staring at.

'Fuck!'

The rain starts to fall in large drops on the chalk picture the street artist has left. Although the picture is much the same as when they went into the antique shop, it differs in two main respects. The first is that the central character, the one Loss had assumed was Icarus, is now a tumbling, black-trousered Gothette in an army shirt. She is quite clearly the girl from the CCTV and the video sent to his computer. The second is that the drawing now has a title written beneath it, beginning to blur and run in the rain:

TUESDAY FALLING

'Take a picture of that before it washes away, for God's sake!'

Stone gets out her phone, but, before she can utilize the camera facility, it rings.

'It's the lab, sir,' she clocks the ID window, and pushes the button to accept the call, and puts the phone to her ear.

While his DS deals with the call, Loss pulls out his own phone and snaps a pic of the chalk drawing on the pavement. All the colours have merged into each other and the image is distorted and surreal; a pictorial representation of how he feels. His phone rings.

And that's when DI Loss's world blows apart.

27

Now they know that I'm not just some random fruit shoot, I have to be a bit more inventive. Not too inventive, cos I'm still dealing with empty-headed morons, but a little bit.

I'm not talking about the police here; I'm still playing *Children's' Hour* with them. It's still *Follow the Leader* in that camp, and they haven't got a clue what's going on.

Of course, when I say the police, I mean DI Loss. I couldn't give a fuck about the rest of them.

Poor DI Loss, all at sea and not a boat in sight.

No, I'm talking about the Sparrow Estate boys and girls. The rape merchants and the pain posses.

Really, they think they're living in some film. They think they're gangstas, or hooked-up players. They think they're part of some crew and the world they live in is run by them, for them.

It's almost unbelievable how people can be so stupid.

They all have smartphones they don't understand, which is a joke in itself. Smartphones for stupid people. They all think it's like chatting in their own cribs. All I had to do was send them a phishing email with a hack attachment piggy-backed onto a free game app, and I have a real-time screen on my tablet of all their texts, all their phone calls, emails, everything. They're children, really. They don't trust each other, but they trust a machine.

Heartless, raping robot children, obviously, but children.

Although technically, of course, I'm the child.

Anyhow, since my little run-ins with them, their phones have been on fire, trying to find out who I am. What I want. To begin with, once they knew it wasn't just some psycho gig, they thought I must be some bit of fluff they'd fucked up in the past. Thought I was out for revenge.

They think that way. Like it's all about them. Well, I'll give them something, I suppose. In a way they're right. Just not the way they think they are.

So they started to talk to each other on their little future-machines about all their victims, all the people they'd jumped in the past.

So many it makes you cry. All so casual. All so part of their everyday DNA.

And the way they think. Once they've fucked someone, they think that person has lost the right to refuse to have sex. Not that it is sex. Rape becomes just an assertion of property. Of power.

I've set up a program on my tablet that logs and stores all their messages, and relays them out to the people they've destroyed. It took me about zero seconds to write it. About the same to find the electronic addresses of the people they'd fucked over. Most of them were already on their hand-helds: trophies. Now all the victims know who it was stamped on their lives, and what they think about it. They knew some of it before of course, but now I've connected up all the dots. Opened the curtains and smashed out the window. I'd send it to the police but it wouldn't be as much fun. It wouldn't create the panic and movement that this is going to create.

And I need movement.

I need all the little worker ants to have boiling water spilt on them so I can watch them run.

I need to know where they're running to.

That's why I've decided to give them another little push.

The kebab house looks the same as any other kebab house; all faulty neon and unbelievably bad food pictures. You can tell by its popularity that it is a front for drugs. There are five under-age groom-girls outside, wearing belts that are pretending to be skirts, and a boy, maybe nineteen, standing a few feet away from them, with cold bullet eyes, like he's a gunslinger, or a spook, or a hard-nosed mutha.

What he is, is he's just a prick that someone else pulls, and he's probably got about half an hour left to enjoy his life.

I've been watching them from a doorway next to the tube station. I've got a litre bottle of cider next to me filled with hydrochloric acid, and I've covered myself with a sleeping bag I pulled out of a skip. I'm wearing a Korean army great-coat cos they're the only ones that will fit me, and I've got on a fake-fur trapper's hat.

Frankly, I look how I used to look three years ago, when I'd only just AWOL'd out of the hospital and was back living on the street. When it all got going and everything broke in my head.

But I smell a lot better.

So here I am, in my brilliant tramp disguise, which only works because no one likes to look too closely at a tramp in case they do something tramp-y to you, watching the boy outside of the kebab/drug shop who is looking at the street like it belongs to him.

He doesn't look at me, though. Me, he looks right through as if I'm litter.

Every few minutes Bullet Eyes takes, then makes, a phone call, and a teenager on a pedal bike comes up and goes in the meat shop. After a little time they come out, get on their bike and ride off. They never have a kebab with them, though. I don't blame them.

I've got my tablet resting on my lap, hidden by the sleeping bag, and I've got it connected to the Interzone with a cascade IP router so I can't be traced. I used to use TOR before it got rebooted. TOR stands for The Onion Router, a way of transferring data that has so many layers of relays as to make it untraceable. Really, I don't know why they bother. If someone doesn't want anyone to know where they've been on the interlanes there are a million programs out there that will help them. Shutting one down is like trying to jail a planet.

Or just buy a pre-jacked SIM. They cost about the same as a packet of crisps.

As Bullet Eyes makes his phone calls and takes his IMS's, I get an instant copy of it on my screen. I've also got a program running that converts speech to text, so I don't have to worry about any audio leakage or spook-y ear-pieces. The conversations are so boring it's unreal. Two grams of this. One wrap of that. Twenty pills of zip-a-dee-doo-dah. Crack, Special K, Bubble, cheese and crackers, blah blah blah. Drugs are so dull.

Occasionally he takes a different kind of call, and a car comes and picks up one of the girls. Before she gets in the car, Bullet Eyes slips a little something into her tiny girl hand to make the night ahead more bearable. All bleeding heart; I'm surprised he doesn't give her a rose as well.

Those girls think they're so big and grown up, with their micro-clothes and their trowel make-up, but they're just broken children getting serial-raped in slow motion; their brains so groomed and loomed that they don't even know what's being done to them is wrong. Except when they're alone and can't find any drugs to numb themselves, of course.

If I wasn't so full of snow, and black, and pain I'd probably feel something for them.

I wish I did.

But then I couldn't do what I do. So I don't.

This goes on for fifteen minutes before he gets a call on a different phone. I look at my screen and see that the caller's ID is withheld. Double withheld, as even I can't trace it.

Of course it is. That's why I'm here.

28

The email that Lily-Rose received painted her soul red. It contained the names of the boys who had raped her, and the name of the girl who had filmed it on her camera phone and then distributed it around the estate. Around the school. Around the dark corners of the Interweb. It told her who was there when she was assaulted, and where everybody lived.

It gave her a list of other victims who had also been abused by the same people, cross-referencing with times and places.

Then it listed an address of a youth centre situated next to the Docklands Light Railway, along with a set of directions and a time.

Underneath was written:

Lily-Rose
I understand if you want to hide away forever, but it's your body, and you shouldn't have to turn your gaze from it. A life with a black hole at the centre of it allows nothing out, and everything in. It is a vessel for pain
Set yourself free.

As she makes her way off the estate, there's a hard wire inside her, tingling with electricity. It is keeping her upright and stopping her screaming at shadows. Inside her pockets her hands are clamped so tight that if she'd had any nails left they would have pierced her skin.

When she finally reaches the Youth Centre she is drenched in sweat, and there is a buzzing in her head like a time-shifted scream. The scream she hasn't let out yet. And then she sees, spray painted across the front of the building

TUESDAY

She takes a deep breath, crosses the road, and walks inside.

29

The phone call to Bullet Eyes is from his boss, and it's to do with what's happening on the estate. There's quite a lot of colourful language being used. The girls pick up on the tone of his voice and disappear into the kebab shop. Honestly, they're as stupid as they look, seeking safety in a drug shop. On the plus side it means they're out of the way. On the down side it means I can't blow it up now.

I take the taser out of my bag and grab the bottle of acid. I'm halfway across the road, walking my staggery tramp-walk before he sees me. He's distracted by what he's hearing on the phone and doesn't look at me properly. Just sees some street plant on his patch. He doesn't give me his full attention. Oh dear.

'Hey. Fuck off, yeah?' he shouts at me. 'Go and find some other street to shit on.'

He's so full of empathy for the homeless he should work for Shelter. I take the lid off the bottle and keep coming. When I'm four metres away I shoot him with the taser. He goes completely rigid. 100 thousand volts of electricity running through your body will do that. I run forward and catch him before he crumples. Not because I give a toss about him. I just don't want the phone to get broken. I fire a flare high into the kebab shop so it doesn't lodge in the pointless brain of one of the skin-girls, not that you'd notice a difference, and put his phone to my ear. Mr Boss-man is still talking.

'Remus? Are you still there, bro? What the fuck's going on?'

I hold the phone away from my ear so he can hear the flare go off in the drug shop along with the girls' satisfying oral accompaniment, and then bring it back.

'I'm afraid Remus has had a bit of a shock.' I know it's a crap joke but I just can't help it. Years of Bank Holiday Bond films on TV have affected my brain.

He's not out, Remus. But he can't move. The taser fires so much juice into the body that it scrambles the neural connectors.

You can still feel, though. I pour the acid onto his crotch. I'm quite impressed that he manages to scream.

'Who the fuck is this?'

The voice is cold. This isn't Remus, all cock-front and gangland. This is the real deal.

'Hello, Mr Man. I'm the one who's been kicking you in the balls.'

'*Tuesday.*' I think the voice is meant to frighten me. It's about as scary as Scooby Doo.

'But I'm bored with that, so now I've decided to cut out your heart, instead.'

And then I take a picture of Remus screaming on the ground, his crotch a smoking ruin, and tweet it to all his contacts. Tweet. Who the fuck thinks these things up? Then I pocket the phone and walk back towards the tube station. There's shouting and screaming going on behind me but it might as well be birdsong.

30

While DS Stone is talking to the lab, DI Loss's phone rings. He answers it and listens to his boss telling him that there's a full-blown riot happening on the Sparrow Estate, and he'd better get his arse down there, yesterday. They both finish their calls at the same time.

'Come on. All hell's broken out on the Sparrow Estate.'

She puts her phone in her pocket and holds her hand up, palm facing him.

'Hang on a minute, sir. That was the lab.' There is something in her face that makes him slow down.

'What? What is it?'

'They've analysed the DNA on the filter of the cigarette butt that was picked up in the alley. They ran it through their database and came up with a positive match'

Loss nods impatiently.

'Yes? Well come on. Don't keep me in suspense. There's an all-out war going on that we've got to walk into.'

'According to their records the DNA is a 100 per cent match for a Miss Suzanne Loss.' She stares at him, bewildered. Loss looks back at her, the colour draining rapidly from his face.

'Your daughter, sir.'

He sits down as though he's been unplugged.

'I'm sorry, sir.'

'It can't be.' Loss's gaze turns inward. And backward.

'I have to put out a call for her, sir.'

Loss realizes his colleague hasn't been around long enough to know.

'You don't understand. It can't be. My daughter was murdered three years ago.'

31

'Sir? Sir, can you hear me?'

DI Loss is sitting in the chair outside the Marquis of Granby, but he is three years away, his mind wrapped in the shadows of his past. He's standing in the entrance to Bleeding Heart Yard. The police strobes from the patrol cars blocking it from the main road are nightmaring the brick walls, and the rain running down the mortar lines is black.

Uniformed officers are taking measurements on the ground; running tape, and sticking down coloured markers, but Loss barely registers them. All he can focus on is the light-fractured body of his daughter lying; a thrown-away toy. One metre away from her is another body, but the Inspector doesn't look at it, doesn't give space in his brain to acknowledge it as he stares at Suzanne. The London rain is lit up in sheets by the strobes. He is hot and cold at the same time and completely indifferent to the scene in front of him. The Victorian yard smells of death, and pain, and broken promises, shattered futures, and failure.

Loss falls to his knees next to his daughter, not feeling his trousers tear or his skin rip open as he slams to the ground. Not feeling the rain slicking his hair, sticking to his skull. The blood running out of her means she is not long dead; the blood is thick and slow-moving, but not yet congealed. It leaves her body in ribbons and rags, and mixes with the blood trickling from his knees. He cannot quite believe that it is his daughter. He feels he is in several places at once: here in front of the body of this girl who was his daughter; sitting at his desk and answering the phone, receiving the call; a rabbit punch of pain that brought him over to this yard. The dead man who has been walking around for the last five minutes, a mapped-out non-future of a non-life without a daughter who had stopped talking to him months ago.

All the things he cannot say to her.

All the hugs and holding he cannot give to her.

All the crying and healing he will not do with her.

DI Loss kneels beside his dead daughter and feels his own life drain out of him.

Leaving him empty

Alone.

Lost.

32

There are six tube tunnels running under Earl's Court, and in my opinion the whole bloody structure could collapse at any minute. This is why the Mayor of London has given his consent for the thing to be torn down. What they're thinking of doing is getting rid of the flyover, digging up the tunnels, and having one massive underpass for all the cars.

A fly-under.

Like that's going to work. What with the super sewer, the new cross-London underground, and the trillion-tonne skyscrapers, they haven't got a fucking prayer.

Still, all that's in the future, so it won't affect me. What I'm concerned about is the Antique Arms Fair that's held there every year. All the antique dealers specialising in military artefacts go there and display their prize pieces. Sometimes it's held at the Earl's Court Exhibition Centre itself, and sometimes at one of the workbot hotels just outside it.

I heard about it when I was pavement-surfing in Soho. All the street children get to hear about the big events in London. That's where there would be surplus food thrown out at the end of the day. Where there might be casual work where you don't need a pimp or a gang-hand. Where people are where they want to be, seeing something they want to see, so might be kinder.

Me, I never went there. After the hospital, I went somewhere else instead. Somewhere snowbound and hidden where I couldn't be touched. Underground and in my head at the same time.

Later on, when I couldn't find a safe way into the Imperial War Museum, when I was looking for a weapon fit for purpose, I remembered.

Of course, it's not just Transport for London who have a stake in the ground beneath Earl's Court. The National Grid recently put in more tunnelling for new power supplies as well. If they keep going on like this they'll have to move Brompton Cemetery.

It's all good for me, though. Each night, when the exhibition is shut, all the pieces are stored in the basement of Earl's Court.

Really, it's very safe down there: security guards on the doors and CCTV all around the curving corridors of the massive building. Absolutely no one would be able to break in.

Absolute fucking doddle to break *up*, though. I shadow my way to Hammersmith, which is one of the busiest stations going, and make my way into the part of the station closed for construction. It's simple. Everyone is so busy no one notices the little Goth girl. I've even put on a hoodie so I tick all the boxes.

Once I'm through the construction site, I slip into the old tunnels that take me under the Exhibition Centre proper, then into the power conduits that let me go right up under the basement. All the plans for the building are available online, and all the tunnel schematics I lifted from the TFL Inter-site. The National Grid stuff is a bit harder to get hold of after the London bombings, but, unbelievably, the civil engineering surveys for where the tunnels are going to be, and all the tunnels that are there already, are easy to access. It's amazing there's any London left. I guess the whole system is so disorganized that most terrorists just can't be arsed to wade through it all.

Once I'm in the Earl's Court sub-station it's easy to access the room where the artefacts are stored. I'd looked at the online catalogue and knew exactly what I wanted. I'd been practising with a sport crossbow and a dart gun I'd taken from a department store, but I'm sure this is going to be much more fun. As for the flare pistol, well what can you say?

Every girl should have one.

33

The Sparrow Estate is in meltdown. Following the phone calls in Brydges Place, DI Loss and DS Stone were picked up by an unmarked police car that was fitted with a live feed from the bomb-disposal vehicle at the scene.

'The sodding bomb squad! It's one teenage girl, not the Taliban!' Loss's thought processes are in tatters. The information from the police lab has thrown him into a vortex of pain. Memory pain of his daughter alive and happy, older and sad, suddenly never getting any older. Never getting anything at all. And memories of his daughter bring back memories of his wife.

Thin. Thinner. Thinnest.

The kebab shop is in ruins. All the windows have been blown out, and the stuttering neon sign is hanging by one wire and spitting sparks onto the pavement. Flames can be seen dancing in the back of the shop.

'Well, at least the doner meat will be cooked for a change,' Stone says. Loss isn't really looking at the chaos on the monitor in front of him; he is looking at a scene from three years ago, when he is holding his dead daughter's hand, unable to see her face properly through the blood and the tears.

'Bloody hell.'

His attention is pulled back to the present by Stone's tight voice. He rubs his eyes and looks at the monitor. It takes him a moment to understand what he is looking at. It takes him another to believe it.

'Get onto the Super. We're going to need the riot squad down there right *now*.'

34

Lily-Rose is on the swing in the Sparrow Estate courtyard, swaying gently backwards and forwards, when the detectives arrive. The swing has been used so little that there are weeds under her feet. She is one of fifty-seven people quietly occupying the area bordered by the four concrete housing blocks. There are candles lit everywhere, and a great sense of stillness. The lights from smartphones screens are giving the scene a surreal quality, like a medieval science fiction film. All around them the estate is electric. The kind of electric that builds and builds, before arcing to ground. There is screaming, and slamming of doors, and the silent sound of fear filling up every gap in between.

DI Loss picks his way through the crowd in the courtyard and sits down on the swing next to Lily-Rose. It has not rained in this part of London yet, and the air feels as though it could ignite with the flick of a lighter. The detective rubs his face and wonders if he will ever sleep again. Both he and Lily-Rose gaze at the messages that have been spray-painted onto the side of the building in front of them.

'Well this is something, isn't it?' he says gently. Lily-Rose has not looked at him. She rocks gently back and forth. After a minute, she begins to talk in a quiet voice.

'All the people sitting here, yeah? Every single one of them has been raped and shat on by someone on this estate. They've lived in shame, shut away in their own heads, hurting themselves over and over again, trying to make sense of what happened to their lives.'

'She brought you together, didn't she? Tuesday hooked you up?'

Lily-Rose spits on the floor in contempt and then grins at nothing, looking straight ahead. The grin contains no mirth.

'*They* hooked us up. *They* put us together when they taped us and raped us. *They* lit the fuse. They just didn't realize they'd made a bomb.'

Loss doesn't really know what to do so he continues to swing gently. The motion is making him feel as if he's made of air.

'But where did you get all the names, Lily-Rose? All the . . . ?' he points at the crowd around them, at all the phones showing the same awful things. Lily-Rose sighs.

'Look, Detective Loss. You've had your go, yeah? You've had your chance, and I couldn't even leave my flat. I was gang-raped and beaten unconscious, and it was filmed and shown all round school, and the only thing I wanted to do was find a way to kill myself without breaking my mum. I was fucked up so bad that I was ashamed of my own flesh, as if there was something wrong with *me*.' She emphasizes her point by punching her own thin frame.

Loss doesn't look at her. If he looks at her he will fall down at her feet, or try to take her in his arms and protect her. Try to turn her into his daughter, to ease the pain that is threatening to split his head open. Do something that will not help either of them.

'I hated my body so much I began to think it was a separate thing from me. That it somehow belonged to *them*. That I had to punish it, or cut it off, so it didn't infect me.' Lily-Rose is crying, but her eyes are hard.

'Half the people here cut themselves to try to feel something other than the pain of what happened. They do it in secret, as though it's way dirtier than anything that happened to them. They do it so much that it becomes the only way they can feel. Fucking hell, *Detective*, what do you expect us to do? Therapy? That's therapy.' She tosses him her phone, showing the footage from behind Candy's. Loss looks at it for a moment, then hands it back.

'Those weren't the boys who attacked you, though, were they?'

'Me. Her. Whoever. They all belong in the same gang. They're all part of the same crew.' Loss doesn't know which 'her' Lily-Rose is referring to, but looking round at all the girls in the courtyard he guesses it doesn't matter.

'Well, I have to say this approach is novel.' Loss focuses on what's in front of him. 'I guess you knew most of the names, between you all, but where did you get the phone conversations from?'

They both stare at the tag of Tuesday sprayed on the wall in front of them, until DS Stone catches Loss's eye. He places his feet on the ground, stopping the swing.

'Stay strong, Lily-Rose. There's a storm coming, and I don't think it's going to stop for anything.'

Lily-Rose smiles at nothing straight ahead of her.

'That's the bare truth, Detective.'

He gets up and threads his way to his DS.

'Well?'

'At approximately nine o'clock this evening Lily-Rose and all these others left the Cross-Harbour Community Centre, and walked *en masse* back to the estate. It seems that all

87

the people at the Centre had at some time been raped or brutalized by one or more of the gang members that run the estate. At the Centre was a list of names, mobile phone numbers, addresses, and alleged crimes, from sexual assault through to drug-dealing and fire-arm supply. All in all, a complete shit storm.'

'Shit storm?'

'Absolutely. Also supplied were various social media accounts, from Facebook to Flickr and everything in between, on which are what appears to be recorded conversations of the alleged rapists boasting about their prowess to other gang members, and generally being complete bastards. Also given were the phone numbers of the local radio stations, both pirate and legitimate, and the telephone numbers and email addresses of all the alleged rapists' relatives and work colleagues.' Stone pauses to allow her boss to take in everything she has said.

'OK. Shit storm,' agrees Loss. Police officers in riot uniform are milling around nervously, not sure quite what to do, but knowing that, whatever they do, it is almost certainly going to be the wrong thing. Above them a press helicopter is visible between the tower blocks.

'When the group arrived back at the estate, they spray-stencilled the names of the alleged rapists, along with their phone numbers, Twitter accounts, Skype numbers, *hang-out* addresses and everything, plus links to the recorded conversations of them bragging about what they'd done.'

'Jesus.'

'Quite. These stupid pain-merchants actually filmed themselves talking about this stuff!'

'And now none of it admissible in court.'

The detective is interrupted by a commotion above them.

'I swear it wasn't me, Gran!'

Stone watches as a woman of about sixty hurls a laptop over the balcony, closely following it with a bin bag full of clothes. The laptop shatters as it hits the tarmac.

'I don't want you ever coming back here. Ever. Some of what you did happened in my house! In my house!' The woman is screaming as she slams the door shut.

'I don't think they give a toss about the courts, sir. In about five minutes we're going to have a mob of very angry brothers and sisters gunning for this lot. I'd say the balance of power has taken a bit of a swing.'

All around the estate young men and women are quietly leaving their flats and coming to stand with the girls in the courtyard.

'Sir?' a young officer approaches the two detectives. She is holding a piece of paper and looking nervously at the growing group of people next to them.

'What is it, Officer?'

'The weapons used in the attack outside Candy's, sir? The blindings and the fatality?'

'Yes?'

'Well, the report has just come back, sir. The crossbow pistol was made in the early nineteenth century by a Frederic Siber, and the flare gun was made in 1941, and was last used by the Luftwaffe in the Second World War. It looks as if this might have been the same weapon that was used on the kebab house.'

'Brilliant. Doesn't this girl like the twenty-first century or something?' Stone takes the report from the officer.

'If you're not connected to gangs then it's quite hard to buy guns, round here. And I don't think they'd like to sell her one, do you?' But she isn't listening. She is scan-reading the report.

'Sir, both these guns were stolen from the Antique Arms

Fair at Earl's Court last year, and prior to that had been loaned to the Imperial War Museum.'

Something clicks into place in Loss's brain, and then clicks out again.

'I'm too bloody tired for this,' he says, desperately searching his pockets for the cigarette packet that hasn't been there for three years.

'Right. Officer . . .' He looks fixedly at her badge, shining in the light from the fires being made from all the clothing thrown off the balconies. 'Swallow, I want you to liaise with the righteous vigilantes gathering over there,' he indicates the young men and women standing by the people sitting in the play area, 'and explain to them that the last thing we want is the riot police, but due to some soon-to-be-fucked-off drug dealers, we have to leave them here for their protection.' Officer Swallow looks scared stiff, but nods and moves towards the armoured vans. He turns to DS Stone, a disconnected look in his eye. 'And I want *you* to get back on to the lab and find out what the hell's going on with my daughter's records. I will not have her dragged into this.' He points at the unmarked police car that had brought them here. 'Right now I'm going to go to that car and get some sleep. I want you to wake me up in two hours, and I want you to make us an appointment with someone at the British Museum who can show me those knives. Is that understood?'

'Yes, sir.'

'Fine.' Stone watches as her boss dead-walks to the car and gets in. She signals to the driver leaning against the bonnet smoking a cigarette. He flicks it away and walks over to her. 'Once he's asleep, drive him home, and don't let him come back to me until morning, OK?' The driver nods, walks back to the car, gets in and drives away. DS Stone watches the car go, white plumes of diesel smoke snaking out of the exhaust, and drifting behind it, clear and distinct in the ionised air. Then she looks back at Lily-Rose and the other girls sitting in the courtyard.

Then she feels a drop of rain hit her forehead, and the sky opens up.

35

I wake up to the shipping forecast running out of the speakers like honey. I love the way I have absolutely, one hundred per cent, no idea what they're talking about, yet everything they say makes perfect sense. The voice echoes around the station like a ghost, filling the space with names and places from a shadow world. I stare at the tiny tiles in the ceiling, letting my body tick back into focus. When the forecast is over I get up and set the laptop to scan for any mention of me on media networks, both on the Interzone and in the physical world.

It doesn't take long.

I'm all over it. I practically *am* it.

I drink a protein shake, and do my business. I try not to eat any real food. I need to keep my body fat index under twenty-two, or I'll start having periods, and there's no way I'm going to let that happen. No chance. I've still got to stay healthy, though. Well, functioning healthy, anyway.

When I lived upstairs, on the street, it was all about scavenging.

Scraping off Mcwrappers. Kebab boxes from bins. Turned fruit left behind from Soho market. Endless chips and pizzas bought with beggar money.

Now, compared to then, I'm tip top. I drink nutritionally balanced health shakes designed for people recovering from illness. I don't smoke, drink, take drugs, or eat shit fast food. I don't sleep on cold pavements where you can actually see your life expectancy shedding off you, and fuck knows what living in a city with four million fume-spewing cars and buses does to you.

Then again, my lungs are probably full of micro-particles of metal from the tunnel dust and the nearest thing I get to a vegetable tends to wear a hood.

Still, it's not like I'm planning a long future, is it?

When I'm done, I strip and sponge myself down and catch up with what's happening on the ground.

The news footage looks like Ukraine. Fires all over East London. It seems that there was a riot in Docklands last night.

Well who'd've thought?

There's an interview with a girl from the Sparrow Estate on an internet radio station, where the programme plays an audio clip of her rapists bragging about what they had done, then laughing about it. The girl names the boys, shouting their street tags down the microphone, and challenging them to get her arrested for slander.

There are pictures on the BBC, taken from a helicopter, of fires all over the estate, lock-ups being broken into and the contents doused in petrol and set alight. Mothers and grandmothers are in front of the burning buildings, their eyes screaming, talking about cleaning out the drug gangs. Talking about not taking any more. Talking about taking back control.

'But surely this is a job for the police?' a bewildered reporter asks a woman in her early forties. Oh dear.

'The police? Fuck the police! The police had pictures of my daughter being tortured by these bastards! And they didn't do nothing! Didn't do f-all while my baby couldn't even leave her room! Well let me tell you. We're doing it!' The woman punches her rigid finger into her chest. 'Us and our children!' There was more but the woman was unintelligible. Never mind. Plenty of others.

On and on it goes. Channel after channel. People in a state of disbelief at what their children were doing. Are doing. What had been done to their children. Was still being done. As the night wears on, the more vocal and focused everyone becomes. Tapes played. Audios aired. Victims interviewed. It was as if, once the secrecy had been blown away, and the predators' identity plastered all over everywhere, the floodgates were opened.

And it didn't just stop at the Sparrow Estate. Names started cropping up all over East London. Written on walls and on buildings. And in other cities and towns too.

Names, dates, personal details. It was insane.

And mixed in it all was the tag *TUESDAY*.

Me.

It was visible on the walls behind the reporters. Sometimes spray-painted in giant cartoon letters. Sometimes written dozens of times on doors and pillars.

It was all over the chat-rooms and in the scar-bars of the Interzone.

It was on the lips and in the hearts of all the fucked-up boys and girls on the battle-field.

It warms a girl's cockles. It really does.

They'll definitely be gunning for me now.

Even the police might start getting a clue.

Well, some of them.

Probably not.

I turn everything off and just lie there, listening to the dripping water finding its way through my home. Watching the shadows on the curved roof and the slowly spinning motes of dust in the air.

Not thinking of anything.

Not thinking at all.

Not thinking.

36

DI Loss's house is a house of ghosts. The ghosts of his wife and daughter. The ghost of himself as he used to be. He stands in the living room of his small but unfeasibly expensive Victorian terraced cottage, looking out onto Cassland Road. The driver who brought him home is long gone, having promised to return again in the morning.

He looks out of the bay window at the street, the night lit orange by the lamp opposite. Even at this time the road is busy; it is often used as a cut-through to the main east trunk road, or into Hackney. When Suzanne was very young he and his wife had been terrified of the road, of all the cars parked against the kerb, blocking the view of drivers travelling too fast in vehicles containing too many distractions. No worries now. Just pain and emptiness and the grey, hard wall of an existence without them.

He turns away from the window and shambles out of the room, knocking to the floor weeks of unread post from a small table. No amount of drinking. No amount of crying. Nothing stops the snatches of past cutting into his brain.

The buzzing of the London traffic recedes as he passes through the hall and enters the kitchen at the back of the house. He takes a cup from the draining board and fills it with water from the tap. There is always a cup on the draining board. Loss never puts the cup in the cupboard: he does not look in cupboards. They are full of the past: plates that won't be eaten off, glasses that won't be drunk from. DI Loss's interaction with his house consists of putting the take-away cartons in the bin and doing the laundry. He has a bed made up on the couch.

Upstairs, two bedrooms; one at the front and one at the back. Loss never goes upstairs: the ghosts are too present up there. But, even downstairs, he can still hear his wife crying. He can still hear his daughter's nightmares.

Loss rinses the cup, places it back on the draining board, and goes out of the back door to what was the garden. He has had everything that grows removed and replaced with paving slabs. He sits down on the back step and doesn't smoke a cigarette.

37

The man sits in his chair and looks at the various screens on his wall.

He monitors the destruction of his business streaming out across the media in front of him. His phones are hot from the news. Most of his workforce have been thrown out of their homes by their own families, and have gone into hiding. Their faces are on the sides of buildings and all over the Interworld.

Across the East End his stashes of drugs and guns are being trashed. He'd actually seen some of his drug money being incinerated by a mad-looking old bat of a woman in slippers, screaming that she'd found it under her grandson's bed, that he'd filmed himself putting it there on his phone, bragging about what a player he was, and that the link had been sent to her. At least the fool hadn't mentioned his name.

His mobile is on fire with questions from his soldiers, asking him what the fuck they should do.

He can't comprehend how his power, the power he has held for so long, has slipped; how it is that the ordinary people have somehow gained strength and courage, when before they were the three blind monkeys.

Hear no evil. See no evil. Speak no evil.

He can't understand it, but he has a name and a face at which to direct his fury.

He opens his desk and takes out a phone he has used only once before, and speed-dials a number. When it is answered he says one word.

'Tuesday.'

He attaches a photo of the graffiti tag appearing all over London, and a picture of the small Goth girl who tore apart his boys on the tube train, and then he sits back and focuses on a still of the girl as she stares up at the camera, a scythe in each hand, eyes bright with madness.

'You're dead, little girl,' he whispers.

38

By the time DI Loss and DS Stone arrive at the British Museum it has been raining heavily for three hours. The building appears to be floating as all the streets surrounding it are flooded.

'It's the sewerage system,' Stone shouts over the noise of the water bouncing off the umbrella they're sharing. 'Every time it rains hard there's a back-up. There's talk of a super-sewer tunnel being built, but they're afraid that if they did that, half of London would collapse!'

'What?' Loss yells. He is still angry about being sent home. He knows it was the right thing to do but he resents it.

'Because of all the old tunnels, and underground rivers and stuff! It's like a whole other city down there, apparently!'

'Right.' Loss isn't really paying attention. He has things on his mind other than a history lesson. Like who is tampering with the memory of his daughter. 'Have we heard any news back from the lab?'

'Not yet, sir. I explained the situation, and requested that they do another check on the DNA from the cigarette. They said they'd rapid it through and give me the results later today.'

'Fine.'

They walk up the stone steps in Montague Street to an unassuming green metal door in an annexe to the main building, and ring the bell. After a few moments the door is opened by a smartly dressed woman in her early sixties wearing a tweed suit.

'Yes, can I help you?'

'We're here to see Professor Mummer. We're expected.' The police officers show their ID, and then follow the woman into a small room with a polished wooden floor. Loss feels the urge to whisper. They are shown to a pair of high-backed chairs, and she excuses herself, saying that the professor will be along in a moment. As she leaves the room, her court shoes make a crisp tapping on the hardwood floor. They sit side by side, not looking at each other.

After a time Loss clears his throat. 'You didn't have to send me home. I was completely fine.'

'You looked as if you were about to collapse, sir.'

'I admit I was tired, but a cup of coffee would have sorted me out.'

Stone snorts in derision.

'A *skip* of coffee wouldn't have sorted you out, sir. You were dead on your feet.'

'I was fine.'

'By the time the driver got in the car you were snoring.'

'I was just resting my eyes.'

'Asleep.'

'Resting my eyes.'

They fall into a tense silence. Loss has the distinct impression that his partner is smirking, but does not turn his head to check. After a couple of minutes the door is opened and a thin woman walks in and shakes their hands. She has a firm grip and reminds Loss vaguely of his primary school teacher. She is wearing a smart two-piece skirt suit, and smells of old books.

101

'Professor Mummer,' the woman speaks in a clipped, RP voice. 'Awfully sorry to have kept you waiting.'

'No problem, professor. I understand you've been told why we're here?'

'Absolutely. I was informed last night. In fact, I half expected someone to come immediately, once I saw on the news what had happened.'

Stone winces at the waves of triumphant vindication washing over her from her boss's direction.

'Still, never mind. You're here now. It gave me time to locate the items. Please, follow me.'

Loss and Stone follow Professor Mummer out of the room and through the corridor. Loss is surprised when, instead of entering the museum proper, the professor leads them to an ancient-looking lift, and presses the brass call button. There's a clunk of machinery from somewhere within the building as the mechanism comes to life.

'Actually, this is quite exciting for me. One gets so wrapped up in the day-to-day running of the museum that one forgets that it's even there.'

The detectives have no idea what she is talking about, but aren't worried by this. They are worried by the lift. It doesn't have any doors, and they can see into the shaft, where the cables supporting the carriage are writhing like snakes. It seems so old that Stone suspects the museum was built around it. As the lift arrives they don't feel any better. The contraption is made out of wood, and has a dim light protected by coarse meshing attached to its wall.

'Isn't it marvellous?' Professor Mummer steps into the cab. As she walks in it dips slightly.

Tentatively, they enter. Stone is appalled to discover there are no buttons; just a large brass handle, with 'up' and down' written either side of its ambit. Once inside, the professor beams at them, and then slams the handle into the 'down' position. There is a sickening lurch, and then the cab begins to descend with a worrying grating sound. It is a few moments before the detectives can take their eyes off the wall in front of them and pay attention to what the professor is saying.

'I suppose it's obvious, really. We get so many artefacts that we simply haven't the room to display them all. Also, fashion being what it is, some things just go out of vogue, as it were.'

'So they're not just stored in some back-room?' Stone asks.

'Oh, goodness, no. These chaps are in the catacombs! Underneath the museum are several basements where we keep all the exhibits not currently needed. There are literally miles of tunnels down here.'

Something fires once more in Loss's brain, but doesn't catch. The wall in front of them disappears upwards, and is replaced by a dimly lit stone corridor, and the lift stops abruptly. As they all get out of the lift, Loss makes a private promise to himself never to get in it again.

'In fact, many of these tunnels were here before the museum. As you know, London has been in existence for over a thousand years, building over and over itself. There are underground rivers, the Fleet, for instance, that were once above ground, and tunnels under London that were once streets.'

There is a small buzzing in the back of Loss's brain, like a thought-mosquito, a relentless whine that is beginning to whirr its way forward. A short trill from his sergeant's phone indicates that she has received a message.

'How come your phone works down here?' he asks.

'Oh, the entire museum is Wi-Fi bubbled,' the professor replies airily, before Stone can answer. 'All the mod cons here.'

'It's the boss, sir,' says Stone, an unconscious look of mild disgust on her face. 'Apparently, he's found some expert in gesture interpretation and,' she squints at her phone, "emotion categorisation of the image". Whatever that is. He wants us to go there once we have finished up here.'

'Ah, here we are!' The professor opens a door, and the three of them enter another tunnel. Stone gives a low whistle. The tunnel walls are lined with grey metal storage cabinets crammed together with roller handles on the side, and the floor is trammed with rails to allow the cabinets to be separated, granting access to both sides.

'Bloody hell, there's thousands of them!'

'Quite. We store them this way because it's easier to catalogue. There are over a million individual items down here, from suits of armour to shrunken heads. Really, it's a tribute to the archiving team that we haven't lost anything. Ah! This is the one we want.'

They stop beside a cabinet, which is identical to all the other cabinets, bar the ID number on the front. The professor consults her clipboard, and then pulls open the second drawer down.

'Well, would you look at that?' Stone says quietly.

Inside the drawer are the two Burmese hand scythes that caused so much mayhem on the Underground. Resting between them on the green baize is a business card with the word 'Tuesday' written on it, and on top of the card is a glass specimen slide. Stone takes a pair of nitrile gloves out of her pocket and puts them on. Gingerly she lifts out the business card and turns it over. On the back is a hand-drawn smiley face. Next she lifts out the specimen slide. Even in the low-watt overhead light in the bunker basement of the museum, the whorls and friction ridges of the single fingerprint are visible.

39

A woman on the *World Service* is talking about earwigs. Apparently in French, they're called 'ear piercers'. Only in *French*, obviously. The reason they got their name was because people used to believe that they went in through the ear, burrowed through to the brain, and laid their eggs.

I fucking love the *World Service*. Here I am, living in the tunnels under the city, and I have a radio station that's more bizarre than I am. One moment it will be talking about child soldiers in the Sudan, and the next it's all about the earwig. Priceless.

I get up from my cot and swipe the keypad, silencing the radio, and tuning into what's happening above.

London is a war zone.

All the rape machines are on the run, and victim-news has spread from the East End to the whole of London and beyond. All over the capital, gangs of young girls are roaming the streets armed with spray paint. It's like slut-shaming in reverse. Names and dates are being painted on walls in letters of red four-feet high.

I love it.

If you fuck people over you're going to get fucked over. Hard fact.

At least these girls have clawed back a little bit of respect. Now, what happened to them is not hidden. Now, they don't think it's their fault. It's not going to make them better, nothing can do that. Once you've had your soul ripped out you can't put it back in again.

But at least they might be able to live inside their own skins.

Start thinking of their bodies as their own again.

A drop in the ocean. But a drop.

I can't even get that.

The bad people are going to start coming for me soon. I've fucked them up good and proper; embarrassed them in front of their peers. They're going to start taking me seriously now. I've fucked up their business. I've scattered their worker drones. All in all, they're not going to be happy bunnies.

They'll get someone from outside. They'll have to. Someone who is not connected.

Not connected to the man.

Not connected to the police the man must pay to let him stay in business.

Someone who takes murder seriously.

Someone like me, really.

40

'Right. She's just rubbing our noses in it now.'

'I have absolutely no idea how this could have happened.' Professor Mummer says, clearly upset.

After DS Stone placed the specimen slide in a plastic evidence bag, they put away the knives, ready to be picked up and catalogued in situ by the lab rats. As they walked out, they could clearly see another calling card blu-tacked to the inside of the door, with 'Tuesday' boldly embossed on it. Loss feels he is having the piss taken out of him.

'And you're telling me you have no CCTV down here whatsoever?' he is incredulous.

'I'm afraid not, Inspector.'

'So anyone can come down here, take some of this stuff, and then just waltz out with no one being any the wiser?'

Professor Mummer looks shocked. 'Absolutely not! The British Museum contains some of the rarest, and most valu-able, artefacts from Britain's past and across the world. Many of the exhibits are irreplaceable. All the staff are security-checked. There are guards on every exit, both electronic and human. On the floor above there are cameras just about everywhere. It would be absolutely impossible for someone to steal any of these items.'

The three of them stare at Tuesday's calling card for an awkward moment, and then Stone says, 'So who *does* have access down here?'

'Oh. Well, the back-room staff, of course. The people who take the material from front of house to storage. And the cleaners need to keep things dust-free. Make sure there's no mould and whatnot. Security personnel, I imagine.'

'Quite a lot, then.'

'I suppose. The Museum is a small village, really.'

Loss is growing tired. More tired. Stone puts on another pair of nitrile gloves, carefully removes the calling card from the door, and places it with the other in the evidence bag.

'Well, would it be OK if we called in *our* back-room staff? You know, just to search for prints, check for magic dust. See if *Mission Impossible* paid a visit.'

'There's no need for sarcasm,' says Professor Mummer, her lips straightening in disapproval. 'Judging by the news, you don't seem to be doing too well yourself!'

Loss sighs. 'Point taken.' They begin to walk back through the dim corridors. The professor mutters to herself. Loss doesn't blame her; her castle has been breached and she has no explanation how. He knows how she feels.

With a jolt he bumps into Stone, who has stopped abruptly.

'I thought you said you didn't have any CCTV down here?' she says.

'We don't.'

'What's that then?' Loss looks to where she is pointing. Hidden in a dark well of shadow, angled at a dull grey metal door, is a tiny security camera, its red 'active' light glowing. There's no wire leading from it, so he guesses it's the type that relays its information wirelessly. He looks at the door.

Although it's battered and looks as if it hasn't been used for years, it has been fitted with a brand-new mortice lock.

'Tell me, professor, if the goods lift is the only way in or out of here, where does this door lead to?'

'Ah! Well, that's very interesting. Did you know that the British Museum used to have its very own tube station?'

Click. And a light goes on in DI Loss's brain.

41

The world is moving too fast for Lily-Rose, but that's ok.

She is curled up on the sofa with her mum, watching TV. Watching programmes on an actual television is quite a novel experience for her. She is used to consuming media on her phone, or on her laptop or tablet. Having to sit in one place, watching TV adds a level of oddness that fits her present state of mind.

Between them is a large bowl of 'skinny popcorn'; popcorn with no sugar or fat in it. Just salt. They are both drinking Pepsi Max.

Every talk show. Every news and current affairs programme headlines the consequences of what they are calling the 'victims reclaiming of the city'. On the digital news channels it isn't just the bulletins, it's the entire news. Nothing else. Just a rolling programme showing the same footage over and over again. Interviewing more and more people. And they're all asking the same questions.

How could this have happened?

Where were the parents, the grandparents?

Where was the church, the mosque, the synagogue?

Where were the schools, the social services?

The government?

London is in a fire-storm. The gang-bangers are getting thrown out of their homes, barred from shops. Their names are all over the media, with blacked-out faces and dark hints of gangland atrocities.

The schools are ghost buildings; parents keeping their children away, saying that they're not safe. That their children are at risk.

Lily-Rose and her mother watch as borough after borough starts to join in the movement. Images of young girls marching down the street armed with spray cans. Names tagged on school walls. On the side of bridges.

And then there are the homeless.

Not the mad drunks. Not the confused ranters or the bag ladies that smell of urine. Not the ones the media portray as a different species, and so don't feel morally responsible for, but the kids. The runaways. The grifters. The lost boys and girls. The media is all over them. They are interviewed at night in underpasses, with stuttering neon street light scattering their expressions. They are interviewed in midnight cafes, where the smoking ban never happened, and the only purpose of the food is to remind you not to eat. They are interviewed in abandoned barges-cum-dosshouses, the waves from the Thames *snucking* hollowly against the metal hull.

And they are made to look almost attractive, these homeless. These children, with their faces in half darkness, and their streetwise looks: a secret society that sees everything happening on the street that we don't. The media loves these children. It makes them out to be extras from Oliver! Happy Baker Street irregulars. It doesn't mention the home abuse or the frostbite from a winter on concrete. It doesn't mention the reek of trench foot, or the casual brutality that happens in the hostels. It makes them look like they want to be there. As if they are what they are on purpose.

111

The media wants them because they all say they know Tuesday. They're all over her. They've all seen her, with her knives and her tag paint. They've all watched her with her antique crossbow pistol and her army shirts. And they all know who she is, and they can't wait to tell us.

Tuesday is a street kid who got raped by the gang drones, and is out for revenge.

Tuesday is a pistol for hire, cleaning up the city for the kids.

Tuesday is an escapee from a mental hospital.

Tuesday is a ghost, roaming night-time London in search of her killers.

Tuesday is the daughter of a policeman, and was the subject of an atrocity he failed to stop.

Tuesday is this. Tuesday is that.

As Lily-Rose and her mother watch the street-dwellers paraded in front of them on the screen, an atrocity exhibition being branded as a lifestyle choice, a voice-over asks if perhaps they hold the key to the identity of Tuesday. The whereabouts of her base.

Lily-Rose can barely stop laughing through the tears.

42

DI Loss and DS Stone are sitting in a small room on the sixth floor of the London Metropolitan University. The room is institutional yellow, and couldn't be more of a contrast from their last surroundings. After they left the British Museum they'd taken the tube to Holland Park and presented themselves at the front desk of the main university building. Five minutes later they are sitting in front of a twenty-five-year-old teenager who can't seem to stop staring at DS Stone's chest. The room has more high tech in it than seems physically possible. Loss sighs and wishes he was somewhere else, possibly even someone else.

'And your PhD is in what exactly, Mr . . . ?' Stone asks.

'Drake,' the student replies. 'The deconstruction of movement as pertaining to psychological profiling in abnormal behaviour categories.'

The young man has his hair tied back in a ponytail and wears rimless glasses reminiscent of John Lennon's, although Loss suspects he might very well not know who John Lennon was.

Or indeed what music is.

He has the look of someone who rarely strays from his

work. Even now, between furtive glances at Stone's cleavage, he can barely take his eyes off the screens showing multiple Tuesdays doing terrible things to multiple gang boys. He seems to have been given access to every image of Tuesday they have.

'And this means . . . ?' Loss tries not to sound sceptical.

The student clicks a few buttons on the laptop in front of him, freezing on a frame of Tuesday in mid-slash, and turns to face them.

'Basically, it means that I've analysed thousands of prison fights, street brawls, football fracas, school beatings – anything, really, that's been caught on camera and recorded, and then I've looked into the psychological profiles and histories of the subjects, and cross-referenced to everything that we have discovered thus far within animal behaviour pattern recognition, to see if it is possible to make an emotional map of the subjects by analysing their recorded actions. Unconscious facial movements. Body positioning. That sort of thing.' Drake sits back and smiles at them.

There is a long pause while Loss tries to work out what Drake is saying. Stone folds her hands across her chest, pushing her breasts up, and grinning at him. 'Subjects? As in social experiments?'

If Drake recognizes the sarcasm he fails to acknowledge it. 'Like the Milgram experiment or Stanford Prison? Well not really, but yes, I have used all the data from the tests conducted by the social psychologists in my analysis.'

'Stanford Prison?' says DI Loss, staring at the frozen image of Tuesday. In one of the images she is looking directly at the camera. She is smiling.

'Brilliant,' says Drake, taking off his glasses and cleaning them. 'It was an attempt to see if so-called normal behaviour can be radically altered by environment.'

'What, *Big Brother-ish*?'

114

Drake grins tightly.

'Not far off. What they did was randomly select twenty-four students to become 'guards' and 'prisoners'. Then they put them in a mocked-up prison, gave the 'guards' uniforms and wooden batons, and strip-searched the 'prisoners' and put them in de-humanising uniforms. Then they sat back and watched what happened.'

'Who's "they"?' asks Stone.

Drake smiles. 'Professor Philip Zimbardo, funded by the US Military.'

'What happened?' Loss is interested now.

'By day two the prisoners had barricaded themselves in and personalized their uniforms. By day three the guards started exhibiting sadistic tendencies. By day six the experiment was halted out of genuine fear for the "prisoners" safety.'

'Jesus. When did this happen?'

'August 14, 1971. You can probably find footage of it on YouTube if you're interested.'

'Not as bad as *Big Brother*, then,' Stone adds. There's an awkward silence, then Loss says, 'And how does this experiment help us with the suspect exactly?' Drake turns back to his computer and starts clicking buttons. Loss feels as though he is living in the future as Drake manipulates the images on the screen and they start zooming in and out.

'With her? Probably doesn't. With them . . . ?' He points at the gang of youths about to enter the train. 'Probably loads. They're like the guards in the experiment. See how they all dress the same?' A superior note slips into his tone, probably unconsciously. The screen flips and is replaced with a still of the alley behind Candy's. 'And here? These guys crave an identity, and acceptance into the group. Not one of them wants to stand apart.' He flips back to the train. 'And see how they position themselves? Definite power structure

115

exhibited in the space they create around each other. Their body language denotes their position in the group just as if they were wearing badges and insignia.'

'Insignia?' Stone obviously finds his use of the word amusing, but Drake ignores her, and flips and zooms, his fingers dancing. Loss doubts he even heard her.

'And here,' he says, the images reflected in reverse on the lenses of his spectacles. 'This was taken from the CCTV outside the kebab shop. 'See how he is looking at the street. Like he owns it.' On the screen is the image of the boy who Tuesday burned with acid, prior to the attack, looking out across the street. 'And look how the girls are staring at him? Power structure through body language, you see.' All that Loss can see is brutality and fear, overlaid with the shroud of his dead daughter. He closes his eyes.

'Now as to your suspect, the girl.'

Loss opens his eyes again, and stares into the face of Tuesday, repeated and fractured on all the screens in front of him. 'Yes? What can you tell us about her?' 'Well she's not trained in martial arts, for a start. See how she moves? More like a gymnast or a dancer. No set or repeated moves or stances.' Stone takes out her tablet and starts tapping.

'Also, look at how she moves the blade? The hand to eye co-ordination is way off.'

'She seems to be doing all right to me,' Stone points at the screen.

'But it's not due to training. At least not the traditional sort.'

'What do you mean?'

'Look, I've studied these types of gang structures on hundreds of hours of CCTV. I've profiled them and talked to their parole officers. These boys get crewed up when they're ten; by the time they're fifteen they're hard as nails, stone cold street thugs.' He gives a nod to the screen. 'By rights your girl should be lying on a slab in the morgue by now, but for two things.'

'Which are?'

Drake holds up one finger. Loss gets the feeling he enjoys holding up his finger.

'Surprise. None of these people saw her coming. They all think she's just a little girl, or a tramp, or a clubber or something. They don't see her as a threat. See how they're standing? None of it is defensive. Jesus, in this one the main guy has even got his hand down his trousers!'

'Yes. That did rather put him at a tactical disadvantage,' says Stone dryly; Drake continues as if she hasn't spoken.

'As soon as she strikes, they go into shock. And then she simply doesn't stop. She takes them apart as if they're toys. It's like it's a play that's already happened in her head.'

'I thought you said she wasn't trained?'

'That's not training. That's something else. See how she's smiling? Also, in the first two, it's the gang who start it. I mean, she definitely seems to be putting herself up as bait, but it's they who actually act as predator.'

'Silly them. What about number two? You said two things.'

Drake turns his face from the screen and looks at them. 'Borderline Personality Disorder; Schizophrenia; Dissociative Identity Disorder; what used to be called Multiple Personality, or Split Personality: all conditions that could explain the re-enactment movement patterns she's displaying. To a certain degree it could also explain the discrepancies between the hand and eye co-ordination. Having a psychological condition also makes it hard to read the motivations behind someone's body stance and facial expressions. Whether they're frightened, lying, happy, and so on.'

Loss considers the young man in front of him. He is probably about the same age as his daughter was when she died.

Was murdered. 'But you don't think she has any of those conditions, do you?'

'No I don't. Look at her movements. Look at her eyes. It's not that she's hard to read, it's more as if there's nothing even there *to* read. I think something terrible happened to her, or to somebody she loved, which produced a massive trauma in her psyche, and now she thinks she is dead.'

There is a long pause as what the student has said sinks in.

'Dead. What do you mean, dead? Look at that one, for Christ sake! In that one she's smiling straight at the camera!'

'Dead. Nothing else to live for, as though she's walking through a play that she's written in her head. And yes, she is smiling, isn't she? I understand, Inspector, that the second, um, incident was sent directly to your police email address, yes?'

'Yes.' They all stare again at the stills on the screens, one from the train and one from outside Candy's. In both of them Tuesday is looking directly at the camera and smiling. Drake brings up all the screens so that they are zoomed in on Tuesday's face.

'Well, I think, Inspector, those smiles could be meant just for you.'

43

The Corinthia Hotel takes up almost one whole side of Trafalgar Square. It is one of the most luxurious hotels in London, since the building was sold by the Ministry of Defence in 2007, and then re-opened as an hotel in 2011. Me and the other scummers used to sit in a doorway opposite, watching all the rich people going in and out. We'd be sitting all squashed together for warmth, the place smelling of piss, with our road-kill pizza slices, and we'd try and guess what those rich people all did. Those people who could spend a thousand pounds to borrow a room for the night.

Don't get me wrong. I'm not saying we were jealous, or resented their money or anything. It's just like we were at a zoo, or in a lab or something. It was just so alien to us.

I know what you're thinking. What was the Ministry of Defence doing owning such a large property in the centre of London?

What the fuck do you think?

I read up about it in a book I found lying abandoned one day; damaged goods at the back of a library skip I was sleeping in. At the outbreak of the First World War, the hotel was called the Metropole, and the government bagged it for the war effort. They did the same thing again during the Second World War, where they set up the SOE; a secret spook-y strand of M19 whose sole purpose was to develop dirty warfare: guns and bombs, and tactics no proper army would ever use. The thinking was, if the Nazis or fascists or whoever didn't follow the conventions of war and committed atrocities, then the British government needed a secret branch that could do the same. Unbelievable, isn't it? You don't even have to delve in hidden offices for secrets to find this stuff out. You can look it up on 'Quickapedia', unless it's been taken down or revised or whatever. Rather handily, the hotel is right above the tunnel that connects Whitehall to the Trafalgar Square tube station that was. What a surprise.

There's all sorts of stuff down here.

When I first started exploring I thought I'd just find the odd relic. Old phones. Gas masks. Medical kits. Harmless stuff from a forgotten time that I could sell at Bermondsey Market. But underneath the Metropole I found all sorts of scary shit. The basement exits to the hotel are sealed up with lime cement so I guess not even the Ministry of Defence has a clue what's down here. Stuff they were using in the trenches. Rifles. Swords. Cannons.

Cannons!

And all of it useless. The Trafalgar Square fountains were originally supplied by a natural spring, and the air down here is heavy and moist, and everything is mainly rusted. I guess it was all stored down here in case the country was invaded, and the capital needed to be protected. Nowadays there are loads of citadels under the city that do that, but I stay away from them. Those places are rammed full of hardware and they'd clock me if I got within fifteen metres of them.

It's beautiful down here. Most of the tunnels are from the 1800s and the bricks that make them up are covered in a pale moss that glows gently when I turn off my torch.

Tiny bricks, made by waist-coated midgets, probably.

It was on my third or fourth visit, not long after I'd started living underground, that I found them. The things I'm going to use. They'd been walled away, and whoever had put them there had completely forgotten about them. Or maybe they were so secret that no one was ever told they were there. Maybe they were just put there by the dirty service, and then, when they were disbanded after the War, no one was left alive who knew anything about them. Who cares? The important thing is I found them and they are exactly what I need now. It was when I'd turned my torch off that I saw where the door had been walled up. The moss had grown into the seam, so I could see the outline of the door-frame.

It took me a while to break through. I had to go back under Oxford Street to get a pick-axe from the store, but when I finally smashed my way in and saw what was there, it was completely worth the effort.

Because it had been so thoroughly sealed the air inside the room was dry. The room itself was really not much bigger than a cupboard, and the only thing inside it was a wooden crate with skull and crossbones on it. You know, like there's deadly poison or something inside.

Obviously I opened the crate. Who's not going to open a crate with a skull and crossbones on it?

As I said, inside was exactly what I need now. Even then, way back before all of this got rolling, I think I must have had an inkling that I would use them. Alongside the pain, when my head never stopped humming and my brain only worked in stutters, I think I must have had this plan, under the surface.

A wreck under the ocean. A ghost inside me.

I took a picture of the contents on one of my phones, and then I went about packing them up in my army bag, and taking them back to my crib.

44

DI Loss is sitting with DS Stone at a table drinking Coke again, proper Coke this time, from glass bottles rather than soda-stream. They are back outside the Marquis of Granby, in Brydges Place. Since the very public explosion of the case, the incident room has been taken over by top-notch investigators from the drugs squad, the anti-terrorist unit, the young offenders division, the serious sexual crime unit and any other department that could possibly have a shout in what the girl Tuesday had brought to the authorities' doorstep. Although the whole thing was being overseen by their boss, the detectives were beginning to feel sidelined. Little people hanging around the edges of the in-crowd.

'They've even convened a meeting of COBRA.' Stone shakes her head and stares at the entrance to Brooks' antique shop. The last time the government called a meeting of COBRA was when the capital was under an imminent terrorist threat. Loss sips his drink, which he has poured into a glass that already contains ice and a slice of lemon. The pavement painting of Tuesday has completely disappeared.

'Do you know, Charles Dickens used to drink here?' he says, his gaze drifting over the steam leaking out of the walls.

'What, *the* Charles Dickens?'

'The very one. He used to come here with his mistress. Not his proper mistress, mind, but his other mistress, his secretary, who incidentally was his sister-in-law.'

'What a bastard.'

'Oh, his wife knew. She just weighed up the pros and cons, and then decided to turn a blind eye. Or at least, that's the theory. On the plus side, Dickens helped set up the first home for homeless women. What did the lab say?'

Stone takes a sip of her full fat, four-star Coke. When it comes to Coca Cola she doesn't give a damn. It's full fat or nothing. 'Well, it's definitely your daughter.'

'Dead daughter.' Loss's voice is tight.

'Your dead daughter, yes . . . The prints and DNA from the cigarette and knives all match. Also from the specimen slide she kindly left. Also from the cabinet, and from the handle of the door to the British Museum Secret Station that I, for one, had never even heard about. All the physical evidence points to the conclusion that the girl who calls herself Tuesday is your daughter Suzanne, who was murdered three years ago, and is now walking around London taking out pointy vengeance on evil gang-bangers.'

They sip their drinks. Above them the river of sky that can be seen running between the two buildings that shape the street is murky and the colour of a two-day-old bruise.

'And you went back and checked outside Candy's?'

'Yes, sir. You were right. Underneath the bins there's a manhole leading to the sewer system, which leads to an amount of tunnels, and bunkers, and God knows what else that I also never knew existed.'

'And some of those lead to the underground train network?'

'Possibly. No one seems to know. And incidentally *which* underground network? The network we're using now, or the

123

miles and miles of redundant underground that I was also completely unaware of? Frankly, I'm horrified by my lack of knowledge of the city I live and work in.'

A waiter comes out and clears away the empty glasses from the table next to them. Loss sighs and closes his eyes. He is seriously thinking of retiring; possibly from life, his heart hurts so much.

Eventually he forces himself to ask: 'Could the DNA have been faked?'

'Apparently impossible. The NKNAD . . .'

'English, please.' Loss interrupts her.

'Sorry. The national DNA data storage facility for the UK took a sample of your daughter's DNA when she worked at the hospital. They say it *might* be possible to plant a cigarette butt with her DNA on it, but not on the knives and slide and everything. Plus the fingerprints are a match.'

'Right. So how did she do it? How did this girl steal my daughter's identity?'

'According to everyone, she didn't. Even the tech guys are saying it's impossible to hack into the database and falsify the results. As far as the evidence goes, sir, your dead daughter is going around messing up gang boys and creating the biggest civil unrest in London since the riots of 2011. Possibly since Cromwell.'

Loss misses his daughter so much; he can only look at what is happening sideways. He misses his daughter so much, with such guilt, that he doesn't even have enough room to miss his wife. Stone puts her drink down and looks at her boss. He is un-stitching in front of her eyes.

'You know what they're saying, don't you, sir?'

Yes, he knew what they were saying. He'd seen the TV. He'd read the papers. One of the rumours was that Tuesday was the daughter of a policeman. That she was a ghost on a haunting mission. Just one of the stories that were scurrying around the city, yes, but considering the DNA samples, one that was hitting Loss like a night terror.

'What a fucking mess. Half of London believing in ghosts. Teenage rapists running scared. Victim posses roaming the streets with spray cans and the police can't do anything because they're *victims*, for Christ's sake! And God knows what's happening with the drug lords. They must be pissing in their Jacuzzis wondering what's going to happen next.'

Like a child, Loss takes several breaths before asking his next question. 'You know it can't be her, Stone, don't you?'

Stone stares at the brick wall in front of her. The mortar is old, and beginning to crumble. Since the DNA sample result she has looked into her boss's personal history. Asked around about what happened three years ago. 'Of course it can't be her, sir. Your daughter died in horrible circumstances, and that's awful. But ghosts don't steal weapons or show up on film. Don't send emails or spray-paint walls. Don't create puzzles to mess with lowly police officers.'

Loss smiles a little. Stone drains the last of her Coke, chewing the lemon and swallowing the rind.

'No,' she continues, 'nothing supernatural here. What we have here is some whacked-out ninja super emo, roaming the streets, killing bad guys, and fucking with our heads.'

45

Next to the Mandarin Oriental Hotel, to the south of Knightsbridge tube station, is Number One, Hyde Park – one of the most exclusive apartment blocks in the world. On its lower floors are the accoutrements of the super-rich: the Abu Dhabi Islamic Bank, the premier retail venue for Rolex, and the central London showroom where Formula One racing giants, McLaren, sell their supercars. Above this, behind tinted glass, are eighty-seven apartments that are among the most expensive anywhere on the planet. The apartments are reached by a glass elevator, and the security is beyond compare.

CCTV cameras are everywhere, including the lifts. Each apartment has its own video security link to the entrance, the lift, and outside its own door. The cameras are not linked to a police station, however, but to the management's own security personnel. The security staff are immaculately dressed in £1,000 suits, complete with bowler hats. Each of them carries a side-arm, and all of them are ex-Special Forces. Each of the apartments have bullet-proof glass windows. Many of them have balconies with pools. All of them have safe rooms; rooms designed to keep the occupant free from harm in case of a full assault.

The cheapest one-bedroom apartment costs £3.6 million. The most expensive, with five bedrooms, is £140 million.

Residents are rumoured to include a pop star, a Russian oligarch, a Korean ex-president, and a Japanese software developer who may or may not work for a foreign government. Although all the apartments are sold, most have been sold to corporations registered in different countries, and it is almost impossible to find out who owns them.

The man's apartment is on the west of the building and overlooks the Thames, as opposed to Hyde Park, and among the obscenely expensive furniture on his balcony is a Jacuzzi with fairy lights. No matter how rich the gangster becomes, how re-educated, how far away from his roots, he still needs a Jacuzzi.

He came originally from Brentwood, in Essex, but there was no way he was staying there. He had an extortion racket going on at his primary school when he was eight, and by the time he went to comprehensive school at eleven he was a runner for a local gang. In a few short years he had ripped through the crew until he had runners of his own, and had consolidated the local gang landscape into a new, lethal machine that cut out of Essex and into the city.

Drugs, guns, rape dates, it didn't matter to him. All his lieutenants thought he was so cold he must have walked out of hell itself. He had no friends and all his family were dead – possibly, it was said, killed by him. Now that he was top of the pile, he rarely left his ivory tower, instead conducting his business electronically, or through Caleb, his network liaison man. He had a string of mistresses. Once he had used them up, he either paid off or had them buried on the Isle of Dogs, in a wasteland owned through one of his many shadow corporations.

His head was shaved and oiled, and he worked with a personal trainer every day to keep himself in shape. He never smoked, drank, nor took any drug other than coffee. He did not want to be anything other than in control. He had converted his safe room, which was sound-proofed, into what was euphemistically called an interrogation room, and it was his one true wish to get the girl who called herself Tuesday inside it.

She was ripping up his business as though it was nothing. The business he had dedicated his life to building.

His workforce was in hiding, fuck knows where, because not even their mothers would take them in now. His clientele were going elsewhere, because nothing loves a vacuum like a drug dealer. As soon as his runners were no longer available, the other gangs had moved right in. A junkie has to get his fix, a party girl has to get her pills and thrills, and if his boys aren't there to supply them then someone else sure as shit will.

And it didn't even seem to be about business. It seemed personal. What she'd done to his crew on the tube. Outside the club. On the pavement in front of the kebab shop. That wasn't about money. That was grabbing his head and rubbing his nose in it.

Well, it was over. He had hired someone. He was going to have her caught and thrown into the room next door. He was going to rip her until even her mother wouldn't recognize her. Then he was going to nail her remains up around the boroughs, and tag-spray 'the ghost of Tuesday' under the body parts.

But first, before he killed her, he was going to find out why. Why she had targeted him. How she knew what she knew.

Why him?

Why now?

Why?

46

DS Stone sits by the window in the police cafeteria, looking out over central London. The food hall is situated on the sixth floor, and as she gazes out through the rain she can see cars and buses turning slowly round the statue in Piccadilly Circus. Although she is looking out at London, she is not really seeing it. What she sees are images of her boss. DI Loss is falling apart in front of her. More than that. It is as if he is being washed away. Stone doesn't have many close relationships with men; she has no insight into their mechanisms for dealing with loss and pressure, but she is certain that he is close to breaking point.

She has only been working with Loss for four months, after transferring from Lewisham. When she first arrived in the West End Division off Savile Row, colleagues had tried to draw her into the normal back-stabbing gossip machine that thrives in so many organisations, but Stone had frozen them out, effectively isolating herself. No change for her. She'd been doing the same thing since her school days. She was not the kind of person to succumb to crowd pressure. After the first few failed attempts to co-opt her into their circle her fellow officers marked her as cold and aloof, and left her alone. Which is why she was unaware of the murder of DI Loss's daughter. When she first began working for him it was as if he were hidden in weeds; unseen and unreachable by the outside world. And she never knew why.

Stone sips her coffee and nibbles at the corner of her sandwich. The coffee is lukewarm and the sandwich is so old it probably arrived at the station before she did. Below her a police car pulls in, the lights on its roof making rainbows in the air.

Stone walks over to the sink, where she pours away her coffee, which she considers a mercy killing. She goes to the vending machine, feeds some coins into the slot, and picks out a Red Bull. She walks back to her seat, taking in the London view; rain, and buses, and birds, and neon, and buildings older than some countries.

'I mean he's really beginning to lose it, if you ask me. He's not been right for some time, but now he's really going over.' The voices are coming from behind her. She knows they're talking about her boss. Even more than Stone herself, he is outside of the machine, and the machine does not like outsiders.

Even less so in recent times. Not just because of the Tuesday thing. Stone has felt a weight hanging around the station. Around herself. As if the force is moving away from her.

Then again, the whole of London seems to be changing in front of her eyes. She doesn't know what to make of it. Riots in the street, riots in the home. The power struggles and body battles on the estates. The killings of the drug boys. People taking the law into their own hands. But what was the purpose of the law, if it were not to protect and serve the people, which it had so obviously failed to do?

'I don't think he should even be here. I mean, there's definitely something fishy, don't you think? Between him and the Murder-Goth? Something's not right.'

The hatchet machine behind her is ratcheting up. Stone begins a slow count in her head as she looks out. She reckons she'll get to twelve. She's wrong. She gets to six.

'And the Ice Queen must know something. I mean you can't work with someone and not know, can you? No one can be that thick.'

She takes a deep breath. The silence behind her has a quality of both anticipation and malice. They know she can hear them. Of course they do. Baiting her. Trying to raise a reaction. Ever since the new Commander arrived things had got worse. Difference was less tolerated. Discussion less encouraged. An atmosphere of suspicion and closed ranks seemed to be the order of the day.

'So. Can any of you ladies tell me what that statue is called?' Stone points at the winged messenger in the centre of Piccadilly Circus. The fact that some of the people behind her are men makes her comment perhaps slightly more barbed than is necessary.

'It's Eros, Stone. Surely even you know that. Not,' sniggers one of the detectives, a nasty quality to his laugh, 'that you're ever likely to need him.'

Stone sighs, and finishes her Red Bull. Maybe she's been following Tuesday too long. Or maybe she's had too many years of stupid, bullish men making snide comments about her, but she's had enough for tonight.

'Actually it's Anteros, his brother. The patron of counter-love.' She turns and looks at the man who made the comment. She stares right at him and says, 'Not that I'd expect you to understand, what with keeping your brains in your trousers and everything.'

She walks away, dropping the empty can in the bin as she goes. She is nearly out of the room before the officer realizes she has just called him a dickhead.

47

I love graveyards.

Not in the Gothy-Dracula-floaty-swoon way, but in the 'it's usually just really peaceful and you often get flowers in them' sort of way. Flowers don't grow underground.

Mind you, when I say graveyards, I don't mean all of them. I've been to some fucking grim ones. Inner-city municipal shitholes full of old needles and used condoms, places where you wouldn't even bury a bad dream. No, the ones I mean are the forgotten ones. The ones hidden from the world, full of weeds and weeping angels. Full of ghosts and sweet whispers from history.

Everyone knows Highgate Cemetery. Karl Marx. Ian Dury. Catherine Dickens.

Not Charles, though. He's not buried with his wife.

Anyhow, too bloody highbrow for me. The one that really does it for me is Abney Park, at Stamford Hill.

When I really can't cope with my head then I'll sleep here for a night. It's within an arrow's distance of North London Central Mosque, off Finsbury Park, so you can hear them calling for evening prayer; the sound a spicy scent in the air. It was the first graveyard in London that didn't give a toss what you were. You've got Jews, Christians, and Muslims in here, all rotting next to each other. You've got prostitutes and paupers as well, although they have their own graveyard in Southwark. Hell of a ghost party that place must have.

It's been abandoned by the city for years, and in parts of it all the graves are overgrown with moss and ivy. Cataracts on the dead. There are catacombs that were used by the Hellfire Club back in the day, and I swear there's a wolf living in the Gothic tower.

Anyhow, this is where I come if I just need to tick at a different speed for a time. I can just open the gates into my head, and it makes me happy and sad at the same time.

I sometimes think about Suzanne Loss. All the mess that surrounded her death.

And I sometimes think about my daughter.

I sometimes see all the blood and spit and struggle through the jerky shattered mirror of my memory.

But mostly I just sit here and listen to the sounds of the city, connecting me to a world above ground that I rarely ever see.

I never think about a future that isn't this.

I imagine the person they would have hired to kill me is in London by now. I really fucking hope they've got someone good, so that all the clever clues I've left for them won't be wasted.

Who knows, they might even surprise me and end my short days.

Of course they might.

48

Lily-Rose is back looking out of her bedroom window, down into the war zone between the blocks of flats. It is a little after 3 a.m., and cold in the early morning. A creeping mist blurs the ground in the orange light splaying out from security meshed fluorescent task bulbs that are attached to the side of the buildings. Lily-Rose has not gone to bed, and is still wearing her day clothes. Her armour. The black combat trousers. The Caterpillar boots. The long-sleeved shirt that covers her pressure cuts. Protecting her body from the world. What has happened over the last few days has wired her mind beyond sleeping. The vigils and the meetings. The media cartooning and moral posturing. The destruction of the power structures she has grown up with. From her window she can see the remains of all the candles on the playground. Rape candles, the tabloids called them. Each one representing a violent event, ripples of which seem to be expanding with every passing day.

Lily-Rose doesn't care about that. She stares down at the tags spray-stencilled to the walls and walkways below her. The names and the numbers. The dates and the Q-codes.

The Tuesdays.

Lily-Rose sings softly under her breath.

49

DI Loss is collecting the things he needs from his office. Not that there is much there anymore. The lab technicians still have his computer. The days when he kept his cigarettes in the bottom drawer are long gone.

The Commander has had a quiet word with him, and he has been asked to step down from the investigation. The Tuesday paraphernalia: the pictures and the questions on the whiteboard. The files and the print-outs collaging the desk. Well they were for someone else to fathom, now. Until the exact relationship between Tuesday and his daughter had been established, Loss was officially compromised. Unofficially, of course, he was a much-needed asset. All his years of experience invaluable, et cetera, et cetera.

In some ways Loss isn't surprised. Looked at analytically, it seems that he must have something to do with Tuesday; the girl masquerading in his daughter's identity. How could he not? Why she is doing this to him, to Suzanne, he doesn't know.

But he intends to find out.

As he tidies his drawer a folder catches his eye. It is new, or recently been delivered by the computer tech tracing all instances of Tuesday across the internet. He picks it up and starts to read. Two minutes later he is heading out of the door, all thoughts of leaving the investigation forgotten.

'Stone! Let's go.' She looks up from her terminal. Her desk is an island in the office. There is a tangible space around it, as if it belongs somewhere else.

'Go where, sir?' But Loss is already breezing past, and so is completely oblivious to the smirks and sniggers when he shouts,

'The cinema!'

50

Back in the bad old days – the ones the clockwork steam punk boys and girls are so dreamy about, the toshers – the panhandlers of the city – used to scrim the London sewers, searching for jewellery, and nuggets of loose change that might have been washed down the drains. There were a lot more drains in those days, and the access to them a lot easier. All they needed was an empty alley and an iron bar to lift the metal cover.

Me, I need construction plans, access codes, lock picks, and stealth cameras.

Lucky I'm me, then, isn't it?

I leave my crib, setting up all my traps and snares, and hobo up to Kensington High Street Station. Then I ghost back down the line to Brompton. Brompton Road Station was closed in 1934 but, *surprise surprise*, was bought by the MOD and used for fuck knows what right up to 2014, when they flogged it.

I've got a soft spot for Brompton. A few years ago some bloke staged a play here. All the people who watched it had to climb down the metal stairs because the lifts were long gone. It was way before my time, but one of the older people I was on the streets with told me about it. The play was performed on the derelict platform, and lit by electric candles. It was just these two blokes walking round talking, but they were being followed by Death, waiting to take them away. The character Death, that is. I don't know if it was the full black cloak and dry ice scenario; my mate never said. All he said was that it scared the living shit out of him.

Then again, he was pretty much out of his mind on cider and speed most of the time; crisp packets used to scare the shit out of him. Every now and then I like to come here and try to re-create it. Not the play. The atmosphere. I light up the whole platform with candles. There's no chance of a fire. There's nothing left to burn down here, just oxygen. I like to sit here, watching the tiny flames dance to the tune of the tunnel winds, and look for him.

Death.

Is he stalking me? Following me through the London under?

I'd like to think so.

When I'm not doing what I'm supposed to do. When I'm not focused and allow space to seep in, I get so tired. Sometimes I think I could sit down with my back against the tunnel wall and just stop ticking.

But then again, if I'm not ticking, how can I go bang?

From Brompton Station I enter the sewer system and start working my way north-east, under the Natural History Museum, and across Queen's Gate. Most of the Victorian sewers in this area are redundant or just used for something else; cables and pipelines and fuck knows what, so all in all it's a pretty dry experience. In the reflection from my halogen headlamp the eyes of the rats sparkle blue. Like underground stars. No red light in halogen. The sound in the sewer system is completely different from the sound in the tube. It's all

138

body sounds. Wet and visceral and somehow urgent. Like the sound of a drunken tramp riddled with emphysema.

Or the sound of a drowning girl trying to breathe underwater.

Not this girl, though. Not tonight, anyway.

I've got a way up into the Natural History Museum I made some time ago but that's not where I'm going tonight. I've already got what I want from there, stored back in my crib.

All I need for tonight I've got in my backpack.

51

The London black taxi cab that carried the man through Hyde Park is no longer in commission. It is an old, but lovingly restored 1973 FX4 black hackney with orange roof indicators. The noisy diesel Perkins engine has been replaced with a whisper-quiet electric model, making it the most emission compliant taxi in the city. The interior has been re-upholstered in brown calfskin leather and the bulletproof windows have been tinted president-black.

As the man gazes out at the tourists soaking up the last of the city sunshine he gives quiet instructions on his mobile to the various people he has positioned around and within his destination. It was not often that he agreed to meetings outside of his residence, but Constantine, the assassin whom he had employed to deal with Tuesday, was adamant. The man feels that perhaps he has been *too* adamant. He smiles tightly, replacing the mobile phone in the jacket pocket of his Anderson & Sheppard tailored suit. It could be, he muses, that anyone who thought they could dictate to him where and when a meeting would be held should not leave the city intact. As the cab leaves the park and approaches its destination, the man reconsiders, thinking of the way that Tuesday has sliced through his street gangs. Anyone who had the balls to tell him where and when they could meet could well be someone he might want in his organisation. The black taxi indicates left, and then pulls into a narrow alley between two tall buildings. The ex-boxer whom he employs to be his cabbie turns round in his seat and slides back the partition glass.

'Right you are, Mr Slater,' he says, his grin showing a solid collection of gold teeth. 'Derry Street. Kensington Roof Gardens, back entrance.'

Slater checks out his crew positioned against the building that houses one of the biggest roof gardens in Europe. On a nod from the one closest to him, he opens the door of the cab and steps out into the street.

52

The building supporting the Kensington Roof Gardens is fucking massive. It used to be a department store back in the Victorian era. Now it's just robot offices for plastic people: men and women sitting at computer terminals spending half their time sending pointless information about themselves to other pointless people using emoticons, and non-reflection texting, and Facebook updates. Updates, for fuck's sake. How can you update emptiness?

But it's got a very pretty basement.

I follow the sewer system until I'm under the building. I've got most of the system schematics downloaded onto my tablet, but the people who built it labelled everything anyway, stencilling grid references into their tiny ceramic tiles.

The department-store-that-was had its own access to the sewer system, and getting into the basement is a doddle. Just a forgotten door with a mortise lock and hinges that are barely held by the tunnel wall's crumbling masonry. I put my rucksack on the floor and take out a noise sensor, a cordless hammer drill, and a tube of Concrex paste – the kind used by rock climbers. I drill two holes either side of the door and use the Concrex to fix in two lanyard anchors.

Once the concrete and glue mixture has hardened, I tie a steel-fibre strengthened rope through the anchors and use a short iron jemmy to pop the hinges. The steel door stays motionless for a moment, and then falls against the rope bracings. Slowly, I let out some slack in the rope, lowering the door down until it's resting on the ground in front of me. The sound sensor stays as dead as a tomb.

It's like *Mission Impossible* down here. I may have to steal some sunglasses. The fact that I learnt how to do all this stuff on YouTube from twelve-year-old warheads is not going to dampen my cool-squib.

I pack all my stuff back into my rucksack, shoulder it, and walk in. I'm in an old sump room in a part of the basement that no one's been in for ever, so there's no danger of the door being discovered any time soon. The building is just offices and stuff now so there's no real security. I open the door into the main basement a peek just because I'm feeling all spy-y, but really, there's no danger. Once you're inside a building the chances of being caught are tiny. So many cleaner slaves with not even language in common that, if I carry a duster, I won't even raise an eyebrow. And anyway, there's always some sad bugger working a midnight shift, and there are a million different companies here, so I could be anybody.

Although, because of my black nails, bleached hair, and fuck-off eyes I might not quite fit in as an office girl.

I walk up the south staircase, the motion lights clicking on and off as I pass, until I reach the roof.

53

Slater studies the man sat opposite him by the fountain. He has slicked-back black hair, a face so white it looks as if blood never reaches it, and long fingers with one painted nail. He is wearing a matt black suit with a collarless black cotton shirt, and smoking a distinctive Sobranie cigarette, with its black stem and gold filter. The man is grinning at him. Slater can see the tip of a prison tattoo on the man's neck, partially hidden by the shirt. Slater suspects it is a white rose; symbol for assassin within the Russian prison regime. Although the gardens are open to the public, Slater's crew keeps them at a discreet distance.

'You know,' says Constantine, blowing out a plume of white smoke, 'there are so few places to smoke in this city, yet so many Russians live here. It's really quite a conundrum.' He trails his finger idly in the fountain, his eyes never leaving Slater. Slater is put in mind of a snake. He wonders if he is supposed to be scared. He isn't. He knows all about snakes. He'd skinned enough in his time.

'Will you find her, Constantine?' Slater says flatly. He does not like the theatricality of the man in front of him; he finds it showy, and on some level feels this man is taking the piss out of him.

'Oh yes, I'll find her.' Constantine answers promptly, flicking his cigarette into the water, the hiss of it extinguishing hidden by the sound of the fountain. 'The money you're paying me, I'd find God himself and stop his clock if you wanted me to.' And then his eyes catch something behind Slater.

'In fact it will be a pleasure,' he adds, with a wide smile spreading across his face.

54

The Kensington Roof Gardens are split into three main themes. Spanish, with vine walkways, and fountains, and Moorish arches. Tudor, with hidden doorways that lead nowhere, hanging roses, and little knotted loveseats, and English woodland, complete with ponds, and four pink flamingos. There are even 60-year-old trees up here, their shallow roots spread under only 10 centimetres of soil. Did I mention the flamingos?

This place is madder than I am.

It's four o'clock in the morning when I step out onto the garden and I can see dawn cracking on the horizon. I stop and stare across London for a moment. There's a slight breeze, and the scents from all the different plants make me feel slightly nauseous. It's overloading me.

I turn it off and get on with why I'm here.

After my little soiree at the kebab shop I knew things would start to hot up, to move on. Once I'd decoded Bullet Eyes' mobile, which took about no time whatso-fucking-ever, I started to monitor where all the little drones were going.

Obviously the main man needed to contract an assassin to stop me screwing up his business completely.

An assassin. Please. All ice cold, showboat arrogance, and mafia muggledom.

Or maybe they'd get somebody good. Whatever.

All the worker bees started checking this place out yesterday; exits, safety zones, how to protect their leader if someone tried anything.

They talk on their phones and think they are talking to a mate in the same room. They use their little street codes and have absolutely no idea someone could be listening in and understanding everything they are saying. Someone should just give them a bottle and put them to bed, they're so infantile.

The meeting is going to happen tomorrow. Here.

Shame I'm not a different person, really, otherwise I would blow up the entire roof garden when they have their sit-down. It would look fabulous. A great big bomb taking out the building, debris raining down on the rich like it's the end of the world.

But I couldn't do it. It wouldn't be kind. The flamingos even have names.

I take off my rucksack, open it up, and get to work.

55

'Oh my.' Constantine is staring past Slater, who is suddenly surrounded by his crew, and being hustled out of his seat. Slater shakes them off to see what Constantine is staring at. Projected onto the wall behind him is the video footage from the tube, showing Tuesday slicing her way through his workforce. Dub music seeps out from hidden speakers, the cranked-up reverb making tiny disturbances in the pool. Slater can sense movement all around him as others also turn and stare, members of the public unsure what is happening. The sequence projected onto the wall rolls on. Tuesday walking down the carriage, two wicked blades in her hands. Always in motion. No doubt in her movements. No waste in her actions. Eventually she gets to the end of the carriage, and drops the card on one of the bodies and stares up at the CCTV camera, her face bright and shining.

'Very impressive,' says Constantine, lighting another cigarette and flicking the match into the pool. He turns to Slater and grins at him. 'She's fun, isn't she? For that little display I might even give you a discount.'

Slater is not listening. Slater is so fucked off he is ready to bite the head off the girl known as Tuesday. Not only is

148

she fucking up his business, but she is dissing him in front of the staff. He takes out his phone and punches in a number.

'Caleb? Meet me in my office . . . What?' He stares at the phone, a muscle corded in his neck, a pressure worm of barely restrained violence. 'Fucking yesterday. That's when!'

Constantine takes a leisurely drag from his cigarette and continues to admire the girl projected on the wall. Through the smoke veiling his face Slater can see he is still smiling.

56

Even with the hijab, DI Loss can tell the young woman has fuck-you hair. In fact, she has fuck-you everything: from the DIY tee shirt with its feminist symbol – a circle with a small cross beneath it, the inside filled with the crescent moon of Islam – to The Cure poster on the wall advertising the seventies' single, *Killing an Arab*; from the scuffed army boots and ripped 501 jeans to the Miss Undastood soundtrack ticking in the background; from the reinforced metal door with the hard-core deadlock bolt to the gorilla tape sealing all the cracks in the windows.

DI Loss and DS Stone are in an abandoned cinema off the main road in Hackney. Or at least Loss thought it was abandoned. Now he is not so sure.

'Nice picture.' Stone is looking at a framed poster on the wall depicting a picture of the Koran, stylized to resemble the cover of *The Hitchhikers Guide to the Galaxy*, underneath which is written:

'Don't panic: Everything's Islamic.'

The young woman in front of them lights a cigarette: a real cigarette, and Loss feels a momentary pang of jealousy.

'Ta,' she says, sucking down the smoke. 'Yours for 1200 quid.'

The woman is about twenty-five, and Loss is having trouble with cultural references. She has a strong Northern accent and, with the hijab, appears to be Muslim, but everything else about her screams rebel. There are several laptops in the room, all switched on, and there are books, papers, an old record player with vinyl discs scattered around it like fall-out, and clothes strewn everywhere. Although the place smells clean it is about as messy as it possibly can be and remain just the right side of an artwork. It reminds Loss of Suzanne's room, just before she left home.

'Have a seat, if you can find one,' says the girl, who tells them her name is Five. Loss perches precariously on the edge of a sofa filled with contemporary art magazines and sketch books. In one of the sketch-books he can see a half-finished drawing of a mosque, a line of turban-wearing Daleks leaving it. Loss knows he's in trouble. He looks enviously at Stone, who is leaning against a wall and appears to be enjoying herself. He clears his throat.

'So, er, Miss . . . ?' He raises his eyebrows, and the girl raises hers back at him. Stone makes a noise that Loss thinks is definitely verging on a snigger.

'Just "Five", mate,' the girl says. 'And to put you out of your misery, I've got an older sister called "Four", and a younger brother called "Six".' Five sits cross-legged on the floor, completely at home in her own space. Loss can't tell if he's being laughed at or tested.

'Last name?' he asks.

'Persian, and way too complicated to bother with,' Five replies merrily. 'Unless you're arresting me, and then you'll need a translator, cos I'll only speak Farsi.' Loss definitely feels he is being laughed at. Mainly by his DS. He decides to get straight to the point. He waves a hand at one of the laptop screens.

'Your blog, yes?' On the screen is a picture of the Crossquays Estate, obviously taken in the last few days, with, graffitied across the walkway in massive letters: 'Tuesday's Dreaming'. Five looks at the screen.

'Mine, yeah. Have you read it?'

'Yes we've read it. Really, that's why we're here.'

'No it's not.' Five stubs out her cigarette in a saucer by her knee, grinning up at him. The hijab has some writing on it, but Loss doesn't recognize the language it is written in.

'I beg your pardon?'

'I *said*, Inspector, "No it's not". Now I know I'm from Leeds and everything so you might find it hard to understand me, but surely my accent isn't that broad.' Five still hasn't stopped grinning at him. The hip hop coming from the speakers finishes, and is replaced with some early trance. Portishead, maybe. Or Tricky. Loss can't tell. His daughter would know. He sighs and gathers himself together.

'No. No it's not that broad. Where were you educated, Five?'

'Ah! That's more like it. Tell me, Inspector, is this official or unofficial?'

'As he's not technically on any case at the moment', Stone pipes up 'I'd say he's probably officially unofficial.'

'Excellent answer,' says Five, winking at Loss. 'Well in that case, I studied art at St Martin's College.'

'And since you graduated?'

'This and the other. Freelance work, mainly. Posters for charities and that. And my blog, of course.' Five lights another cigarette. She is not wearing lipstick, but her eyes are heavily made up.

'And before St Martin's?

Five appears to be the happiest person in the world. Her

152

grin gets even wider. DI Loss cannot believe how many teeth she has.

'University of life, mate.'

'According to your blog, you spent some time living on the street.'

'You know how it is, Inspector Loss. Trouble at home. Anonymity of the big city is an attractive alternative. Nothing new. Then I pulled myself together and went back to school. Good, eh?' In one fluid movement Five gets up from the floor and walks over to a flashing screen. She taps a few buttons on the keyboard and the screen goes blank. 'Sorry,' she says. Loss is beginning to wonder if there is something wrong with the muscles in her face, she is smiling too much. She doesn't explain why she is sorry. Neither does she explain why she shuts down her computer.

'Also, according to your blog, you've met the girl who calls herself Tuesday.' Five comes back and sits on the floor again, facing Loss.

'Poetic licence. I'm an artist, yeah? I interpret the world around me.'

'So are you saying that in fact you haven't met her.'

'Bang on.' There is a pause while everyone thinks about this, and then Stone says, 'And so what about the picture?' Five turns and looks at her. Loss thinks her smile fades just a little bit, but he can't be sure.

'What picture?'

'Well, you see, we asked our technical people to look at your blog, and they told us that it had another IP code embedded in it. A kind of door, so to speak. They said it led to a single internet page, which had a picture on it.'

'Oh, that picture,' says Five. 'I thought you meant the one of me eating a bacon sandwich.'

'No, we mean the one where you appear to be sitting on

the steps of some building with your arm around the girl who's brought London to the brink of civil war,' he continues.

Five looks at them for a while, and then says, 'Photoshop.'

'Photoshop,' says Loss, deadpan.

'Or Pixer. I can't remember which,' says Five.

'Pixer,' says Stone, disbelief buttering her voice.

'Pretty certain it was Photoshop, though.'

'So the picture's not real. Is that what you're saying?' Five spreads her hands.

'What's real? Is a painting real? A country?' She touches the corner of her hijab and gives it a little shake. 'A culture? I'm an artist, detectives. I try to create questions with lies. Not answers with truths.'

Loss hasn't got a clue what she is talking about. It must be obvious in his face because Five volunteers, 'Look, say I did know her, yeah, which I didn't by the way, It would have been when I lived on the street, and nobody had names and addresses, you get me? Even the me would have been a different me, if you see what I mean. What passes for knowledge, or history, only works if you all agree. It's an agenda, not a fact.' He feels he has wandered into a gender politics seminar by mistake. Any minute now he's afraid that Five is going to start waggling her fingers, creating air speech-marks. He leans forward, pinning the girl with his eyes. 'Dead people all over London, Five. That isn't an art project.' Five looks at him. She is not smiling now. Now she is staring at him as if he is an intrusion.

The same way that Lily-Rose had stared at him.

'*Everything* is an art project, Detective. Otherwise we're just animals.'

'Bad people are looking for her, Five. And if we found you, then they'll find you. And you really don't want to be found by them,' says Loss. Five gazes at him a little longer, and then picks up a Nexus off the sofa and tosses it to Stone without looking.

'Find it,' she says.

'What?'

'Find it. Find my blog.'

Stone looks at the screen and starts tapping. After a time she looks at her boss and says, 'It's gone.'

'Gone?'

'As if it was never there, sir.'

'Things aren't always what they seem, Inspector.' Five is smiling at him again. She points at the picture on the wall, of the Koran. 'There's a great bit in there about how to fly.'

'What, in the Koran?' Loss is confused by the seeming randomness of Five's conversation.

'No, in the other book. *The Hitchhiker's Guide to the Galaxy*. It says that it's easy to learn how to fly; that all you have to do is follow three easy steps. Climb high, throw yourself at the ground, and then miss.'

Loss is silent for a moment or two. 'Is there something you want to tell us, Five? Some reason why we're here?'

Five tilts her head at him as though he's an exhibit. 'Of course there isn't, Inspector. I wrote a blog as a piece of contemporary art is all, and then deleted it as another piece of contemporary art. It's just that, in between, you saw it and contacted me. The end.'

Out of the corner of his eye Loss sees Stone pick up something from the floor, and place the Nexus on a book tower. He feels as if he is on a conveyor belt with no understanding of where it's going. He feels old, without wishing he was younger. Mainly he feels as if he should be in bed. Or possibly hospital. He stands up.

'Well, thank you for your time, Five I'm not sure what it is you're doing, but I've enjoyed meeting you.'

'Oh, I'm sure we'll meet again, Inspector.' She gives her hijab another little tug. 'After all, we're everywhere.'

As they leave Stone turns. 'Are you any good?' she asks Five. 'At drawing?'

'Well, I tend to keep my talents locked firmly away in the Interworld, these days. Bye-bye, detectives,' says Five, smiling and closing the door quietly on them.

As they cross the road toward the tube station Loss mutters, 'What kind of question is that? Can you draw?' Stone takes a piece of chalk out of her pocket, and hands it to him. It is the object she picked up from Five's floor. It is somewhat larger than the type used in schools. It is the sort of chalk pavement artists might use.

'The kind of question a shit-hot detective might ask when they are going about their shit-hot detecting.'

57

Caleb flicks his cigarette butt out above the edge of the wooden balustrade and watches it spin down, over and over, until it hits the dusty cobbles below, skittering sparks as it impacts. He gazes at the people drinking below him for a moment, then sits back down. He is seated in one of the enclosed wooden galleries above St George's public house near London Bridge. His recent meeting with Slater squats unpleasantly at the front of his thoughts, focusing him on the task he has been ordered to undertake.

Across from him sits a mid-level drug dealer in a dark suit that appears to be Paul Smith, but in fact is a stitch-perfect copy made by Chinese sweatshoppers in a windowless basement in Hackney. *Of course it is*, thinks Caleb. Everything about the drug dealer is fake: from his automatic smile that switches on and off like a mousetrap, to the human disguise he is wearing; from his capped teeth to the slight mockney twang in his vowels.

Caleb has a second-class degree from a minor university, and a past littered with personal violence and first-class professional criminality. He looks thoughtfully at the drug-dealer. He is not a street dealer, but a middleman between the import gangs and the chain-cutters; the crews that chop and crop the product before it gets distributed to the gangs controlling the London boroughs. Working for Slater for five years as a liaison officer, his orders are to put out a bounty on Tuesday, and to offer a reward to anyone who can supply information leading to her whereabouts, or demise.

Drugs. Flesh. Power within the organisation. Whatever lever needs to be pushed.

Or pulled.

Right now, Caleb is sitting in the private gallery of the Old George coaching house, overlooking the courtyard where Chaucer used to drink, pulling the lever of a drug dealer, making Caleb, who has done his fair share of fucking people up, feel like an angel. Below them Londoners sit drinking at the wooden tables, trying to cool themselves in the muggy city heat. Caleb lifts his iced Becherovka, takes a small sip, then he lights another cigarette.

'Did you know this is the only galleried pub left in London?' He is looking past the drug dealer to the domed roof of a mosque poking out from behind a housing estate. The man in front of him says nothing, sips his water. 'In fact', he continues, using a fingernail to pick at the peeling white paint on the rail in front of him, 'it's even believed that Shakespeare used to drink here.' Caleb idly wonders if the paint under his nails contains lead.

'Who the fuck's Shakespeare?' the drug dealer asks. Caleb sighs while the man arranges his artificial face into an aspect of enquiry. He can't quite tell if the dealer, whose name is Lilt, is taking the piss or not. He suspects not. 'Nobody you need to worry about, mate.'

Caleb takes out the Galaxy Note from his inside jacket pocket and places it on the table in front of him. He does this quite slowly; he has been around criminals far too long to make any quick movements: removing things quickly from inside pockets can get you dead, fast. He taps a few buttons and brings up a picture of Tuesday. It is the still from the tube.

'Ever seen her?'

The dealer shakes his head.

'The man I work for wants to find her.'

'I bet he does. The way I hear it she's turned his boys into wall-whores.' Caleb looks confused and the drug-dealer's smile broadens. 'She fucks them just where they stand.' Caleb makes a note inside his head. The damage Tuesday has wreaked on the traditional power structures is beginning to break down the natural order of things. People are losing respect; are not as afraid as they should be. And people who are not afraid of one thing are soon not afraid of lots of things; soon become hard to control. Caleb dips a finger in his drink, and then draws an elaborate 'T' on the table, the moisture vaporising almost before he's finished.

'In many ways, of course, Sunshine, my boss Mr Slater, is your boss.'

'What do you mean?'

'We're not the fucking Russians, are we? We don't want to family-up and control every farthing. My boss likes to run his business in a few choice areas, and allow the economy, the sort of economy we're part of, to do the rest. Mr Slater doesn't want to spend his time importing product, parcelling product, then selling product. Product doesn't stoke his boat, except in the sense that it's criminal confetti. It gets fucking everywhere.' Caleb leans forward, channelling the dealer's attention towards him, to what he is saying. 'He's happy to leave the supply of all the pram toys to you, mate. It's about your fucking level.' The drug-dealer is barely controlling his anger. He is being disrespected. He is being reduced. *Good*, thinks Caleb. *Prick the skin and punch the piper.*

He goes on, holding up his right hand and ticking off his

points. 'But this girl, Tuesday, she's fucking up the drug train. She's fucking up the skin train. She's messing with the whole station and she needs to be stopped. I don't need to tell you what will happen to you if Mr Slater decides to let someone else move into the nursery, do I? Let one of your competitors have top spot? No, I thought not. Mr Slater, he wants this girl found. He wants anyone who has knowledge of this girl found. And you, my slimy fucking friend, are too far up the drug leash to slip back down to the collar and survive, you get me?' Caleb's eyes have gone from urbane businessman to lock-down psycho ward.

The dealer has dealt with some unhinged people in his days, but Caleb's doors seem to have come completely off the frame. He picks up the Galaxy and studies the picture. 'Look, man, she's a fucking ghost, ok? Half the crews I deal to are jumping at shadows, and the other half are quietly thanking fuck that they're not connected to Slater, you know? This girl is like a fucking Goth terminator, yeah? I mean she's a fucking storm.'

Caleb notices that the drug-dealer's hard-man, comedic, probably has a Canary Wharf glass fuckpad, mockney accent has slipped.

'I don't care what she is,' says Caleb, taking back the mini tablet and Bluetoothing the Tuesday data over to the drug-dealer's phone. 'She could be Satan's little lap girl as far as my boss is concerned. He just wants her found, and shut down. He wants anyone who has had contact with her deleted. You, my friend, are hard-wired into all the gangs in the city. You have access straight up their noses to their black little souls. We want you to spread the word.' Caleb leans forward and looks into his eyes. He holds nothing back.

Lilt sees the madness, the violence, the eager chaos that has allowed Caleb to survive in his position for the last five years. He sees it and is frightened. 'Yeah, man. All right. I'll put the word out, OK?'

Caleb tilts back and throws the remainder of his cigarette over the railings. 'Fabulous.' He pauses, looks down at the Londoners below, and then looks back at the drug-dealer . . .

'Well what the fuck are you still doing here then?'

58

Lily-Rose is packing her life away. Her mother, in between bouts of uncontrollable shaking, is packing right next to her.

The night before, Lily-Rose had received an invitation to a chat room on a site that didn't even have a name. She could tell it was from Tuesday by the way the invitation was framed. There she found details of a bitcoin wallet through Armory; internet currency with no borders or traceability. It contained enough money to make her feel physically sick. All it required for the funds to be transferred to a bank account of her choice was for her to tap in a password. Enough money for them to leave everything behind and run. There was also a note, and a list of instructions. Lily-Rose read it through once, printed out the instructions, details of the bitcoin account, and then pressed the button that would erase all trace of the meeting. She then removed the hard-drive from her computer and put it in the oven, and switched it on. Then she went and woke her mother.

'They're coming for us, Mum. The people who raped me. The people who *paid* the people who raped me. They're going to shut Tuesday down, and they're going to try to use us to get to her.'

Her mother contemplates her from the bed: her daughter who has been so abused and whom she has been unable to protect, the daughter who seems to live in a world accelerating beyond her understanding. All she says is 'When?'

'Now. We need to pack now. I've phoned for a minicab.'

59

I used to think about killing myself.

Different times. Different ways.

When I was really young I thought I could just hide in the closet and be safe. Like Narnia.

When I was a little older I tried really hard to stop breathing. Just go to sleep forever.

Then, after the baby started growing inside of me, and I knew I had to leave, I stopped thinking about dying. Stopping. I just started to think about keeping her safe.

Away.

Hidden.

And then when it all went to the fucking wall I started thinking about killing myself again.

That's the difference. That's the difference between the robots and the humans. The robots would never think of killing themselves. Wouldn't even cross their minds.

Nothing's their fault. They can never blame themselves or take responsibility for anything. And anybody else's suffering is a meter against which to measure their power.

Sex. Drugs. Guns. Cars. Souls. It's all just product. Like the perfect capitalist robots they are, all they can do is consume.

Destroy.

Use up and then throw away.

Slash and burn.

Well that's all right.

I don't care if I live or die anymore. All I'm here for now is the movement.

The dance.

The choice.

And they chose me.

60

DI Loss is losing track of which reality he's living through.

After leaving the cinema, DS Stone went back to Savile Row to file a report on their meeting with Five. To attempt to make sense of her motives, and slot what they've learned about her into what they know about Tuesday. They definitely had a connection. In fact, Loss had the feeling that she was almost laughing at them.

But of course, at present he's not in control of the case, only an adviser. Or worse, someone not to be trusted.

There was a time, before Suzanne's murder, when he was fairly certain he had some sort of grasp on the world he occupied, however tenuous. Ever since her death, however, his disconnection has been permanent. It has defined him. Given him structure. Only as an observer, even of himself, was he able to function on a day-to-day basis without breaking down. He was able to give the impression that he was alive, and stagger through without screaming.

But now someone has re-animated the corpse of his daughter, and is making her walk round the basement of London. Tuesday, for reasons unknown, is taking a giant pin and ramming it into his heart and soul again and again.

This morning he was informed that, because of as yet unknown connections he might have to the case, he was being side-lined even further. Benched. Taken off the investigation; given open-ended leave. Yes, he was being retained as an advisor, but effectively in a civilian capacity.

And then he received a phone call from the Commander, who explained that, in the present climate, it would be prudent for DI Loss not to come in at all, that, as he seemed to have a direct link to the girl, Tuesday, it would not be appropriate for him to have access to information pertaining to the case

That was that. Tuesday had somehow, impossibly, stolen his daughter's identity, despoiled her memory, and now lost him the only thing that was keeping him sane.

And he doesn't know why.

Loss sleepwalks round the streets of central London, trying to make sense of the lights, and the smells, and the noise. Trying to.convert the puppet show around him into something with meaning. But he just drifts through the crowds, and the fug, and the mortar of living, and sees nothing.

Nothing but ghosts.

He is pulled back to himself by his phone ringing. It's DS Stone.

'I'm off the case,' he informs her. 'Too much of a security risk.'

'Too much of a self-indulgent old bastard, more like. I don't give a damn if you're off the case or not. Lily-Rose has gone missing.'

Loss stops; becomes a rock in the river of the street.

'What? When?'

'I've just left there. I called round with some follow-ups; see if there'd been any movement. The flat looks as if it's been taken apart with a hatchet. There's no sign of Lily-Rose or her mum, but there's no blood, so I'm hopeful they left before whoever did it arrived. Are you still there?'

Loss tries to get his mind to catch up. He has so many things going on in his head that his thought processes are weeds.

'Yeah, I'm still here. So are you saying someone came for her, but she was already warned?'

'Looks that way, Sherlock. Anyway, their flat is a deadzone, and no one knows anything. What are you doing now?'

'Nothing. as I said, I'm . . .' Stone didn't give him time to finish.

'Good, because I'm on my way to meet the only expert I could find on the lost city of underground London, and I want your help.'

'Why?'

'Well, for one thing, because you're not technically on the case I can be really, really rude to you; calling you "Sherlock".'

Loss sighs deeply.

'And?'

'And? You need an *and*? And this expert I've dug up. The one who knows all about the secret underground network?'

'Yes?'

'When I spoke to him, and mentioned to him the name of my boss, i.e., you, he asked if you were related to Suzanne Loss.' The detective closes his eyes. Behind his lids are tiny pinpricks of burning thought, waiting to be connected up. 'When I confirmed that you were, he wanted to convey to you his belated condolences. It appears that he knew your daughter.'

61

Constantine does not have a last name. If he ever did he has kept it to himself. He is what is known in the underworld as a wet-smith: a man for hire when it comes to the cessation and disposal of human beings.

He is currently sitting in a shitty flat in King's Cross, recently vacated by a prostitute. He has a laptop open in front of him, and for the last few hours has been absorbing all the information that he can find on the girl known as Tuesday. This includes a large selection of media reports, both legitimate and underground, along with stuff from all the social network sites. He also has the footage from the train, and the link sent to DI Loss's computer. He has the audio from the phone conversation outside the kebab shop between his client and the girl, and he has set up a program mapping all references to Tuesday, or the weapons she used, or any internet footprint she might have made. He also has a constant feed of all the information gathered by the street crews that Caleb set in motion. He is very good at what he does. He has already given Lily-Rose's address to Slater's men.

Constantine sits in his chair, in the crappy flat that smells of broken dreams and twisted love, electronically thumbing through the city, until eventually he turns his computer off, packs it away in its Pelican hard case, and leaves, heading across the road, and into King's Cross tube station.

On the tube he is amused to see a 'Tuesday' graffiti tag. He has spotted them all over the city since he arrived. He gets off at Knightsbridge, and enters Number One, Hyde Park. The cold-eyed security guard in a suit and bowler hat takes his card and makes a phone call. He is searched, his weapons expertly found and removed, and then he is escorted to the lift and accompanied up to the top floor. He is walked to the door of his client, who opens it and nods at the security guard. The guard inclines his head and withdraws politely, never taking his hand out of his jacket pocket, or off the gun therein.

Constantine grins at his employer and says,

"'Dear oh dear, what did you do three years ago to piss this girl off so royally?'

Slater glares at him, saying nothing. 'Because up until three years ago, Tuesday didn't exist.'

62

I'm getting ready now.

I've restocked all my supplies out of the Oxford Street shops, and gone round all my cribs making sure everything's ready. I've checked out the feed from the door at the British Museum and seen all the action going on there. Well done, boys and girls.

It shouldn't be too long until everything moves underground. I just need to give them one more little push. I lie down on my bunk and listen to the *World Service*.

Not really listen to it, but let it carry my weight for a while.

Lily-Rose should be on her way to her new home by now. I hope she doesn't hate me. I didn't use her like the gang boys used her, but I still used her.

Still used her to stir things up.

Used her to break things down.

I wonder who'll reach me first: Detective Inspector Loss with his guilt and his questions; the police with their standard issues and their righteousness; or the bad guys, with their lust for revenge and their dreams of girl torture?

Me, I don't fucking care.

63

'Aldwych Tube Station, originally called Strand Tube Station, was opened in 1907, and closed in 1993. In all that time the original lifts were still in use. It was built on the site of the Royal Strand Theatre, which was demolished in 1905. The platform we are standing on is ninety-two feet and six inches below street level. It is interesting to note that the station itself is built on one of the biggest plague pits in London. Indeed, when it was being constructed the workmen commonly saw the ghosts of rotting victims shuffling around the site. So if any of you ladies see something awful shambling around, feel free to hang onto my arm.'

'What bloody century are you living in?' DS Stone mutters under her breath. She and DI Loss are standing with a group of tourists being shown round one of London's 'hidden' tube stations. To get here, they have had to walk down a high, spiral staircase containing more metal steps than DS Stone would have thought possible .. While the guide entertains the group, the two detectives look around. With the tiny ceramic tiles and oak panelling; the whole place has a feel of quietly-collapsing gentility. The door to the station office opens and a smartly dressed man in his early thirties comes out.

'Detectives Loss and Stone?'

The police officers nod. 'How did you spot us?'

'Well, you don't have massive cameras strung round your necks for a start,' he addresses his response to Loss, indicating the tourists receding down the platform in front of them. 'And you just insulted my tour guide in language which I believe is standard police patois,' he tells Stone. 'Please, step into my office.'

As the three of them walk away from the tour party, the man in front of them looks over his shoulder and says, almost apologetically, 'Plus. I can see your daughter in you.' For a moment, Loss thinks he is going to fall over, but he recovers, and makes it through the door into the young man's office and onto a seat. There's a blade fan gently spinning in the ceiling, and the room is occupied – that's the only word Loss can think to use – by a massive mahogany desk with a green leather top, upon which sits a monitor relaying the activity on the station platform. There is a standard lamp in the corner of the room, and an umbrella stand, Stone is pleased to note, containing an umbrella. She thinks of making a comment about the amount of rain falling underground, but doesn't.

'Colin Stevens,' he says, holding out his hand. Stone shakes it.

'How did you know my daughter?' Loss grips the proffered hand a little more than perhaps he needs to. The young man's smile fades.

'I used to work with her at the hospital. Please let me say how sorry I am, Inspector. It was a sad loss. She was very much liked and admired, you know.'

Loss feels tears pricking his eyes, so he bites the inside of his cheek. 'What was your role at the hospital?'

'I was a therapist, Inspector. Part of the patient outreach team. I specialized in alienation problems and depression.'

'How come you're here? This is a long way from being a counsellor.'

'Therapist,' Stevens corrects him. 'Oh, I don't know. Half the tourists who come down here only seem to be able to view the world through a camera lens.'

'Except it isn't a lens, is it?' Stone asks.

'I beg your pardon?'

'Well it's all digital these days, isn't it? No lens involved.'

'Quite.'

'So how come you're here?' Stone repeats the question. Stevens has a look of someone unsure if he's been reprimanded. Stone is unmoved.

'I've always loved the Underground. Ever since I was a kid and we first moved to London I've been fascinated by the stations and the trains. Did you know that originally each line had its own look, its own individual architecture? Right down to the colour of the bricks.' He sits back in his chair. 'Plus, I discovered that I wasn't a very good therapist.' He pauses, and considers the detectives for a second. 'Sorry. It's difficult to explain. All the work I did before becoming attached to Charing Cross, well, it just didn't prepare me.' He fixes his attention on Loss. 'Before I took the post at the hospital where your daughter worked, I was stationed in the suburbs. At the other end of the equation, you might say. I never expected to . . .'

Loss sighs. 'Ok, sir. Tell us about the Secret Underground.'

Stevens seems to lighten with the new direction of their questioning. 'Oh, it's not just the Underground. I mean the Underground is fascinating. All the lines that are still there, a whole forgotten transport network . . .'

Stone breaks in, 'And are they connected to the present one? I mean, could you get from one to the other?'

'Oh, yes. Many of the stations we use now were built to replace the old ones, because as new lines, new outposts,

174

were added it was cheaper, and less structurally problematic, to create new stations above the deep Victorian ones, than to demolish and replace. But yes, the old stations are still there. Sometimes only a door away, in the side of a walkway, or sometimes just a few metres below, connected by a staircase similar to the one you came down today.' The flickering flames of a true fanatic are dancing in his eyes. 'And those stations have the old lines, no longer used, but perfectly navigable! Miles and miles of them down here.'

'You said not just the Underground,' prompts Stone.

'No indeed. There's the Royal Mail mini railway, for a start.'

'I'm sorry?'

'Royal Mail has its own underground train network. It was used to move all the mail around central London, allowing it to cope with the twice-daily delivery service they used to offer.'

'What, its own mail trains under London?' says Stone. Loss turns and looks at her.

'Even I knew that. They had to have it for the second delivery.'

'The *second* delivery?'

'Yes. Amazing, isn't it?' Stevens interjects. 'Then there are all the bunkers, and all the tunnels from private houses and department stores . . .'

'And museums,' adds Loss.

'And museums, yes. And then, during the War, many of these tunnels were connected up in case of bombing or invasion. Did you know it was possible for the Prime Minister to walk from the War Office to Oxford Street without once coming to the surface?'

'Amazing,' says Stone dryly.

'Indeed. In fact, many people living in London houses aren't even aware that there are cellars beneath them, and tunnels leading from the cellars. After the Blitz, when much of London was rebuilt, these things were just, well, sealed off and forgotten. Plans were lost. *People* were lost. Things were forgotten or hidden for another time.' Stevens pauses for a moment, contemplating the past, and then continues with renewed enthusiasm. 'And then there's the sewer system, and the old river sluices, and the smugglers' pubs, and so on and so on.'

He reaches under his desk and starts rummaging in drawers. 'I've been writing a book all about it.'

As he brandishes a detailed hand-drawn map at them Stone tries to keep him on track. 'So are you saying it's possible for our girl to have got off the train at Embankment, say, and then walk through the network of disused tunnels to wherever she wants to be without ever coming to the surface?'

'Oh easily. There are tunnels everywhere. To the stations, yes. But also to the big shops in Oxford Street. To all the old hotels. Government buildings. Hospitals. Churches. If you wanted to, and were determined enough, you could set yourself up and live underground for years.'

And then all the lights snap on in DI Loss's head. His mind palace lights up like Christmas.

'So food, bedding . . . ?'

'The old department stores all have tunnels connecting to the network. Had to, so goods could be safely moved around during the War.'

'Internet? Wi-Fi?'

Stevens thinks for a moment. 'A lot of the stations are Wi-Fi-enabled. You'd have to ask someone technical, but I shouldn't think it's too difficult to set up some sort of relay system, if you could source the power.'

Loss murmurs to himself: 'Christ. She's been living underneath us. Not just using it to get around. It's her world.'

176

The two detectives look at each other, the implications of what they have just learnt fizzing between them

'We need to go.' They get up, thanking Stevens.

As he leads them to the stairs, he says, 'You know, Inspector, I was genuinely sorry to hear of Suzanne's murder. She was very much loved around the hospital.'

Loss isn't sure what to do with the man's sympathy. 'Thank you. We'd grown apart a little, and I wasn't fully aware of her friends. It's nice to know she was so well liked.'

Stevens smiles at him. 'Well it wasn't just me, it was everyone really. And not just at the hospital. All the kids at the refuge loved her too.'

'What refuge?'

'The one off Charing Cross Road, do you know it? That's what I meant by the other end. I was used to seeing where they'd run from. Not to. The refuge for teenage runaways. It was because of what happened there that I left my job.'

64

I never think of my body as becoming something; only staying the same. Only not becoming something else.

Too big.

Too weak.

Fertile.

I turn on my laptop and set up a program to search for any new reference to me. Actually what I'm searching for is any *old* reference to me that's been newly uncovered, but all that's out there is what's happening now. I shut it off and fire up the *World Service*, lie back down and let myself drift away to the shipping forecast. I may have no fucking idea what they are talking about, but it makes me feel safe and warm. I reckon when I die this is what I'll hear; a beautiful voice telling me which way to go.

Or maybe just screams.

Sleepy time now. Shut down. Night night.

When I resurface, the radio is talking about penguins. I listen for a while, taking in the ticks of the station. I can hear the scuttle of rats, and just below hearing, I can feel the slight changes of pressure that indicate the tubes are running. I get off my cot and power up my laptop, opening the window that monitors all the mobile activity of the drones.

Oh dear.

I click to a London news channel and there it is. The Roof Gardens, formally Kensington Roof Gardens. The reporter is standing outside the ground floor entrance, underneath the big brass 99s that sit above the doorway. There is a pop-up box in the corner of the screen showing people running about in confusion. The resolution is terrible. It is obviously footage from somebody's mobile phone. Really, there's no excuse these days. Every mobile phone should have a hi-resolution camera. Ones that don't, the phone companies are just dicking you about. The camera is shaking so much it wouldn't surprise me if one of the flamingos has filmed it. But bad as the pictures are, as stuttered as the images in the corner of the screen come to us, we can clearly see Mr Man being dragged away by some of his drones.

Honestly, between the shuddering camera, the top-notch dub music, and the video wanksta waving his gun about in confusion, I feel the urge to pull up a director's chair and change my name to Quentin Tarentea-time. What a bunch of posturing pricks. I turn off the news and go back to hearing about the penguins. I take off my beach shoes and put on my hiking boots. I wear something on my feet when I'm asleep in case I have to wake up running, and the DMs are just too big. The beach shoes are lightweight but with a solid sole, so they do the job perfectly. I'd wear crocs, but I haven't quite given up on life yet.

I go to my workbench. On top of it are a portable stove and a saucepan I borrowed from the department store. I switch on the stove and there is a satisfying whoosh as the gas ignites when I flip the Zippo I took off the Z-boy outside the nightclub. I close the lid of the lighter and put it in a box on the floor with all the other lighters.

They'll be really gunning for me now. I've embarrassed them. They had their little meeting, like they're James Bond or the mafia or something, and I walked right in and slapped them in the face.

Right through his little army. Right up to him and his assassin and gave them a hug.

He must really hate me now. I bet he's got his drones searching all over London for me, tearing it apart. I bet he's got every low-life drug fuck-up and street tally girl scanning the lanes trying to eyeball me. I bet he's tearing his hair out, trying to get information about where I am.

Except he hasn't got any hair.

I tap out a message on my tablet, and send it to one of the drone's phones. I do it in text-speak so they can understand it. If I wrote it in proper English they wouldn't have a clue what it said. I send it via a free text app rather than SMS, and beg them to let me in to their gang.

Or at least let me have some free coke or some smack.

I tell them that I've seen this girl, the one they're looking for. I tell them that she's just sitting there, like she's waiting for someone, and if they want her, come and get her, but remember that it was me who told them where she was and I want paying.

I make up a name and sign off. I do a couple more on the same theme then store them ready to send. I weigh out an amount of potassium nitrate and sugar, mix them together, and throw them in the pan. Potassium nitrate used to be given to prisoners in their tea to reduce their sex drive. It also used to be a main ingredient in gunpowder. Now you can buy it in most garden centres as fertilizer.

Or you can steal it from a large department store.

Once the mixture has turned brown, the sugar caramelizing and the whole thing becoming syrupy, I take it off the heat and let it cool. From under the desk I bring out a few cardboard tubes I've saved from the centre of toilet paper rolls and use black Gaffa tape to seal up one end. I love Gaffa tape. I love the sound it makes when you pull a length off. A kind of ripping sound. On the radio the penguins have been replaced by a programme about plants growing round an active volcano. Apparently these plants have such a high level of silicates in them they should not exist.

I fill the tubes with the gloopy substance and use a palette knife to level it off. Then I seal the ends with some more Gaffa tape, and stick a fuse in. I took the fuses from some fireworks.

Actually I took the fireworks as well, then just cut the fuses in half.

I never could resist a pretty firework.

After everything's cooled down I pack all the stuff I need in my rucksack, set up all my alarms, and head out, a ghost girl in an underground city made for ghosts.

To get into Seething Lane Gardens you have to go down four stone steps, worn concave by the feet of the dead. It's a medieval street next to a medieval church in a medieval town. St Olave's has three skulls above its entrance, just so you know it's not fucking about. It also has the tomb of the original Mother Goose.

I love this city. It's a thousand years old with more blood in its mortar, more history in its stone, and more stories in its streets than anywhere else I can think of.

It's been half an hour since I sent the texts so I imagine the gang boys should be here any time now. I'm sitting in a cherry tree, hidden by white, genetically modified forever-blossom. I've got my rucksack strung over a broken branch just above me and I'm looking down through the petals at the street below. I'm loving the view.

Seething Lane attracts a lot of tourists. It's one of the few remaining streets that survived from the Great Fire of London, and people enjoy coming here and feeling all olde-worlde, as if they're living in a film or something. People of all nationalities are walking backwards and forwards taking pictures and videos of themselves and the street. Really, the amount of ambience and culture they're soaking up, they could just take one photo of themselves against a white background and Photoshop in the scenery. Still, you never know, there might be something interesting to film a little later on.

I spot a few city boys and girls having a quiet toke on their crack pipes. They're not too difficult to pick out; expensive suits on ghosts waiting to hatch. Since the introduction of e-cigarettes some clever entrepreneur has made an adaptation for our little drug addicts. You put your rock in and suck away and no one can really tell the difference.

At least, not until you fall over dead.

I stare at the entrance to the street. It's not a real street anymore. More like a mock-up. It's like a street island: it leads nowhere and comes from nowhere. A street shipwreck, with me in its mast. A boy walks into the street. He's got on Diesel jeans, £300 sneakers and a Weird Fish hoodie. He's talking into an android phone, and he's scanning the street as though he's the fucking Terminator. I nearly fall out of the tree with fear. He sits on a bench. The woman who's sitting there takes one look at him, gets up and leaves. Smart girl.

He's looking for the informant, or for me, or for trouble, and he's looking hard. The tourists are moving around him like he's a disease. I bet he's loving it. Actually, maybe I'm being hasty. Maybe he's a nice boy. Maybe he's looking for Wally. I see he hasn't bent his right leg when he sits down and guess he's probably got an iron bar down his trousers.

Maybe not a nice boy, then. Maybe a fuck up merchant.

Five more come in and start working their way up the street. The assassin's not with them. He'll be doing something cool and assassiny somewhere else. I haven't set up any cameras because every tourist is a filmographer these days, ready to upload straight to the inter-grid and on into a million brains.

I don't have to wait for them to start something, this time. Just turning up is enough. I watch as one of them grabs a little Goth girl by the chin and stares hard into her face. She's Japanese, and could be anything from seventeen to thirty years old. He pushes her away and she falls to the ground.

All the tourists are heading for the street exit, being clocked by a couple of hard boys guarding the arch above the stone steps. Once the street is empty they start checking everywhere, looking for the informant, or me. After a while they stop trying to look hard and kind of mill about, not knowing what to do next.

Jesus fucking Christ. Here I am, sitting in a bloody tree, on a street walked down by Samuel Pepys, looking down on a bunch of rape machines disguised as hurt robots, wondering how I can make them notice me without actually shouting 'Cooee!'

Fuck it.

I pull on my extremely cool aviator goggles and face mask. I light the fuse and throw down my first smoke bomb.

Tally-ho.

65

'Well, I hope you still feel special, even though she didn't send it to *you* this time.'

DI Loss and DS Stone are watching footage from Seething Lane Gardens on the TV set up in the incident room. They are sitting at the back, no longer central to the investigation. Since Suzanne's DNA was uncovered on the cigarette butt found outside Candy's, Loss has been in a box; a spectacle for speculation.

The viewpoint of the street is from the entrance. It has been taken by a tourist and the quality is just about as good as the BBC. Loss guesses it has been taken by a Japanese tourist, and then wonders if he is being racist. It shows a group of hooded youths, some carrying iron bars, milling around, looking both menacing and bewildered at the same time. Nothing happens for a few moments, then a slight movement of something spinning, and then thick white smoke starts spilling out of the ground, as though it's just been opened up and steam is coming out.

'She's in the tree,' Stone mutters. The youths stare at the smoke bomb as though it just magically appeared there. Slowly, they edge towards it and then jump back when another one appears a few feet away.

'She's in the tree, fuckheads. Jesus. Did these boys forget their brains or what?' Loss takes his eyes off the screen and looks at the detective by his side, possibly for the first time. At least, properly.

'Is everything all right, Stone?'

'Sir?'

Stone is transfixed by the action on the TV. He is grateful for the 'sir'. His role, somewhere between expert witness and involved party, has thrown his identity crisis into overdrive. The fact that Stone is treating him just the same is helping him stay on the ground.

'Only I've noticed that you seem to be swearing quite a lot and I wondered if everything's all right?' When she silently turns and looks back at him for a moment, Loss wonders if he has crossed a line. He can't get his daughter out of his mind, and he has an urge to hit something and go to sleep at the same time. He suspects he's having some form of breakdown. Then Stone smiles at him. 'No sir. Everything's fine.' Loss can't work out the sentence. Does that mean everything is not fine, but she'll be all right? Or everything is fine and stop asking? He stops thinking about it as another three smoke bombs hit the ground and the gang of hooded youths start coughing.

And then one of them screams and falls to the ground.

'Here we go again,' Loss whispers, reaching into his pocket for a cigarette that isn't there. A ghost cigarette.

185

66

I'm not very good with the throwing knife: all I did was smash him in the head with the hilt. Oh well. There go my cool points. I light the fuse that connects up to the fireworks then jump down to the ground. As I land, the tree above me explodes. Twenty exhibition fireworks all going off at once makes quite a spectacle. The bad boy nearest me looks up and I slash him across the throat with my knuckle knife, circa 1914 vintage. While he's gurgling away I kick the next one in the crotch and start running. There's swearing and spluttering all around me and I can hear the sound of police sirens a few streets away. I pick up the throwing knife. The drone I threw it at is still on the ground. I stick it in his thigh and move on. There's sparks raining down everywhere, mingling with the smoke, and the screams, and the coughing.

Lucky I'm wearing my mask and goggles really, isn't it? There are two left in front of me so I start running towards them.

67

'Bloody hell, it's *Apocalypse Now*.' The team gathered in the police incident room have gone quiet as they watch the carnage unfold on the screen. It's hard to see anything clearly after the tree explodes, even with the expensive equipment that was used to film it. The whole scene is wreathed in white swirling smoke and shimmering crackling stars.

'I'm pretty sure I saw a rocket,' quips Stone. Loss ignores her, concentrating on the figure running around the gang members. In the oversized goggles her face could be an insect's, or some alien being's.

'One swipe and she'll be down. That's all it would take. Why would she risk it?' he mutters.

'Well that's obvious,' Stone says. 'She's laughing at them. She's making them look ridiculous in the eyes of their peers.' On the screen, two of the gang boys dive to the ground as Tuesday runs towards them. 'Plus, according to our friend Drake, she thinks she's dead already. Who could possibly touch her?'.

68

I run past the tourists and into the church. Outside, the police car screeches to a stop. Very macho. Very Flying Squad. Perhaps I should swoon.

I love St Olave's. I run through the church and out through the cemetery arch. The cemetery is exactly as you'd hope it to be; all Gothy, and sinister, and crumbly.

In fact it's so Gothy that Charles Dickens used it in one of his books, renaming it St Ghastly Grim. Nice one, Charles.

I lift the grate hidden next to a plague grave and drop down into the sewer system. Since the church got bombed in the Second World War the sewer system round here has been replaced with a newer one, but the structures of the old one are pretty much intact.

Enough to get me back into the main system, and allow me to lose myself below London, anyway.

Bye bye police.

Bye bye thieves

Bye bye.

69

'Last year, according to government records, only six children under the age of seventeen were found living on the streets in central London. They were, of course, immediately placed under the ward of the city, found shelter, and put onto a programme of rehabilitation.' The man in front of DI Loss and DS Stone looks tired. Not tired as if he's ready to drop; tired, as though he's ready to throw it all in and sod off. They are all cramped together in a small office above a sex shop in a tiny lane off Brewers Street in Soho. The room reeks of decay and mildew and the walls appear to be sweating. The window is grimy, filtering the neon lights, making them almost pretty. Behind the man is an A5 poster of a naked girl kneeling, facing away from the camera but looking back over her shoulder. The photograph has a sleazy sheen to it. Underneath is the caption 'Your daughter, your partner, your friend: never an object.' The girl's lips are parted slightly. Loss feels sick inside.

'Not seen that one on the tube adverts,' says Stone, nodding at the poster. The man turns round and looks at it.

'No,' he says, turning back to them, barely registering their presence. 'Bit too hard-hitting for the Mayor, that one.'

After all the media interest in the homeless, and the video footage of Tuesday, the new CIC has sent Stone to glean information from the various agencies that dealt with homelessness in central London.

'So there are no children living on the street at present? All the homeless are over eighteen?'

'Consenting,' Stone adds, still looking at the picture. The smartphone sitting on the desk beeps discreetly. Loss takes in the desk and thinks it has not just seen better days, but better years. It looks as though it has been liberated from a skip. So does the man. He has greying black hair, and his eyes are whisky-veined and look as if they have seen far too much, for far too long.

'No, as you are no doubt well aware, I'm not telling you that. All I'm telling you is what the government says.' The man picks up his phone and reads the IM scrolling across the screen like ticker-tape.

'So how does it work then? What's the deal?' Stone leans against the wall. Loss grimaces at the thought of what her shoulder might be touching. 'Where do the stats come from?'

'Every year Westminster Council commissions an audit of all the homeless in Soho, Chinatown, and the surrounding areas.' The man does not look at them as he tells them this. He continues to read the texts on his phone. 'This comprises two teams going out on one specified night at 11 p.m. and checking the doorways, subways, and such and doing a head-count. If they think an individual looks under eighteen they are reported and taken in to the appropriate juvenile authorities. They do not, however, check the bedsits for sofa surfers, the abandoned buildings where the junkies squat, the container hotels, or the myriad other places that technically don't count as "the street".' The man stops speaking and looks up at them. 'Basically, it's the three monkeys.'

The man's name is Tam, and he works for an outreach

190

charity for the homeless. He is obviously severely overworked, minimally paid, and very angry. The DI doesn't blame him. It's hard to watch a city eat people up, and then pretend that nothing is wrong.

'So it *is* possible for an underage girl to be living on the streets, then?' Stone asks, with just a hint of sarcasm in her voice.

'Oh yes, depending on your definition. I could take you to brothels with 16 to 18-year-old illegal immigrants, boys and girls, who are working for nothing except the promise of the return of their passports. I could take you to a house across the river where 14-year-old Somali girls, whose parents have sold them, are being rented out as maids. It's not so much as it was fifteen years ago, with Cardboard City. It's more hidden now.'

'Cardboard City?' Stone finally takes her eyes off the picture on the wall. Tam looks at her. 'How old are you? OK. Cardboard city was near Waterloo Station, in all the old underpasses there: around 250 homeless people living in tiny cubes made out of cardboard boxes; runaways, ex-cons, mental patients, rubbing together in a happy Third World wonderland of drugs, rape, and random violence.'

'It's where the IMAX is,' says Loss, wearily. 'Tell me, Mr Tam, what's a container hotel?'

'Old shipping containers put on pre-development land, owned by gang lords masquerading as human beings, and stuffed full of street kids who are then used to run drugs around the city,' says Tam, reading a new message on his phone. 'It's a win-win situation. Less homeless on the streets, with no squatting damage to public buildings. But all this is by the by. What you really want to know about is Tuesday, yes?'

'According to the media interviews with the homeless kids, they all say they knew the girl known as Tuesday,' says Stone.

'I've seen the news, yes. Tuesday the street warrior. Tuesday the ghost.' Tam looks up from his phone to DI Loss. 'Tuesday the policeman's daughter. I'm sorry, Inspector Loss. I never met her myself, but those in the field talk very highly of Suzanne.' There's something slightly strange about the way that Tam is looking at him, but Loss can't put his finger on what it is. Outside the room the neon is fractured by strobes from a passing police car, shuttering his concentration. For a moment, he can't distinguish between the sirens outside and the sirens from three years ago. The before-sirens and before-strobe lighting that ripped his life into jagged little strips of pain, and loneliness, and guilt.

Tam begins counting off organisations on his fingers. 'Streets of London. Railway Kids. Thames Reach. Crisis. There a dozen or more charities working the London streets. And that's not including the hospitals and the faith agencies. There's the old-school homeless; the mentally ill who have slipped through a very ragged net; the armed forces burn-outs with battle fatigue syndrome who stagger the streets of London but see the streets of Basra; there's the benefit losers who can no longer afford their council flats, who've handed over their kids to the state and are trying to drink away the memory; and all the immigrants who aren't even entitled to benefits, stuck in the cogs of a system that's not kept up with how the world is now.' Tam's fingers have stopped counting and are clamped tight to his phone. Loss wouldn't be surprised if he threw it through the filthy window. He is not telling them anything they didn't already know, but he is saying it with such venom that it's like hearing it for the first time.

'And there's the runaways,' Stone adds.

Tam looks at her. 'Yes. And there are the runaways.'

'You are aware of the refuge centre my daughter worked at?' Loss asks. Tam nods. 'Colin Stevens, whom I believe you *did* know, said the refuge dealt with teenage runaways. He also said that a high proportion of the girls were pregnant.'

Stone is concentrating on the wall poster again.

'The more you look, the more you see, yes?' says Tam. 'Notice the old track marks on her left arm? And look at her eyes. No hope left. A whole book of sorrows.'

'The runaways?' prompts Loss again.

Tam sighs and plays with his phone for a while, and then looks at the two detectives.

'Some kids get kicked out of their homes, and just don't have the skills to sort themselves out. First they sleep on friends' sofas, jumping from flat to flat. Sofa surfing, it's called. And then eventually . . .' he shrugs his shoulders. 'They don't. They feel they've used up their welcome and they just come to the capital and disappear.' He puts down his phone.

'And then some get sexually abused, or suffer physical violence, either from a new parental figure, or a long-standing situation that the victim is now old enough to walk away from. Or there's bullying at school, or by a sibling. Or there's drugs and alcohol in the home. Or neglect. Or psychological problems.' Tam sighs, then looks up at them. 'Dr Stevens could probably give you a lecture. The whole system is not hermetic. There's not one agency that has a handle on when they leave home to when they end up with pavement sores and alcohol dependence. I only really deal with the practical problems once they're here. And once they're here, the race is on.'

'What do you mean?'

'Statistics will tell you that the average life expectancy of a long-term street-dweller is 40, but shocking as that is, that doesn't tell even half the story. This city is full of sharks. Drugs. Prostitution. Criminal fodder. Unless we can get to them first, and persuade them to get back into normal life, then they're just oil for the machine, really.'

'How long have you been doing this work?' Stone asks.

Tam gazes at her. 'Too long for me. Not long enough for

them.' What he is saying hangs in the air for a moment, while they all think about it.

'And so you know a lot of the street people. Have any of them been talking about Tuesday. Have you met anyone who knows Tuesday?' Stone persists.

Tam smiles widely. 'Everyone knows Tuesday. They talk about her as though she's some sort of talisman.'

'What do you mean?'

'I mean that, young people living on the street, sooner or later the drug gangs sweep them up, use them as runners, or for prostitution, whatever. When your girl Tuesday started knocking out gang members as if they were toys, then the rumours started slithering up and down the lanes. I mean, she didn't just fight back and hurt one of them. She humili-ated them. She made them look stupid and weak. Before Tuesday, these street kids thought the world was fixed. That nothing could change. Now you've got rape girls telling their story to the BBC. You've got the bad boys and girls running around like chickens, not even welcome in their mothers' homes. And you've got the homeless kids being sought after. Their opinions asked. As if they're human beings. Really, it's a brave new world.'

'Whereabouts?' Stone asks. 'Where could she be holed up?'

Tam opens his arms wide, as if to encompass the whole city. 'The wreck of the Temperance Hospital. An old cinema. Under the Thames in an abandoned tunnel. In the sewers. In a penthouse in Canary Wharf, from which she emerges like sodding Batman. In the shell of the old refuge. In hell. Take your pick.'

'And what about you, Tam,' Loss says, gently. 'Have you ever seen her?'

Tam returns his gaze, unblinking and clear-eyed. Loss can't tell what Tam is thinking, but he knows they're not happy thoughts.

'What a shitty job you have, Inspector. Always having to push people further. No, I have never met Tuesday. If your daughter were still alive she might have been able to tell you where Tuesday is. From what I picked up, Suzanne seemed to have the trust of all the young street kids. The pregnant runaways were her special thing. That's one of the reasons the refuge was set up. There was nowhere else for them to go, except gang flats or the breeder dorms.'

'The what?' asks Stone.

Tam sighs. His phone beeps again and he picks it up. 'The gang boys knock up a girl so she gets a flat if, and it's a big if, she survives the hostels, and then once she has an abode they move in, use it as a safe house for drugs, as a brothel. Whatever. Look, detectives. I'm sorry I can't be of any more help, but I don't know who Tuesday is, where she lives, or how she does what she does. But I promise, if I get any information you'll be the first to know, OK? Now I've really got to go.' Tam gets up and goes to the door, opens it, and raises his eyebrows at the detectives. They thank him and leave.

Out on the Soho streets they gaze at the lights and the displays of erotic ephemera in the shop windows.

'Not a happy bunny,' says Loss.

'Not even an unhappy bunny,' Stone agrees. 'More like a fucked-off social worker with anger issues. Did you notice the screen saver on his phone?'

'The picture of *Tuesday Falling* from outside the Marquis? Of course I did. Contrary to popular belief, I'm a detective.'

DS Stone smiles slyly. 'But not a good looking shit-hot one, like me.'

They walk through the Soho streets to Leicester Square, and disappear down into the tube station.

70

When I started getting my mind back together, and unhooked myself from the street islands, I just let myself float. Suzanne was gone. My daughter, gone. All the earlier things, all the things that had happened before, I'd packed away and thrown down a rabbit hole. I just let myself drift through the city. Letting it know me. I knew I'd have to fuck him up, when I was ready.

Mr Man.

Not just fuck him up into next week, or next year, but forever. I didn't know how, but the how wasn't important, not then. If I didn't want to just curl up and scream until I was dead, or deader, then it wasn't the how. It was the why.

The question DI Loss is asking. Has been asking for three years. Everything's coming to an end now. Everything is slowing down, but back then everything was black and white. The past was dead zone black and the present was static-white.

I used to come up at night, onto the streets. I had an *A to Z* on my tablet, and I used to just slide through the night, getting to know how London was stitched together.

People think that when you're living on the street you

know it; that you know all the alleys, and cracks, and corners of the city. That's just bollocks. When you're living on the street your life is fucking tiny. You know where you can sleep without being beaten up. You know where you can panhandle, or steal food. Your world is doorways and parks. Bins and church basements. Underpasses and graveyards.

Nothing's connected up. It's just little islands where you live, separated by chunks of city that you mist through. Like they don't exist. Once you've established dry, and warm and safe, nothing else registers.

Except people.

When you're on the street you learn to read people. Who can fuck you up. Who can cut you down. Who you can scam. Who you have to run from.

I should have run from Suzanne. I ran from where I grew up to this city. I ran from what had happened, ran so hard and so fast that I was just a spirit, just air. No one could ever find me. Not even myself. Not until Suzanne.

Close it down. Shut it off. Bye bye.

Anyhow, I'd choose a destination on my map, and start walking. It was Diston's tablet, at that time, and I had it connected to a Bluetooth earpiece I kept under my permo-hat. Back then it was hoodies over tramp hats. Anything to keep warm and keep closed. For a while I'd worn headphones, listening to pirate radio. It was good for finding out what was happening in London. Bad for knowing what was going on behind your back.

I mean, who'd beat up a 14-year-old girl-tramp?

Plenty of fucking people, apparently. Gang boys who want to street-mule you. Chav hags out for ethnic cleansing. Dirty police boys on a bit of extra-curricular.

Especially dirty police boys.

Half the fucking city, it felt like.

So I stopped wearing headphones, and moved on to the

Bluetooth. A foot in two worlds, a ghost in both. Night after night I'd come up, and shade through the town, going from random A to random B.

That's when I discovered the honeystreets; when I first started packing up the future.

I was going from Piccadilly Circus to Richmond Mews in the heart of Soho. When I started up Shaftesbury Avenue the theatre crowd were just coming out. *Dance-Boy*. *Sing-Girl*. Some fucking thing. I shoegazed up Great Windmill Street, the buildings getting suitably seedy and run down; girls and boys hung back in piss-ridden doorways, their faces ravaged by drugs. The Windmill Theatre is long wound up, but the meat trade goes on. I slip down Archer's Street then up Rupert Street, past Madam JoJo's, with its impossibly tall transsexuals outside, smoking cigarette after cigarette; their industrial lip-gloss never losing its oil-slick shine. From there I go along Berwick Street and shim down Tyler's Court, past the dopers and the street girls washing their dreams away with little bottles of vodka. Small enough to take down in one slug. Just the right size for mouthwash.

I come out of Tyler's Court with my head down and my hoodie up. You never know if one of the girls' handlers will be with them, tightening the leash with a wrap of this or a rock of that. Up Wardour Street with the London rain beginning to sift down, dancing with the soot and the dust from a million building sites. At The Ship I turn into Flaxman Court, punk music splashing out of the bar windows and crashing onto the street, my right hand in my hoodie pocket, wrapped round the contact taser.

And that's where I find out about the honeystreets of London.

According to my street app I should be able to walk through Cleaver's Passage and end up on Richmond Mews. Except, I ended up at a brick wall. Cleaver's Passage, it would seem, had been cleaved. I just stand there, gazing at the wall like I'm on drugs. It's an old wall, not just been thrown up. It's been there for the duration. To get to where I want to I have to go back round and through St Anne's. It quite fucking freaked me out. Here was a street in London that existed on my *A to Z*, but didn't exist in real life.

A ghost street.

A Lie street.

What I later found out was a honeystreet. As in trap.

When I got back to my underground crib I started doing some research. Trawling the Interzone for information about streets that don't exist. To be honest it was a bit of a head-frack. I'd become so abstracted from the world above that I'd been laying the virtual world on top of it like a skin, thinking it would fit perfectly.

Not just me, of course. Everyone. We all do it. Take things written down as fact. Believe what we see.

That's when I first started working out how I could fuck him up.

There are honeystreets all over London. Streets the mapmakers put in for a laugh. Or for their loves. Or to prove, if the streets turned up in other maps, that their work had been stolen.

There are so many tiny streets in London. Alleys, walks, passages, sidings, courtyards.

A thousand years of fires, bombs, wars, shanty towns, builders, and rotating town planners, so that half the honeystreets were forgotten, and therefore never removed from the maps. Or removed from some editions, but then turn up, like mine, on ripped-off online maps scrimmed off old editions. On the other hand, there are streets in London that don't even have a name anymore. At least not officially.

As far as I can tell. Which is not very bloody far.

Honeytrap. You tempt someone in, and they think that

one thing's happening, when in fact something else entirely is going on. But by the time they realize it, they're locked in.

Shut down.

Switched off.

71

Loss and Stone stand in front of the university lift doors. They are both immensely pleased there *are* doors after their experience at the British Museum, but are happier still when the doors open and they can step out onto the sixth floor. They walk out together into a corridor that reeks of institutional thinking. It is the worst kind of off-white with large squares of florescent lights that buzz just within human hearing. Loss thinks it's a supple form of mind torture, and idly wonders if Drake has set up an elaborate experiment.

'What the hell was that, anyway?' Loss is referring to the music that was playing in the lift.

'Fuck knows. "Price tag"? "Anarchy in the UK"? Everything sounds the same on panpipes. Did he say why he wanted to see us again? I thought we were going back to the British Museum.'

'I don't know. He didn't speak to me directly; it was our Commander,' Loss informs her.

'Oh?' She raises an eyebrow. 'Well we'd better get goose-stepping then, hadn't we?'

'Nice to have you back, officially' Stone says, as they

walked down the corridor. 'How come you're back, anyway? I thought you were too much of a security risk, what with the DNA thing?'

'I don't know. Maybe he just wants me where he can see me. Anyhow I'm back on the case, so you'd better stop being rude to me, and start treating me as a professional.'

'Or maybe he's just all over the sodding place, and has his head up his arse,'

He sighs. 'You do know that your total lack of respect for authority is going to get you in massive trouble, don't you?' He's beginning to feel slightly disorientated. Swirls of prison-school green have begun to appear on the walls.

'Yeah? Well I'm not the one everyone's favourite Murder-Goth has been writing to, am I?'

They arrive at Stevens's door, and knock. Loss examines it.

'Not very original, is it?'.

'What?'

He nods at the door number.

'102. So what?'

'Come in!' The voice is slightly muffled, but it definitely belongs to Drake.

Loss sighs again. He can't tell whether Stone is taking the piss out of him or not; whether she gets the painfully modern reference, but is too tired to pursue it. He pushes the door open and they go inside.

The scene is almost exactly the same as their first visit. Tuesday on the video-walls in various poses; CCTV of underground London run silently around her; Drake with the ponytail trying hard to look at everything apart from DS Stone's breasts. And failing. And focusing on the screen in front of him.

'Hello again, Mr Drake,' Stone smiles, while Loss closes the door behind them, and leans against the wall. That way, he reasons, there's at least one of them he doesn't have to look at. 'You asked to see us again, Mr Drake. Do you have new information for us?' Stone asks.

'Call me Drake, please,' he says, not taking his eyes from the screen. He is using a wireless toggle to move the film backwards and forwards. 'Everyone else does. No Mr, just the one name. Sorry.'

'Your parents were duck lovers?' Loss shoots a warning look at his partner but then sees that Drake is smiling.

'Close. Lovers of English melancholy. There.' He puts the device down, freezing on a single image. It is from the tube train. Tuesday's arms are outstretched at her side, chest height, the scythes pointing downwards. Loss can't look at the scythes without hearing a high-pitched whine in his head. The sound of a razor cutting glass. 'I tried to reach you at the number you left, but had to talk to some stiff-necked authority geek called, ah, Commander Stonebridge, instead. Is he your boss?' Drake takes their silence as an affirmation. 'Thought so. If you like, I can do a complete assassination of his character by doing a speech analysis for you. It would take me about two seconds.'

Loss warms to the young man in front of him. He points at the screen. 'What are we looking at?'

Drake picks up the toggle again and zooms in on Tuesday's arm. 'I've been trying to work out where your girl might be hiding. First of all I thought that maybe she's been living on the street. I mean she's not living in a flat or something, is she? With the exposure she's had in the media someone would have come forward. And then all those interviews with the homeless? Am I the only one who found those a bit creepy, by the way? See there.'

All three survey the screen for a while, and then Loss says, 'It's an arm.'

'Yes, but it's a *clean* arm. Not an arm that's been living rough and not getting washed properly. Also there are no lesions denoting poor diet or disease. Look at the fingernails.'

203

'What fingernails? They couldn't get any more bitten if you tried.'

'Well, fair point,' concedes Drake. 'But you'd still expect to see some dirt build-up, some detritus if she'd been living commando, as it were. Even if she'd been squatting you'd expect to see more dirt than this. In fact, even if she'd been living in suburbia you'd expect to see more dirt than this. Look at her clothes. I mean, yes they're old army stuff; faded, and scarred, and whatnot – but they're not teenage grimy and covered in KFC finger fat, or anything.' Drake plays the images of Tuesday over and over. He's right. The clothes are ripped, and scuffed, and generally teenager fucked-up, but they are clean.

'Are you saying our fine youth are teenage dirtbags who live on fast food?' Stone is smiling almost affectionately at Drake but he is in his own zone now, fingers flying.

'And look here.' He has stills of Tuesday all over the LED wall. Tuesday on the tube. Tuesday outside Candy's. Tuesday running out of Seething Lane Gardens. Streaming down the wall on the right is image after image of teenagers; many with hoodies, all wearing some form of listening device. 'No earbuds. She must be the only teenager in London who isn't wired for sound.'

Loss is surveying the images of Tuesday. Something is bugging him. 'How come she's so white?'

Stone stares at him as if he's an idiot. 'She's a Goth,' she says slowly. 'She wears Goth make-up. Of course she's white.'

'Well done, Inspector. That puzzled me, too.' Drake zooms in on Tuesday's face. 'The hair, of course, is dyed. Here you can see where her real hair is just visible at the join beneath the wig. As there are scarcely any roots showing, I'd say that her hair might be dyed regularly.'

'Professionally? I mean, like at a hairdresser?' says DI Loss, then pulls up. 'Sorry,' he says. An image of Suzanne slams into him: leaning over the sink in a black sports bra and a pair of ripped 501s, a bottle of peroxide in her nitrile-gloved hand. 'Sorry.' He has an urge to sit down. Or perhaps throw up. Stone has taken out her iPad and is tapping notes into it. Drake is still talking, his Oxbridge-modulated voice is a soft tide.

'With most high-matte foundations, such as a Goth might use, the mixture is similar to that of silicone putty, rather than paint, and so can easily blend where the natural tone of the skin converges with that of the product.'

'What on earth does that mean?' says Loss.

'No tan line. Or rather no anti-tan line,' Stone explains.

'Well that's right, isn't it? I mean there's no division line on these images,' Loss squints at the screens.

Drake gives an exasperated snort. 'There are two main reasons for someone wearing foundation at her age: to change the colour of the skin, Goths go for white, Chavs for orange, or to hide a skin blemish, such as scars or acne. Your girl isn't doing either.'

'How do you know?'

'I think, Inspector, that she really is pale. All she has on is a slightly coloured moisturizer, to smooth out the skin. I don't know. It's as if she only comes out at night, or something. Her pigment is almost similar to an albino's.'

'But she's not? An albino, I mean?'

'No. Look at her eye pigment. Even in the crap CCTV you can see she's not albino. It's a shame she was wearing the goggles in Seething Lane. The quality of the camera that caught her there was outstanding. Anyhow. See the neck? And where the wrists are exposed with her arms outstretched. Anyone who spends even a small time exposed to sunlight gets tanned. Our faces and hands are consistently darker than the rest of our bodies. Not this girl, though. I don't think this girl has seen sunlight for quite some time.'

DI Loss and Ds Stone look at each other. 'That's it then. Confirmed. She's living underground.' Loss wipes his hand over his eyes. He thanks Drake, who looks smug, and they leave.

'For what it's worth, detectives,' says Drake as they reach the door. 'Skin that pale, I'd say when she isn't wearing a wig or bleaching her hair, she must be a redhead.'

Loss closes the door.

Stone's phone beeps: a message. She looks at it. 'Well it's never boring. I'll give it that,' she says.

'What?'

'We're needed back at the office. There's a message from Five. Apparently she has some more information for us.'

'I'll meet you there,' Loss says. 'Somewhere I've got to go first.'

72

Lily-Rose and her mother are in a coffee shop on Wilton Road, just outside Victoria Station. They have spent the day in the big department stores on Oxford Street, buying everything they need for their journey: they have brand-new suitcases full of brand-new clothes; they have each had their hair cut and coloured at the salon; they disposed of their old clothes in a charity shop, and now they are unrecognisable, even to themselves.

Lily-Rose stares out of the cafe window at the street outside. She can see a ghost reflection of herself, mingling with the road beyond, and it moves her further away from the reality of her past.

Lily-Rose's mother stirs her coffee, her newly manicured nails still ragged from biting. 'I don't understand why she has done this for us. I mean, what are we to her?'

'I don't know, Mum,' Lily-Rose sighs, trying to make her insides work; make them feel as if she is not in a dream. She knows she needs to talk to her mother. Help her understand. But she doesn't know how. She doesn't have the vocabulary. But she knows she has to try.

'When I was . . . well, when I broken up by what they

did to me, yeah? I used to go online. I didn't do Facebook or any of that, cos I knew it would always get back to them. Everyone was connected, yeah?' Lily-Rose looks at her mother, to see if she understands, and goes on, 'I used to go to these sites. Where people had been messed up. Raped, beaten up. Stuff like that. Anyway, the only way these people had been able to deal with it all was by completely controlling their bodies.' Lily-Rose does not look at her mother, but her mother looks at her, willing her love into the tiny, thin, cracked and scarred body of her daughter. 'And the way they did it was by controlling what they ate. Or by cutting. Or burning. Some of the girls, they hated themselves so much, blamed themselves so much that they deliberately went out to find people to, to *do* them, you know what I mean? To use them. They thought they were so shit that they deserved it, cos that was what they had been told.'

Outside it begins to rain again, and the drops tick against the window. In a doorway opposite the café, Lily-Rose sees a homeless boy with bleached blond hair pull his hoodie tighter around his head.

'So I used to meet these girls in the chat rooms, and we'd give each other tips on how to eat less without dying. How to survive the nights when you can't close your eyes. How to stay off drugs but keep your body separate.'

Lily-Rose's mother can't believe that her daughter is fifteen. She feels as if she has been living in a war zone and not even known it. She feels stupid, and a failure, and wrong.

'Anyhow, this name kept on coming up. Tuesday. Tuesday saves girls who need saving. Tuesday fights rapists and gang-bangers. Tuesday can return your life to you. The girls in the chat rooms, no one had ever met anyone who knew her, but they all knew *of* her. They all had stories about someone they knew who knew someone who knew her.

'Well one night, when my body hurt and I wanted to make

208

a call to . . . to *them* to buy drugs, or give up, or let them have me or whatever, I went to a chat room and put a call out to her, asked everyone in there if they could hook me up, told them I was on my last night and I couldn't take any more. And then this girl asked me to meet her in a private room, and then in another private room. And then on and on. Different IPs, different rooms, until finally she said she'd take me to her, but I had to give up my computer. Let her control it remotely, so she could wipe away the footprints.'

Lily-Rose's mother didn't really know what her daughter was talking about, but she understood enough. 'So you met up with her? In your computer?'

'In the Interzone, yeah. She asked me what had happened. What they did. Who they were. And then she said she'd help me, but that there'd be a price. A price on my soul.' Lily-Rose stares into her coffee cup. 'She said that she'd meet the boys, and whatever they brought to her, she'd bring it back to them full tilt. That if they brought violence they'd get it back double. She said that there would be no going back. That, although the responsibility was theirs, I might try to make it mine, and there would be no way to undo what was started.'

Lily-Rose takes out some money from the pocket of her new cargoes and places it on the table. Her mother reaches across the table and takes her daughter's hand in hers. 'I'm glad you did. I'm glad those boys got stopped. Not just for you, but for all the other girls they've, they've . . .' She doesn't know how to frame it. How to say what has happened to her daughter. 'Fucked up. Would have continued to fuck up.'

Lily-Rose's mum squeezes her daughter's hand, but not too hard. She can feel all the tiny bones, and is afraid of breaking one of them.

Lily-Rose smiles at her mum. 'I don't think I've ever heard you effing before.' Her mum smiles back. 'I'll try not to do it again.'

Lily-Rose stands up. 'Let's catch the train. She told us any time before half past, so it might as well be now.'

Lily-Rose and her mother make their way into Victoria Station, and board the 17.11 fast service to Brighton.

At half past five the first tube station in central London is evacuated.

73

DI Loss is standing outside the cracked remains of the refuge off Charing Cross Road, where his daughter used to work in between shifts at the hospital. It is Victorian, its smoke-damaged brickwork pocked, eroded by 130 years of acid rain. The mortar between the red bricks is similar to scar tissue. The whole structure is being pulled apart in super-slow motion by weeds and some form of mutant city honeysuckle. There are crows flying in and out of the broken roof. The late-afternoon London light seems to get sucked into their feathers, then reflected back, prism-like, through city oil and polluted air. It does nothing to ease the knot of pressure building in his spine. Rather, it feeds into the despair he feels whenever he thinks of Suzanne. There is a thin cloak of cooking smoke drifting around the area, possibly from a squat in one of the adjacent buildings. Since the change in the law prohibiting squatting, a new kind of unauthorized occupation has developed: pop-up squats; people who live in the buildings for a few days, and then move on. Slash and burn.

Survival always finds a path.

The door and windows to the refuge have been covered

by metal security sheeting, bolted, and stapled, making it look as if the building is being tortured. A faint smell of putrefaction seeps out of the garbage bags scattered against the walls, shiny and slick, non-biodegradable and utterly impervious to the march of time.

DI Loss is not surprised to notice 'Tuesday' spray-painted across the scarred metal sheet bolted to the wall that has replaced the door. The lettering is cracked and blistered with at least one year of city heat and cold, and he wonders if Tuesday did it. If this is the first tag she ever wrote.

'Just give me the keys, darling,' says a voice he barely recognizes. He looks round, but nobody is there; impossible shadows in the sunlight. Time is stuttering in front of him. The doorway to the broken building in front of him morphs into the doorway of his flat. His old flat. Suzanne is standing in front of him, seven years old. She is wearing black jeans and a sweatshirt. Her hair is tied back in a loose ponytail because that's all he can do, and she is blocking the door her mother will never walk through again.

And she has hidden his car keys. She doesn't want him to leave for work. She has had too much leaving. You can see it in her too pale face and her too old eyes. He wants to hold her and tell her it's all right. But it isn't all right. It won't ever be all right again.

'Don't leave, Daddy.'

But leaving is all he can do. He can't stay here in this flat.

'I need to go to work, Suzanne.'

Loss wipes his hand in front of his eyes. The determined look on his daughter's face falls apart, and the past disappears.

The street in which the refuge is situated is run-down. London is endlessly amazing, he thinks, his mind cartwheeling, trying to find something to cling on to: poverty and prosperity lie next to each other, with only a courtyard or a side street between them: the past and the present. In the gutter outside the building he can see used disposable lighters, crumpled squares of blackened tin-foil, and deflated balloons, which would, he knows, have been filled recently with nitrous oxide. For a moment his mind stutters again and the black garbage bags become morgue bags, the contents too awful for him to face.

He thinks about the children at the refuge whom his daughter tried to help. Children being destroyed by circumstance. Imprisoned by culture. Children for whom 'family' was the word for pain rather than love. Children who would rather live on the streets of London, with the gutter-men and drug dealers, with the skin-girls and hobos, than with their own parents. Loss looks at the building and thinks of the girl known as Tuesday.

'What happened?' he whispers. Even to himself it is unclear who he means: Suzanne or Tuesday.

He thinks of his daughter. He sees her life staggering in front of his eyes. The withdrawal when her mother died, like the cutting of a flower. The betrayal when he left for work, again and again, for longer and longer, unable to cope with the pain in his own body. More withdrawal as his job took him to desperate places. Vice. Drugs. Gangs. The work getting darker and darker. The distance between him and his daughter growing each day.

Suzanne's resolution to become a doctor; to make sure no other son or daughter had to lose a mother as she had, and his inability to hold her because, year after year, she was moving toward the likeness, inside and out, of his wife, and it made him want to scream. Scream at himself. Scream at the world.

'I'm so sorry, Suzanne.' Loss leans his head against the door of the refuge, trying to fill what remains of his daughter's spirit with his love.

Too late.

All that is left are ghosts.

His phone beeps. Detective Loss keeps his eyes closed and his hands clenched, trying to stop time. Trying to find the space between the seconds where his daughter might live.

His phone beeps again, and he takes a deep breath and pulls it out of his pocket. It's a text from his DS, telling him she's at Euston tube station, but in his head he is so far away he can barely see it.

74

Hacking into the national database that collates the DNA of over 10 per cent of the population of Britain is not an easy task. There are security protocols that are rock hard, even for me. And it's not as if all you'd have to do is replace one set of data with another. Sometimes they go back to the original samples. You'd have to set up a rolling program that would Trojan in behind, and return to a request and *shiv* in your false reading each and every time. It would be an absolute nightmare.

Lucky I don't have to bother then, isn't it?

By the time I've set up everything I want to do, it's two o'clock in the afternoon, or at least that's what my watch tells me. Down here it doesn't matter what time it is. It's always my time.

I keep my watch set to GMT, cos that's what the *World Service* runs on. I don't fuck about with British Summer Time. I'm not a farmer, or Scottish. I live underground. I don't have friends, only clients.

I don't have appointments, I just find out what appointments others have, and make sure I'm there too.

The last time I cared about time was when my daughter's was stolen.

Stopped.

Taken.

Since then. Well since then, who cares? I'm awake, I'm asleep. I hear the water in the sewers and rivers. I hear the air compressing and releasing in the tunnels. I hear the rats and the bats and the tunnel foxes with no eyes, and I know some sort of time passes.

One day it will stop passing for me, but in my world down here it will carry on, become less human and stranger. I like that.

I hit the button on my laptop and start shutting down the tube system. Really, people are so closed in their little worlds. They create this entire network; tubes, signal boxes, escalators, air flow, and then instead of employing loads of people to run it, they computerize it. And then they allow remote access because it's so fucking complicated when you go out to fix this or that you need to access the whole system. And that means there are laptops that are live.

Hooked in.

Connected and open on the tunnel Wi-Fi.

They make it too easy. I just slide in behind a hot laptop and ease myself into the train-web, copy all the access protocols, and ghost out.

Easy.

The first station I shut down is Leicester Square.

I don't want any panic and trampled babies; I just want the station empty.

First I shut down the timetable screens, and replace the train information with a message to leave the station as quickly as possible. From the pop-up box in the top corner of my screen showing the CCTV feed I can see everyone looking confused. The staff are talking into their radios, but nobody's saying the T word yet.

That's terrorist, not Tuesday. I'm not some egomaniac who

thinks, just cos she's shut down London, she should get top billing.

Next I send a system-wide message for no trains to stop at the station. Now I can see the staff running, and people are beginning to head out. The staff are really doing very well. I hope they get some sort of bonus for today, I really do.

I press a button and all the lights in the station black out.

Ta-daa! OK, I might be a *bit* egomaniacal, in my James Bond underground bunker.

I'm not sure, but I think I can hear the screams from here.

75

'So. Tell me again why we aren't going to the cinema?' DI Loss enquires as he and DS Stone tramp along the road, their clothes sticking to their bodies in the heat.

'Are you asking me out on a date?'

Loss wipes his face; he is too tired for this. 'The abandoned cinema where Five lives, as you well know. By the way, is that even legal? I thought the squatting laws had changed. And what about fire regs and stuff?'

'Well, if you're worried about that you're going to brick yourself about this.'

He sighs; his feet hurt and he has a headache caused, he has decided, by too much caffeine and too little nicotine. 'What's "this"?'

' "This" is this,' says Stone, coming to a halt. 'The Temperance Hospital. Five's new home, apparently.'

They have walked the short distance from Euston underground to the derelict hospital on Hampstead Road. The London sky is midnight blue, lit up and time-fractured by lightning. It is impossible to tell from which direction the thunder is coming. To Loss it sounds as if it is coming from everywhere. Or maybe just from his head. Everything seems to be moving to a beat that he can't quite hear: the rape riots, as certain parts of the media had begun to call them; the feeling that his city is ready to erupt in flames; the confusion of the gang world, its handles on power being blown away, the tension in the office, not just because of him. The case seems to be affecting the entire staff.

At least on the surface. Loss is not so naive as to think people as cold-hearted and vicious as those in control of the East London estates were just going to shut up shop and walk away, all because of a girl called Tuesday.

No. They would be out searching for her, and anyone who knew her.

And now Five. The art terrorist. He was also fairly confident that she would know Tam, who had not only mentioned the cinema, but also the derelict hospital. That she was somehow connected to Tuesday, Loss had absolutely no doubt. When he looked her up on the NCDB he found that she had been arrested several times as a student, involved in various different protests: Gaza; corporate control; Militant Pride; arrested but never charged.

The arrests hadn't shed any light on who she was. As part of her art degree, she had apparently wiped her personal history from the college records, creating the 'Five' persona as an expression of 'art as real in an art-ificial world'. Her reasoning, according to her teachers, was she had wanted to show that modern life was an imitation, or construct, of a perceived reality that was the past. That modern-day living was, in effect, nothing more than an art project imitating a reality that in all probability never existed. She had written an essay on how easy it was, both legally and illegally, to not only change one's identity, but to make it virtually impossible for anyone to discover the prime identity. As her final dissertation piece she had handed in a valid British passport containing her new name.

'So, do you get her? Five?' Loss asks as they turn the corner into Cardington Street, following the decrepit, hulking building round to its entrance. The day has become so dark that the cars have all switched on their lights and the automatic street lighting has activated.

Stone shrugs. 'Not really. I like her, though. Don't trust her, but like her. I like the fact that she just sees us as people. Not the enemy, not the ally. She's just in her own world doing her own thing.'

'Except, she's not, is she?' Loss protests. 'She's not just some experimental artist; I don't know, Stick, or Banksy, or someone messing about with what we think. Putting creative things into the public space.'

'Isn't she? I thought that's exactly what she said she was doing', Stone pauses, then adds, 'the dangerous thing is that, maybe she thinks that's what Tuesday is doing too.'

They walk up the stone steps leading into the hospital entrance, and are unsurprised to find that there is a brand-new security door with a camera intercom. Loss presses the button, and waits. Stencilled onto the door in black and white ink is a stylized representation of the planets in their orbit around the sun. There is something wrong with the picture, but Loss can't put his finger on what it is. He's just about to ask Stone when there is a buzzing and the door swings open.

'Jesus.'

Inside is exactly as one would expect the inside of a derelict building to be. Exposed wires everywhere, and the high odour of rat urine. Broken glass and pieces of ceramic tiles on the floor, and because the windows have been boarded up there is very little light. By the door, is a small table with a Nitecore flashlight, which Stone picks up. She turns it on.

'Bloody hell. You could light up the moon with this.'

The beam is as bright as a helicopter searchlight. It picks

up every detail in the lobby and throws it into nightmare, horror-film relief. To the left of the curving staircase, treads missing like broken teeth, is a door with '5' sprayed on it in red. They pick their way over. From all around comes the sound of whispering and muttering, as if the place is filled with spirits. Stone notices tiny speakers placed around the lobby.

'OK,' says Loss. 'This is officially very creepy.'

Under the large number on the door is a neatly stencilled notice: 'please knock'. They knock.

'Who is it?' Five's voice rings out from behind the door.

'Oh she's funny. I'll give her that,' mutters Stone. The police officers identify themselves, there is the sound of bolts being thrown, and then the door is opened. In front of them stands Five. She is wearing a black hijab, a long-sleeved canvas grandfather shirt with 'Conceived in Heaven: Designed in Nature: Made in Britain' written across it, and her ripped 501s. On her feet are a pair of brown military fur-lined boots. On her face is the ever-present grin.

'Why hello, Detectives! How nice of you to drop by.'

'Yes, er, Five.' DI Loss hasn't managed to acclimatize himself to the single-name format yet. 'What with you asking us, and everything, it's amazing. What happened with the Cinema, anyway?' Five moves to the side to allow them in, shutting the door behind them. The whispering is immediately cut off. Loss and Stone find themselves in a space very similar to Five's last room: vinyl records strewn across the floor; on the turntable, David Byrne's 'My Life in the Bush of Ghosts' is playing quietly; an old poster of the band Tubeway Army advertising the single 'Me: I disconnect from you!' is on the wall, together with a frame containing strips of text in English, Hebrew, and Farsi, woven together to form a pattern.

'The problem with abandoned buildings, detectives, is that you occasionally have to abandon them.' Five waves her hand toward a sofa futon covered with books and sketchpads. Even from the door, Loss can make out the picture of the three monkeys in their traditional poses, each wearing a tee shirt with a symbol of a major religion on it. Loss is not going anywhere near it. Loss walks up to the picture on the wall, hoping it is safer.

'What is this?' he enquires.

'The Serenity Prayer in three languages, woven together to make a point. Yours for 1200 quid.' Loss looks at it for a moment. The way the strips cross over and under each other making a new design, almost a new language when viewed as a whole, for some reason creates an emotional response in him. He makes a mental note to look up the Serenity Prayer when he has a moment. He turns and faces the artist, who is grinning at him.

'I'm sure I can arrest you, just for living here.'

'Actually you can't. I am officially a Building Angel.' Five pulls out a laminated card from a pocket on her sleeve and holds it out to him between her slender fingers, waggling it back and forth. He nods at Stone, who walks over, takes the card, and examines it.

'Looks legit, sir.'

'Good. Now, can you tell me what a "Building Angel" is?' Loss feels somewhat stupid as the two women look at him, obviously amazed that he hasn't heard of Building Angels. Then Stone tells him, 'Building Angels are people employed by equity firms, banks, people like that. The people who either own the buildings, or manage them. Surely you've heard of them?' Loss shakes his head.

'Well, to stop squatters, or tramps, or gangs or whatever, they employ a kind of security guard, called an angel. They set them up with a refurbished bit of the building, and let them live there for free, and in return, they kind of keep an eye on the property. Ring if anyone breaks in, that sort of thing. Really, are you sure you don't know about this? I mean it's not as obscure as the second post.'

'What's the second post?' asks Five.

'Don't.' Loss glares at Stone. 'Don't even go there.' He turns to Five. 'Fine. Whatever. You can live here. You can do your art experiments, mess about with our heads. I don't care. I just want to find Tuesday. Stop what's happening out there.' He jerks his finger at the wall, indicating the city beyond the room. 'Maybe find some answers. Why are we here, Five? Again. I'm fairly certain, no matter what you say, that you know who Tuesday is. What is it you want to say to us?'

'Nothing really, detectives, It's just that you said if I knew anything, then I should get in touch with you.'

'So what is it? What do you know?'

Five turns on an award-winning, full-toothed smile, and fires up a cigarette. She sucks the smoke deep into her lungs, then blows it out in a long straight line.

'How about where she lives?'

76

In the train window Lily-Rose's face is half reflected back at her, and half not. It is an exact representation of how she feels.

Her mother is sitting beside her pretending to read a magazine, but she is not fooling anyone. Her hands are holding the copy so tight it is a wonder she hasn't ripped it in two. Lily-Rose can't help her. Not at the moment. It is all she can do just to not go to curl up under the seat and never come out.

Outside, London slips away like a dream, the train slicing through it at ever-changing heights, changing its perspective in clicks and clacks. Gradually the mobile phones start ringing. From all around her the fear starts to ramp up, as news begins to filter in.

77

'What do you mean she's shut down the tube network?' DS Stone has just come off the phone to the Commander in charge of the Tuesday case. She and DI Loss are back at the British Museum, heading towards the tunnel, which Five has told them leads to Tuesday's crib. Of course it does.

'Well, somehow she's hacked into the London Transport system and given instructions that no trains are to stop at Leicester Square, Piccadilly, Covent Garden, Goodge Street, or Tottenham Court Road.'

Loss can picture the chaos she has caused. Many London streets are already in semi-riot mode. Having the underground shut down will push everything into full-scale meltdown.

'Brilliant. Two square miles of completely buggered London, then.'

Stone isn't finished. 'Also, only the emergency lights are running, and all the announcement boards are saying one word: "Tuesday".'

'Very arty. Sounds as though it's something Five would do. When we get back out of here, I want her arrested!'

'On what charge? All she's said is that when she lived on the street she used to come down to the tunnels for shelter.'

225

'Bollocks. I don't care what we arrest her for. How about inappropriate use of Daleks? Or crimes against modern art?'

'I think that's the nature of modern art, sir,' says Stone, smiling gently.

The skeleton lift arrives, and the two detectives step gingerly onto it.

'The Commander said to me that if we find anything down here we're to report it directly to him. He also told me to keep a quiet eye on you.' She raises an eyebrow, and Loss is almost certain she has been practising the movement in front of a mirror.

'Nice to have our esteemed boss's complete faith. Have you found out any more information about my daughter yet?'

Stone digs out her phone again, and punches up her emails. 'Well, as you discovered, while Suzanne was working at the hospital, she and a few other doctors also helped out at the St Martin's Refuge. A place for street kids; children who ran away from home and lived rough. It's closed down now.' The image of the burnt-out Refuge they have just left slips behind his eyes, and he blinks it away.

'I didn't even know Suzanne was working at the Refuge. We'd had an argument a year or so before, and we'd hardly been in contact,' he murmurs.

Stone continues, more gently, 'The reason your daughter got involved, it seems, was because she was getting a lot of referrals to the hospital from the Refuge.'

'Why was that?' The lift stops with a shudder, and they step out with relief.

'It was one of the few places equipped to deal with pregnant teenagers. In fact it had quite a reputation for it. A lot of these children were in the shadow of the drug gangs, and were used for prostitution. Either openly, or groomed into it.'

'Bloody hell.'

'When you're low and unprotected, anything looks up, I guess. Anyhow, that seems to have been the set-up. The girls would come into the refuge, and then be sent to the hospital to be checked out.' She pauses, then seems to gird herself to go on. 'Now here's a weird thing. Your daughter was murdered three years ago. She was coming back from a night at the refuge, and was brutally attacked and killed. Nothing was taken, and it was assumed to be a random killing, as you know. But it seems that same night something strange happened at the refuge. Some girl's baby was killed, and its body was stolen. I couldn't find any more information on it, but I've got some people digging. Do you know what date your daughter was killed?'

They arrive at the door to the closed-down tube station. The tech team had strung festoon lighting from the entrance down to the door leading to the connecting tunnel between the museum and the old tube station, but no further. The area is so vast that the force is liaising with the Army. As there is a major incident ongoing in central London, DI Loss guesses they won't be here any time soon. He turns and looks hard at his DS.

'What a fucking thing to ask, Stone. Of course I know the bloody date. The twenty-third of June. I wish I didn't. I wish there was no date to know. Why?'

Stone returns his stare. She looks at him, clear-eyed and unapologetic. 'She died on the twenty-third, just after midnight, but was attacked on the twenty-second, which was the day that the baby at the refuge was taken.'

Loss is blank, not comprehending what she is telling him. 'So what?'

'It was a Tuesday.'

78

The expression on Constantine's face is unreadable as the blinged-up Hummer pulls up at the kerb outside Number One, Hyde Park, and the side door slides open.

'What the fuck are we now, The gangsta A-Team?' He climbs in and the door slides shut as the van sets off towards the West End. Inside the vehicle is more guns than you'd find in a rap video and the crew have taken enough amphetamines between them to waken a corpse. Constantine sighs inwardly. They have a radio set up in the back, tuned to the central police channel, and he is not at all surprised to hear from it that the thin blue line is to open to allow them through.

He had explained to his employer how he'd extrapolated all he could find out about Tuesday, and her possible connections to Slater's business operations, from the recent events. He'd examined all the information he could access, and used several sophisticated algorithms to establish whether there were any correlations.

'Her name isn't Tuesday, or at least I don't think it is. The first time we see this name in connection to your boys is three years ago, written on the dude who rubbered the policeman's daughter. It was written on his palm with a marker pen. Like it was a memo or something.'

'Suzanne Loss,' says Slater, glaring at a point on the wall.

'Yeah, her. I don't know what business you had with her, but whatever it was, this girl calling herself Tuesday was in on it too. I'm guessing it has something to do with your Eastern European venture. The next time we see the name 'Tuesday' is in a school, but I don't think it's connected. I mean it's her, for definite, but I don't believe it's anything to do with you.'

His employer rises and walks out onto the balcony. He takes a shallow breath and gazes out, across the London cityscape. He is impressed that Constantine knows so much. In the distance he can see Harrods in all its chocolate-box splendour, and further on, an absence of light marks the Thames snaking its way through the city. His city.

'Don't worry. I'll deal with that.'

'Oh, I'm sure you will,' says Constantine. 'I'm sure with your, ah, special relationship with members of the fine British constabulary you'll be able to put things back on track, once our business is concluded.'

' What about now? Where is she now?'

'Oh, that's easy,' he smirks, joining him on the balcony, and lighting a cigar. 'She's in the Underground. That's how she can shine her way in and out of your world. She's very good, actually. She'd put up some smoke-screens in the interzone, but I managed to blow through them. She's been chatting with some of the girls your people had messed up. Building them up in chat rooms. I chased her footprint back to the IP in the underground. Looks as if she's been piggy-backing off their Wi-Fi. Quite sophisticated stuff. I reckon she's an educated girl, your Tuesday.'

'What, so she's living down there?'

'Yes. From what I've found she's been breaking into the

229

big department stores on Oxford Street for her food and equipment, and according to the police report she got the blades from the British Museum and the antique guns from some arms fair. Apparently she tunnelled her way up and just stole them from under their noses.'

Slater is silent but his jaw tightens.

Constantine laughs. 'Fabulous, isn't it? She, my friend, has been tearing holes in your operation using weapons from the British Museum. Priceless! I can't wait to meet this girl.'

'And put her down, yes?'

The assassin nods. 'As you say.'

Slater's mobile rings discreetly. He answers it and listens for a moment, and then hangs up.

'It looks as if you'll get your chance now. She's just shut down a major section of the tube system. There'll be a car downstairs for you in two minutes.'

79

DI Loss and DS Stone walk down the tunnel which connects the British Museum to its old station. They have passed beyond where the festoon lighting vines from the ceiling, and their way is now lit by the powerful halogen torches they are carrying. The beams cross and re-cross each other as they stumble forward. Loss feels as if he's underwater.

'So how come you were out of touch with your daughter?'

'The Commander told you to watch me, Stone, not to quiz me about my life story. Do you think that's an appropriate question to be asking a senior officer?'

'Yes'

He smiles to himself in the dark behind his torch. The new information about what happened three years ago has made him feel closer to his daughter.

He shrugs. 'Fair enough. When she went away to college, I was working with the drug squad. It was fucking horrible. Horrible policemen. Horrible gangsters. Horrible drug addicts. There was nothing nice about the job. Not for me anyhow. Then one day I got a phone call from Brighton, where Suzanne was studying.'

'I can see where this is going.' A small amount of water

is dripping from the ceiling, and pooling around their boots as they walk. Stone guesses that this tunnel must be beneath one of the hidden rivers. The Fleet, maybe, or the Tyburn.

'Yeah. Suzanne, and a few of her medical student mates, had been arrested at a house party. Public nuisance. It seems that everybody there was on some smiley drug or other. Ecstasy, GBH, Ketamine. Bubble. Anyhow, once she'd been ID'd, the duty sergeant gave me a call, and I drove down and collected her. I got rid of the charge sheet for her and her mates, otherwise they'd never have been able to qualify, and took her back to her place.'

The detectives come to a set of stairs, which Loss assumes lead down into the old tube station. As they descend, Stone says, 'She was only partying, sir. Everyone gets into trouble when they're young.'

'Yeah I know, and I know I over-reacted, but I'd been walking through so much shit that all I could see when I looked at Suzanne was the drugs. The lies about what they do to you. Anyhow, I lost it. We had a blazing row; I told her she was wasting her life, throwing her career away, and treating me like dirt, and she'd better change her ways or she was going to end up in a serious mess.'

'Very subtle, sir. Let me guess; she threw herself upon your mercy?'

Loss smiles. 'No. She threw my cigarettes out of the window to make a point, said that I was a hypocrite, and told me to fuck off.'

'Ah, so she took your loving intervention well, then.'

Loss sighs heavily, happy he no longer smokes, but wishing once again that he had a cigarette. 'I just cocked it up, basically. The only excuse I have is I did so with good intentions.'

'But it worked. She graduated.' The stairs come to an end and they start walking cautiously forward into an access tunnel.

'Without me going to the graduation ceremony. Then she got a job at Charing Cross Hospital, and we'd just started building bridges again, when I got the phone call telling me she'd been attacked. By the time I got there she was dead. All I could do was hold her dead body and tell her I was sorry.' Loss is glad that it is dark, that the only illumination is the beams from their torches bleeding on the walls. He is crying, letting out the pressure that has built up over three years. It is just a little hole in his shell, but it feels good, nonetheless. They walk on in silence, their footsteps echoing around them. Loss feels her hand on his shoulder. He halts at once.

'What's that noise?' she whispers.

He sniffs hard, pulling back the past inside himself, and listens.

'It sounds like someone talking,' he whispers back, switching off the past as he kills the light from his torch. He motions to Stone to do the same. They can make out a dim light ahead of them. There is a corner in the tunnel, and the spectral reflection of colours plays on the wall. As they inch round the voice gets louder. It is a man's voice, but because of the acoustics in the tunnel they can't work out what he is saying. When they turn the corner, it opens up into a tube platform.

'This must be the old station,' Stone is still whispering. Tentatively, they step out onto the platform. Hundreds of strands of fairy lights hang from the ceiling. Loss feels as if he's underwater. Submerged.

'Wow. It's an emo Narnia.' Stone steps onto the station platform. He follows her. A warm airflow, which makes the bulbs sway slightly, is creating patterns on the tiled walls. He nudges his partner, pointing out a camp bed against the wall, and a crate of protein drinks on the floor next to it. The crate is embossed with a skull and crossbones symbol. The voices are coming out of speakers attached to the walls. The talking stops and is replaced with a soft tune.

'Is that the *World Service*?' Stone asks, snatching at a memory of a camping holiday in Greece, with a transistor radio clamped to her ear. The tune is the station tag. On the curved, tiled tube wall, next to an information poster left over from the Second World War warning people that walls have ears, is a massive poster of the old punk band, The Clash. The guitarist is smashing his instrument against the ground, the words 'London Calling' are written above him.

'This must be where she lives,' whispers Stone.

'Lived,' Loss corrects her, looking around them. 'This place has been wrapped up and left for us as a present. Look.' He points to a table against the station wall, with a milk bottle containing a single yellow rose, and next to it, a framed photograph. He walks along the platform, his footsteps loud in the silence, and picks up the frame. It is a picture of Suzanne. She is smiling, and has her arm around a young girl, maybe fourteen years old. The girl is also smiling. She is as street-thin as if a blown kiss would snap her, but she is smiling.

'That's her, isn't it?' Stone joins him. 'That's Tuesday.' The picture was taken in what appears to be a hospital room. Loss supposes it must be Charing Cross Hospital. Where Suzanne worked.

And in the girl's arms, held as if the world depended on it, is a tiny new-born baby. The baby who, a few hours after the photograph is taken, will be stolen, and possibly killed. Along with his daughter. Loss stares at the picture. Two daughters, murdered. He feels as though he is being rocked. Above him, the fairy lights sway gently.

'Yeah, that's her. No ghost. Just a girl holding a baby.'

Stone moves away from her colleague and starts examining the station. Loss examines the photograph more closely. There is obviously a great deal of trust between Suzanne and

234

Tuesday. He can't stand up any longer, so he sits on the cot and tries to breathe. To keep breathing.

Stone is focusing on the station wall. 'What are these?' she asks.

Loss takes the picture of his daughter and Tuesday out of the frame, folds it, and pushes it carefully into his pocket, before turning his attention to his partner.

'What?'

'These.'

He joins her in front of the wall. It is covered with tiny porcelain tiles, just as in many of the old tube stations, but on this wall the tiles have writing on them.

'It looks like a list.' On each tile is a name, a date, and a QR code, the type of code a smartphone can read to connect to a web page.

'There must be thirty names here,' says Stone, counting the tiles. Loss reads the name at the bottom of the wall, presumably the last one written. It is no surprise to him that he recognizes the name of the boy who was tasered and had acid poured on him outside of the kebab shop. On the tile above, is the name of the boy who was shot through the eye. Loss lets his gaze wander up the wall. Some of the names he has read before, in social workers' reports and offenders' photo-shots. Some he has seen in morgues.

'Hey. Weren't they the gang who tried to do over that boy at the school?'

Loss looks at the names his DS is pointing at. He feels his heart breaking and floating away from his body. So many names. 'Yeah, that was about two years ago.'

'Almost exactly two years ago,' says Stone, noting the date next to the name, and taking her phone out of her pocket. 'I remember, cos I was at Henley just about to graduate. It looks as if our girl got some practice in before she moved onto the main event.'

'What are you doing?'

Stone points her phone at the QR code and snaps the camera button. She looks at Loss, her eyes clear and wide, 'Going to the movies?'

'You've been practising that in front of a mirror, haven't you?' She grins at him and nods her head towards the phone. The screen on her phone goes blank for a second, and then it is filled with what appears to be a school gymnasium.

80

They come into the gym in a tight pack. There are six of them, all about fifteen, and in front, pushed and stumbling, his tie all crooked and his shirt untucked, is the boy who's been talking to me. No one's putting on any lights and the squeak from their stupid-expensive trainers echoes around the hall, setting the air on edge.

I found him on a self-help suicide site, this boy. He's thirteen years old and he's had enough. Once his parents are asleep, he spends his nights trawling the Interzone, finding places that will tell him how to kill himself.

He wakes up an extra hour early so that he can empty himself of tears before his mother comes into his bedroom.

That's on the nights he can go to sleep at all.

'Hey, Derrick, what's it like to be a *meatspinner*?' The pack snigger, and the boy cringes, trying to make himself disappear inside his own body.

Derrick. That's his name. The pack has decided he's gay, and has fucked him over so much that the pain of living is just too much for him. Me, I don't care if he's gay or not. I check that the camera sitting on the bleacher in front of me is on.

237

The pack makes a rough circle around the boy. They're in their school uniforms, but the older boys all have hooded sweatshirts.

It's a big sports hall in a big school. It's got climbing bars running up one wall, and, running along the opposite wall are tiered benches that retract for storage when there isn't some event on.

Well there's an event on now. I'm all cosy underneath those benches, in the area where the retracting mechanics are. I can see out between them. The pack are pushing Derrick like a pinball between them. It's hard to tell from this distance, but I'm pretty certain he's crying. I don't blame him. If all my tears hadn't been ripped out of my body, I'd be crying too.

It's seven o'clock at night, and the only other people in school are the illegal immigrant cleaners who get paid below minimum wage, which they give over to their handlers, and other packs of kids like this one. Not quite old enough to own the streets, but big enough to own the school. They know all the alarm codes and they have all the keys. The teachers can't wait for the working day to be over so they can leave the war zone.

During the day they've got CCTV and metal-detecting machines like you'd see at an airport. At night, though, they've got fuck all. All I had to do was stroll in.

Pathetic. During the day it's a prison, but at night it's a pain park patrolled by torture drones. I look at my tablet to make sure I have what I need, then turn my attention back to Derrick.

Derrick's not doing too well. They've got him down on the floor and are making dog sounds at him. Barking and yapping.

'Hey Derrick, why don't you show us some tricks? Why don't you show us what you do with your boyfriends?' The pack can smell blood now. They've worked themselves up, and there's no turning back. They can smell it, and they've got all jittery, jumping from foot to foot, as if they've taken too much speed.

Actually, they probably have. These brothers have speed eyes; all hard and shiny, like a frozen piece of filthy water.

Derrick can sense it too. He knows it's going to be worse than the other times. He looks round wildly. The pack laugh, thinking he's looking for a way out.

What he's really looking for, though, is me.

When I found him on the suicide site, he'd been there for a while, trying to find a way to snuff himself out without hurting his parents. Not possible. Not if they care. Then again, if they cared, why hadn't they noticed what was happening to their son? Anyhow, we get to it, and sooner rather than later I have a client.

The pack have their heads up now, egging each other on. The only light comes from the safety lighting in the corner of the big room, and the shadows dance and stagger around the walls. They're going to rape him. They don't even admit it to themselves but you can see it in their body language.

Derrick knows it too, and has stopped struggling. He's trying to make himself dead inside so the pain won't reach him.

The body pain. The head pain. The soul pain.

The pack won't even think of it as rape. It's just about power to them. About controlling someone completely. They're so fucking boring. They never even try to think about what they are doing.

Quietly, I come out from beneath the benches.

'Leave him alone!'

Everybody freezes.

'What's he ever done to you?' I walk further into the room so the drones can get a good look at me. I'm wearing my grey cargoes with the Burmese army shirt, collar ripped off. On the uniform front, I've got them stone-fucking-cold.

The pack stares at me. Slowly the surprise leaves their faces to be replaced with a look of pleasure. As if someone handed them a bag of crack for free.

'Well, Derrick my man, it looks like you've got a little fag-hag as a fan! Come over here, *Valentine,* help your girlfriend out.' He starts walking towards me. I reach down under the bench, and pick up the wooden relay baton and throw it at his head. It hits with a satisfying clunk, and he goes down. I'm quite surprised. Normally my aim's not that good.

'Fucking Christ! What did you do that for?' Blood is pouring from his eye as he stands up. His crew leave Derrick and start towards me.

'Because you're going to hurt my friend, shitheads.' I think it would probably be the wrong time to tell them that Derrick isn't a friend. It might overload them.

'Yeah, bitch,' Bleeding Eye snarls, 'we're going to do your friend, and then we're going to turn you inside out!'

Wow. He's so scary I might fall asleep. Still, he did threaten me, so bingo. I throw another baton at them for good measure then duck back under the benches. Derrick runs for the door, as if I'd told him to, and once he's out I pick up the camera.

It's brilliant. They're going to follow me under the tiered benches, two going one way and two the other. That way they'll trap me in a pincer movement. I go to the middle and climb up the ladder that leads to the top tier. It's super-dark under here but, unlike the drones, I know what the fuck I'm doing.

When I hear them under me I drop the flash bomb and climb down to the centre of the gym. When it goes off, I can hear them screaming that they've gone blind.

Calm down, boys, it's only temporary.

I take out my tablet and touch the screen. The benches begin to retract back against the wall. It will take about ten seconds for them to retract to the point where there will be no space left under them. Now that's what I call a fighting chance.

I put the camera on the floor, press the button that fires it up, and walk out of the gym, my electric blue DMs not making one fucking squeak.

The phone fades to black, and Stone silently puts it back in her pocket.

'Jesus.' Loss takes the photograph of Suzanne and Tuesday and her daughter out of his pocket and stares at it. 'What happened? What the hell happened to you?'

81

It's just a matter of waiting now.

I'm used to waiting. Waiting till I was old enough to walk. Waiting till I was old enough to run. Always waiting. If you don't wait, you don't watch. And if you don't watch, you get fucked. Stone cold fact. When I lived on the street, waiting was mainly what you did. Hours and hours of waiting for nothing. Just ticking. When I was pregnant there was more waiting, but that was a scared waiting. Hard waiting. Not knowing if it was going to go wrong. Or be wrong when it was born. Or if I could love her. A rape baby is not a planned event.

I needn't have worried. Of course I loved her. I loved her more than it is possible to say. I loved her so much that I started thinking of a future. Started thinking of forgetting a past. I couldn't believe anyone could do anything but love their child with every strand of their being.

Except, of course, I'd seen it. Felt it with my own skin. Anti-love.

There's a poem by some dead bloke that begins: 'They fuck you up, your mum and dad'.

Too right.

And even me. I couldn't save her. I couldn't save her with my body, and I couldn't save her with my heart, and I just couldn't save her, period.

Stop thinking. Just live in the present. Make the future a play you've seen before.

I've chosen Leicester Square. I was toying with leading them to an abandoned tunnel under the Thames and drowning the fucking lot, but it's really not my style. Plus there's no escape route if something goes wrong. Not that something's going to go wrong. No way. Leicester Square has got really deep tunnels, and the sound down here is like the sea. An empty sea with just me in it. Everyone else has been cleared out. The air is warm on my face and the walls vibrate. I just sit against the tunnel wall and tick. I can feel the smoothness of the tiny ceramic rectangles behind my back. I have really got to find out what they're all about. I'm wearing my black pilot trousers, my black collarless British army shirt, and black nail varnish. I've sacked the wigs and re-bleached my hair, put on my silver, steel toe-capped DMs, and have more weapons down here than Russia.

Well, you've got to make an effort, haven't you?

There's no sirens anymore and I've shut the Tannoy down, at least until later. The emergency red lighting is on and I love it. I've made the whole station into a ghost.

I turn my head to the side. Above me, I can hear them walking down the escalator, the sound echoing back on itself. They're coming for me now. Gang boys and killers who want to shut me down.

Listening to the noises of death creeping towards me in the dark should make me scared, I suppose, but after I lost my daughter it got too hard to feel anything.

Anything at all.

Here they come, with their guns and their animal hate.
They think they're in control.
They think they're in control and are hunting me.
Don't they know I live here?

82

The Hummer pulls up outside the tube entrance on Charing Cross Road. The whole station has been cordoned off, and is being patrolled by the police. There are uniformed officers everywhere, and the strobing from all the police cars appears to be doing nothing to calm the situation down. The street is alive with people. Tourists and locals pack together as though it's a free show – which, Constantine muses, it is.

The fact that there are uniformed officers everywhere doesn't bother Constantine. Together with the other people who have been sent with him, he gets out of the back of the vehicle where all the guns are hidden away in two large FILA hold-alls. He weaves his way through the crowd and ducks under the black and yellow hazard tape that cordons off the tube entrance. He approaches the policeman planted right outside the stairs leading to the station and whispers something in his ear. The policeman nods, and steps aside. Constantine and the others walk past him and descend below street level.

'What did you say to him, man?' Constantine doesn't answer him. He understands that knowledge is power. Plus, if they're too stupid to know that his employer has bribed their way in here, or perhaps even had a conversation with some bent officer further up the food chain, then the less conversation they have, the happier he is.

'Right. I'm going to give each of you a gun. Now I want you to pay close attention to me. The bit with the hole at the end, that's the barrel. That's what you point at the girl. The bit with the trigger, that's the end you hold.'

'There's no need to take the piss, man.' Constantine looks at him as though he's nothing, which is in fact what he is. 'I'm not "taking the piss", he says, jabbing the man in the chest for emphasis, 'I'm just making absolutely certain you don't do Tuesday's job for her, and shoot your own empty fucking head off. Or mine. Now follow me and don't make any noise.'

Constantine and his gang walk through the silent ticket hall. Emergency lights cast a sickly glow over everything. The turnstiles are open and the escalators are shut down. Strange shadows animate the walls as the murder crew walk around the hall.

'This is freaky man,' says one of the gang as they head for the escalators. The emergency lights stutter and hum, making the shadows flick and fracture.

'Which line, Northern or Piccadilly?'

Constantine breathes deeply. He thinks it is absolutely incredible that his employer has managed to build a criminal empire with such a bunch of subhuman, screen-drunk, skunk-ridden, crack-frazzled fuckheads.

'Both, you idiot. We split up.'

'Right. I knew that.' The four gang members start walking down the stationary escalator towards the Piccadilly Line platforms. Constantine watches them go, smiling gently. He takes a quiet pleasure in having absolutely no expectation of seeing them again. At least not alive.

'Come on', he whispers, 'and don't make any bloody noise.'

Along with the remaining two members of the gang, he begins to walk quietly down the escalator towards the Northern Line platform.

83

'Where the hell is Cranbourn Station? I've never heard of it.' DI Loss is finding it difficult to keep up. The picture of his daughter, and Tuesday and *her* daughter, is a weight in his pocket threatening to sink him. The *World Service* is talking about the melting of the ice-caps, and DS Stone feels she is in the middle of a David Lynch film; one of the earlier ones that make no sense, but scare the crap out of you.

On the table, under the milk bottle containing the rose, was a scrap of paper with a smiley face drawn on it in blue felt-tip, and the name of the tube station Loss has never heard of. Stone pulls off her rucksack and gets out the augmented map of underground London that Colin Stevens gave her. She spreads it out on Tuesday's camp bed, the slight indentation where Loss sat on it still visible, and peers at it. After a moment she stabs her finger on a section near the centre.

'There. It's the original name for Leicester Square, back in the 1800s.' She studies the map, her fingers drumming on the makeshift table. 'You know, Tuesday might as well be a ghost for the amount of past she lives in.' Loss draws near and looks at the map with her, taking in the scratches and scribbles for a moment, deciphering them into something he can understand.

'OK. So to get from here to there we're going to – what? – go through first the sewer system, then an abandoned tube tunnel, then an actual *live* tube tunnel and . . . what is that, anyway?' He points to a section of the map cross-hatched in red.

'A stretch of private subterranean canal, sir, which frankly I find a bit of a head-fuck.'

'OK. And then we reach Leicester Square.'

'Well, then we reach the old lift shaft in Leicester Square that used to contain, surprise, the lift, before the escalators were put in, and for some unknown reason still exists as a ventilation shaft, and has an exit into the ticket office.'

'Brilliant. And tell me again, why aren't we just going back up here and taking a nice police car across town?'

'Well, mainly because of this note, I suppose, sir,' says Stone dryly.

'Ah yes, the note.' They look at the scrap of paper that Tuesday left behind. On the one side are the smiley face and the name of the ghost station, on the back is a single sentence.

'Yes sir.'

'That would be the note that says that some police officers were involved in my daughter's murder, and not to trust them, yes?'

'That's the one.'

DI Loss stares at Tuesday's home: the crate bed, and the yellow rose, and the old punk poster.

'And we're feeling that it puts a slightly different slant on what the Commander said to you, about reporting anything we find straight back to him, are we?'

'We are.'

'And we're thinking that, perhaps the investigation into my

249

daughter's murder might have been somewhat compromised, if what this girl is saying is true?'

'In a nutshell, yes.'

Stone puts her rucksack back on, and hands a halogen torch to Loss. The detective feels that the information on the note has finally pushed him over into a new state of being. He takes a deep breath and looks at his DS.

'Right then. After you, Sergeant.'

They walk away from Tuesday's home; from the *World Service*, and the fairy lights, from the sad camp bed, and The Clash poster. They walk through the station to the old platform, jump off and onto the tracks, the metal rails long since removed, switch on their torches, and enter the black tunnel.

84

Smartphones are like tracking devices you can make calls on. They're like little homing beacons; a GPS tag you want to wear cos it's cool. Really, considering these boys are meant to be scary, mean bad guys, they're a walking joke. Seven of them coming down the escalators, another six coming up the tunnels from the stations down the line, and according to my police feed, the boys in blue have sealed everything off so I can't run away. I'm shaking in my silver boots. I just sit here for a while, looking at the little dots on my tablet, showing me the GPS from their phones. Because of the station Wi-Fi, it even works underground. Who'd 've fucking thought?

I think a little bit about Suzanne, and I think a little bit about my daughter, and I think a little bit about the man who lives in the flat at Hyde Park, and about what he did, and then I stop thinking for a little bit. I don't think about the people coming down the escalator to kill me. What's the point? They're going to be dead soon. Not as dead as my daughter, cos they're not real human beings, but definitely stopped-clock, run-down dead. After a time I start thinking again, and press a few buttons on my computer.

Time to get to it.

85

'Jesus fucking Christ!'

All the LED smart-signs that line the walls adjacent to the escalators have switched on. Every one of them is showing the same identical thing. It is footage of Tuesday, on a loop. Tuesday running towards the screen, her oversize goggles giving her that insectile, alien quality. Tuesday on the tube, walking through the gang boys as if she's spring cleaning. Tuesday outside Candy's. Over and over again, the image of the boy being shot in the eye with the crossbow pistol plays out on the screen. The gang members walking down to the Piccadilly Line are mesmerized. So much so that, when the escalator comes screeching to life, they are caught unawares, and fall over.

Cursing and swearing, they scramble to their feet and point their guns at the open space below them. Although the escalator is working there are no lights. The low illumination comes from the electronic posters on the walls, flashing the name 'Tuesday' in carnival-red lettering, and the stuttering emergency lights high in the ceiling. The foyer below is a gloomy pool of unknown menace, and the tunnels leading off from them toward the platforms are black holes.

'This is seriously fucking me up, man,' says one of the gangboys. They arrive at the bottom and step onto the tiled floor. The overhead lights come on with a metallic snap.

'Shit!'

Although the lights have come on there is nothing to see. The crew point their weapons everywhere but there's no one to hit. No one there. The place is still empty.

Two of them take the Eastbound platform and the other two take the Westbound. However freaky the situation is they take heart from the fact that it's just one teenage girl, and they are hardened bad boy criminals. That plus the fact that they've got some serious guns.

86

I have no compunction in taking out these boys. They have come to kill me. Look at them, walking down the empty platform holding their guns out in front of them, but turned sideways like they're all Mr. Black. Like they're some gang-banger SWAT posse. Stupid, stupid gun bunnies. Don't they know you can't aim if you hold a gun like that? That there's a reason the sighting bar is on the top? I mean, I'm not an expert or anything, but even I know that. Mind you, if they hit me then I'm dead. I'm not stupid, or so blasé that I think I'm indestructible.

If they see me and shoot at me, it's game over.

Not that there's anything to aim at anyway. I'm not on the platform. They're looking around, stealth-walking just like in the films, pointing their toys at any shadow their tiny gang minds think is moving.

But they can't see me.

Of course they can't see me; I'm not on the platform.

I'm not on the platform, boys.

I'm under it.

87

'How can you get an email down here?'

DI Loss and DS Stone have been getting an education. They have walked through underground London. They have been amazed at the beautiful stone arches in the Victorian sewers. They have seen bats, and rats, and blind foxes with milk-coloured eyes. On the underground canal section they had quietly walked past a narrowboat that seemed to be being used as a bordello. The deck of the boat had been festooned with Chinese lanterns, and Billie Holiday's cracked voice was seeping out of the windows, singing about love and pain. The moment was so bizarre and broken-heartedly beautiful, that Loss would have taken up smoking again right there and then, if someone had offered him a cigarette.

'I don't know. I guess because we're near Leicester Square we're picking up its Wi-Fi.'

'OK. But it's quite weird, getting it down here.'

'Not as weird as having post delivered twice a day,' says Stone. She looks at her phone, and reads the email. 'It's from Professor Mummer. She says that following the break-in, they've done a complete inventory of the artefacts stored in the basement. It seems some other stuff was taken.'

'Like what?'

'You're not going to like it.'

'What?' Loss stops and glares at her. 'What?'

'Where's Borneo?'

88

The traditional poison used with the big game dart gun that I borrowed, i.e. nicked, from the British Museum is curare. Well, they should have better security, shouldn't they? But I'm not fucking about here; I've gone straight for the sting from the Iraqi red scorpion. Once the poison hits the bloodstream you've got about three seconds, then you're dead.

Thank you, the basement of the Natural History Museum.

Well, there's more than one museum in this city built by tunnel-mad Victorians.

As the first drone walks over the grate above me, I shoot a dart into the underside of his chin, in the soft area beside the jaw-bone. I walk on to where I can hear the next one before the first puppet has even fallen to the ground.

'Jed! What the fuck's happened, man?'

Jed's dead. That's what the fuck has happened. As his partner runs over me to see what's wrong with his mate, I stab him in the shin through the grate with the poisoned tip of my knife. He lets out one surprised little yelp, a bit like a small dog, and then he falls over for good. Puppet strings cut. Really, if these people weren't sent to kill me I'd feel sorry for them. I can hear their friends coming from the other platform, running to find out what is causing all the noise. I move on and climb the steps that lead up to the air-conditioning shaft behind the wall. It's like some old stately home down here, with service tunnels behind every wall so the public don't have to see how the machine functions. I have a good view of them through the access door grille as they look at the bodies of their scummy little buddies.

89

The two gang boys skid to a stop when they see the bodies in front of them. The one at the back takes out his mobile and punches the speed button.

'Constantine! She's down here, man, and she's zeroed Jed and Lem. What? I don't *know* how she did it. Shit, she's a freaking ghost! Look.' The boy swipes on the camera app and shows his boss the area in front of him. 'See. There's no one here! No!' In front of him his partner drops to the ground as if he's been rabbit-punched in the head. His body spasms once, then is still.

'Did you get that? He just died in front of me, man. No bullet or nothing! I'm getting out of here!' And then he feels a small prick in his neck, and the world goes numb. The phone drops from his hand.

Three seconds later he's dead.

90

The phone in Constantine's hand shows the boy falling to the ground, then the sender screaming, 'He died in front of me!', and then the image vanishes as the phone drops and, by chance, lands pointing at the boy who was holding it. It shows an image of his head, a bubble of blood in his mouth, and a slug of red oozing from his nose. The eyes are staring past anything a living person can see.

'Fucking hell,' mutters one of the gang boys next to him. Suddenly the phone is picked up and turned round. Constantine stares into the face of a girl with short choppy hair, bleached white. She smiles at him.

'Hello, boys. Stay right where you are. I'll be with you in a minute.' She stares at them for a moment longer, and then ends the call, turning the screen black.

91

'You'll need to get out of the ventilation shaft in about three minutes.' DS Stone's phone has just rung, nearly making her jump out of her skin, and the girl known as Tuesday looks out at her, smiling serenely.

As Stone and DI Loss look at the image on her phone, she can't believe that this young girl has caused so much mayhem in her city. Has killed all those people. She is just a girl. Her black eye-liner has run a little, giving her a slightly frazzled look, but other than that she could be one of any counter-culture emo Gothy types you can see around the city.

'Tuesday. You need to come in, Tuesday. You need to let us come and get you and take you in.'

The girl on the phone goes on smiling at them, showing two rows of slightly gapped, but perfectly maintained teeth. Loss wonders how she has managed it; whether there might be dental records somewhere, with her real name attached.

'Sorry Detective Sergeant Stone, but you're not in charge here. The gang boys are in charge. The rape-drones and the bodysnatchers, they're the ones who are calling the shots. I'm just reacting to them.'

'You can't believe that,' says Loss, staring at her. He feels as though he is living in the future. The image is crystal clear.

Tuesday shifts her gaze to look at him. 'Hello, Inspector. You know, I really loved your daughter. When I first came into the Refuge she didn't look at me as if I was shit. As if I'd just fucked myself up out of spite. She looked at me as if she was my mum. A proper mum, that is. Not the one who raised me. I'm really, really sorry she is dead.'

'How did you do it? How did you steal her DNA profile? *Why* did you steal it?' He clenches his fists by his side in the dark.

The girl stares back at him for a moment, not smiling now. And then she seems to relax. 'Tick-tock, detectives,' she says, holding up a thin wrist and shaking it, as if to show them an invisible watch. 'Well, the "how" is easy. Really, everyone tries to look for complicated systems, when everything is simply not that hard. Everyone who worked at the hospital had to have his or her DNA added to the database, yeah? They had some high-security cases going through there, so I think it was just standard procedure. So was taking DNA samples of the runaways. Talk about a police state! How can it even be legal? Anyway, I was in for a late scan when Suzanne was giving her DNA sample, and they took mine at the same time: a saliva swab and a fingerprint on a square of glass. Well, there was some sort of doctory thing, some emergency next door, and everyone had to rush out. And I was left alone for a couple of minutes.' Tuesday pauses and winks at the detectives. 'So I swapped them. Hers for mine. Simple.' The girl stops looking at Loss for a second, and gazes at the past. Then she snaps back, causing a spasm of electricity to surge through him. 'I was 14-years-old. I didn't want anyone to find me. I *specifically* didn't want anyone to find me. So I swapped them.' The girl who calls herself Tuesday glares defiantly out of the screen at them.

'And then, when they took my baby and killed your daughter, it became a sort of talisman for me. As I staggered about in the dark, it was one of the things that kept me alive. Knowing my daughter was taken and killed. I was going mad, and being part of Suzanne kept me sane.' The girl pauses for a moment, and then smiles brightly. 'Well, fairly sane.'

'But why? Why did they kill your daughter? Why did they kill Suzanne? And what do you mean in the note, about the police being involved?'

Tuesday holds his gaze for a moment, her eyes unblinking. 'Have you ever wondered, detective, how come I haven't been caught? How come, with algorithms being used to hunt for terrorists, and metadata being sieved by pattern-recognition software, that I haven't been stopped before now? I mean, you've seen my wall, yeah?' An image of the wall with all the names and QR codes stencilled to it skims across Loss's brain. He nods.

'Well If all that was working as it should, even someone as clever as me should have been put down long ago.'

'Someone's been fucking with the data,' whispers Stone. Tuesday looks at her and grins.

'Bingo! Time's up, I'm afraid, detectives. I really hope you're near the shaft exit.'

Stone looks down the tunnel ahead at the entrance to the shaft. From there they will need to climb up the internal ladder for a minute or so to reach the ticket office. 'Why? What's so bloody important about getting out of the shaft?'

Tuesday glances at her tablet. 'I see Professor Mummer has sent you another email, DS Stone. I'd open it if I were you. It looks as though she's found something she wants to tell you about.' And then Tuesday gives them a little finger wave with the hand that isn't holding the phone, and severs the connection.

Stone presses some buttons and opens up her email and quickly scans the contents. 'Oh God.'

Loss is still numb from the information Tuesday has and has not given him.

'We've got to get out of here. Right now,'

Loss picks up on the urgency in her tone. And the fear. 'What is it? What has she stolen?'

'Professor Mummer says that they've found a crate in the lower basement that has absolutely no right being in the Museum.'

Loss thinks of the crate in Tuesday's strange home, with the skull and crossbones embossed on it. He feels a block of dread whiting out his brain. 'Go on then, tell me. It's a bomb, isn't it?'

The phone in Stone's hand gives a merry 'ping': an Instagram. 'No, sir. The crate contains a yellow rose and a bromide gas grenade. Professor Mummer says that if the crate had been full it would have contained twenty grenades.' Stone turns the phone around to show a picture of a small room, somewhere underground: an open crate showing the grenades nestling on a bed of straw. The photo is tagged 'Tuesday'.

'Like this one in the photo Tuesday has just sent through.'

92

It's surprising what useful information you can pick up from books people throw away. Bromide gas was used in the trenches to temporarily blind and disorientate the soldiers. It was dropped onto the battlefield in canisters fired from mortars. So, blind and disorientated is just about what the boys and girls coming up the tunnels will be. After all this time the likelihood of the gas sealed inside their metal sheaves still being full-strength is quite small, but it's going to give them a world of pain. The effects are really quite nasty. As well as temporary blindness, there's vomiting, internal blisters to the throat and lungs. I've put two canisters in the entrance to each of the tunnels, and one in the lower hallway, just for fun. In fact, just so my little friends get the full effect I've turned on all the lights and put some hardcore psycho-dub over the Tannoy system. After all, I've got a reputation to uphold.

93

The men and women coming up the tunnels to the station are a mixture of Metropolitan Police specialist fire-arms command and hardboiled criminal muscle. Each one of them is armed with a selection of assault rifles and handguns. Many of the criminals have killed before. Of the police contingent, each of them, to a greater or lesser degree, is corrupt. It had not taken Slater and his collaborator in the Met long to pull their little army together. Nor is it the first time they've done so. Over the years it had been necessary for Slater to have someone high up in law enforcement to facilitate his growing business interests. Doors needing to be opened, or kicked in. Borders needing to be crossed covertly. People difficult for him to get to needing to be retired, so to speak. Now, with Tuesday ripping up the criminal carpet from beneath them, the stakes were very high, and neither of them could afford any mistakes. Any leakage.

When the station lights go on ahead of them, the leader of each group holds up his hand, and converses with his equivalent by mobile phone. One group has just emerged from the Westbound tunnel of the Piccadilly line. It is obvious that one splinter of Constantine's group has failed to neutralize the girl, as they are dead, lying on the platform. No matter. The people sliding out of the tunnel towards the station are not East London gang-bangers who think violence and attitude are enough. These boys and girls are professionals: hired mercenaries in the gang wars of the most diverse city in the world. They start to move forward again, slowly. They are not in a rush. The station is sealed from above, and with every step they make the cornering, and then killing, of Tuesday more of a certainty.

The tripwire, which is snapped as they make their way out of the tunnel and onto the platforms, is so thin that they don't even feel it. Only when the green-brown gas starts to roll out of the blackness behind them do the hard-nosed, dead-eyed professional killing machines have any idea that something is wrong.

Five seconds later, as the gas envelopes them, it's too late.

94

DS Stone and DI Loss start to hear the screaming as they scramble up the ladder in the ventilation shaft.

'That'll be the mustard gas, then,' wheezes Loss. Even though he hasn't smoked for three years the effects of all the years before make him short of breath and dizzy.

'Bromide gas,' Stone corrects him. 'If she'd stolen mustard gas we really would be in sodding trouble.'

'You know you swear too much, right?' says Loss in between rungs. 'You never used to swear this much, did you?'

'Yes, sir. And sir?'

'Yes?'

'Could you hurry the fuck up, cos this is a ventilation shaft.'

'What's your point?'

'Well, judging by the screaming, I'd say Tuesday has just let off her little weapons of mass destruction on the platform below.'

'Yes?'

'Well, not to put too fine a point on it, sir, the gas has to go somewhere once it's been released, and *this is a ventilation shaft!*'

Realisation dawns swiftly. Loss looks down past her. At the bottom of the shaft, but rising quickly, is a muddy brown cloud that even looks as if it's bad news.

'Shit!' He shouts, quickly clambering up the last few rungs of the ladder. In front of him is a metal door with a simple sliding lock-bar keeping it shut. Loss throws the lever, kicks open the door and flings himself out onto the floor of the ticket office. He rolls aside to let Stone tumble out, and then slams the door shut.

95

Constantine and his remaining crew stumble up the escalators to the next level. They are half blind and retching, blisters erupting from any exposed skin. It was lucky that they were on the Northern line platform, as it is less deep than the Piccadilly one. By the time they reach the escalators below the ticket concourse the gas has thinned out. It now forms a swirling, viscous pool about their feet. Constantine is the least affected. When the canisters blew, and he saw the gas rolling towards them, he immediately drew his tee shirt up over his mouth and nose, and then he held his breath, and smashed a vending machine and snatched a bottle of water. Taking the cap off, he poured the water over the cloth round his mouth. After that, he grabbed the people with him, and pulled them off the platform and up the escalators. Behind them people stagger out of the tunnel, blind and firing indiscriminately. Constantine is amazed that neither he nor his crew are hit by random bullets as they stagger through the arch into the escalator hall.

They travel up the final set of moving stairs below the ticket concourse. The LED posters on the walls are showing scenes from the station below them. Tuesday must have set up remote cameras and patched them into the station network, thinks Constantine, one part of his brain grudgingly admiring. The screens show people lurching around, screaming, and firing at anything that moves. Down near the tunnels the gas is like a river, with the would-be murderers wading through it, scratching at their eyes, and shooting each other.

'Well at least the fucking dub music has finished,' Constantine mutters, pushing his men onto the final escalator. He waits till they're a third of the way up, gets on, then lies down on the cold, metal steps.

96

All things considered, I think it's gone rather well. After I'd said bye-bye to the boys on the Piccadilly line, I scoobied up to the ticket concourse and waited for the fun to start. Don't get me wrong, it's not that I get pleasure from the death and destruction of those who want to kill me. Just because they're murderers, rapists, peddlers of drugs and despair, and all-round soulless deadheads, it doesn't make it fun. What makes it fun is they're so fucking shit at it. They think they're something special, with their guns and power.

Well, look at them. They're not fucking special; they're just dying, and dying badly. In fact, if they weren't dying, they should just blow their brains out in embarrassment, for being made to look like playschool tossers by a girl.

I look at my tablet. I can see from the phone tags on my screen that some of them have made it to the escalator in front of me.

Clap clap.

I pull the 1934 Russian PB 9mm silenced pistol from my thigh holster and point it at the top of the escalator, feeling very *Resident Evil*. Didn't find that one did you, Professor?

As the first hoodlum comes in sight, appearing like a toy

272

on a fairground game, I shoot him through the mouth. I don't want him screaming to his baby-killing cronies. The only noise from the gun is a tiny *phutt*. As the first one falls to his knees the second one comes into sight. I shoot him in the heart while he's still rubbing his eyes, trying to get the bromide sting out of them, wondering what the hell is happening. I walk over to the top of the descending escalator and crouch down between the scarred metal sides. The machinery driving the stairs is old and in need of a service. With no other ambient noise going on I can hear the grating and the grinding of it. I crouch there and wait for the third bad boy. There is a whining in my head and the snow storm behind my eyes is at full blow. There is a slight possibility that I may be losing it a bit. As he steps over his dead buddies, gun held out in front of him pointed at where I was, I shoot him in the side of his head.

Bang bang. Everyone's dead. Boo-hoo. All that's left is the metal stairs, grinding their way to forever.

I get up and walk back to where my bag is. I sense rather than hear something. Maybe a slight difference in the tone of the escalator as it turns. Maybe a shadow, or a shadow of a shadow. I'm spinning round and pointing the pistol but I'm too late. Of course I am. In my head I'm three years too late, but right now I'm just too late, period. I can see him lying on the metal floor of the escalator, cloth round his mouth and a big, never-wake-up gun extended in front of him. I see him squeeze the trigger and I feel something punch me in the shoulder. I know it's a bullet but it doesn't feel like a little slug of metal. It feels like a sledge-hammer. There's no sound accompanying the shot, but I don't know if that's because he has fitted a silencer, or the detonation is so fucking loud I've gone deaf. It doesn't matter. I'm spun round, and then suddenly I'm spun round the other way as a second bullet hits me in the leg. Nice shooting, fuck-face.

273

I fall down and stay down. Not on purpose. I just can't move. I can feel my heart accelerating, giving my body adrenalin to keep it working. To stop it shutting down and dying. The man points his gun at me a bit longer, to see if I've got anything left. His arm is extended past the end of the escalator, and his shoulders are where the flattened steps disappear into the heart of the machine. Then he gets up and walks towards me.

No. No, I haven't got anything left.

Nothing at all.

97

Constantine steps over the three dead bodies of his gang members and walks towards Tuesday. She is still on the floor, her body looks like a thrown doll. Her legs are splayed out, blood seeping from her left thigh, and her right shoulder is just plain wrong where the bullet has shattered the bone. She is breathing quickly, but with no depth. Constantine keeps the gun pointed at her, but he can tell she's got nothing left. Nothing left inside her. Now she's just a little girl, trying to stay alive. Constantine smiles.

'Hello, Tuesday. We've had some fun today, haven't we?' He walks over, kicks her gun out of reach, and body-searches her. He is not gentle as he pats her down. He takes her tablet out of the pocket of her pilot trousers. It takes him a little while because there are so many pockets. Amazingly, the tablet is still working. Constantine notes the GPS glympse tags of all the people down in the station, stumbling about in the bromide fog, and the unmoving tags of the gang boys six metres away.

'Very clever, little girl. You've done some truly amazing things over the last few weeks.' He taps a few keys on the tablet, changing the screen to the control panel. He taps the buttons a few more times and the images that were on the LED posters cease. The station is now still, except for Constantine, who has stood up and is pacing back and forth. After a moment he stops and looks again at the broken girl lying at his feet.

'You know I've been told not to kill you, don't you, little girl? You know I've got to cut your hands off and then take you back to Mr Slater? The money and resources you've cost him, I think he might want to make an example of you.' Constantine is clearly enjoying this. His pulls an elegant silver cigarette case out of his pocket and removes a black-papered Sobranie. He places the gold-tipped cigarette in the corner of his mouth and removes a Zippo from his pocket.

'You'll never get me out of here. The police will stop you,' says Tuesday, panting slightly, spit hanging out of the corner of her mouth.

Constantine laughs, lighting his cigarette with the Zippo, which he fires up by flipping it open and scrimming the cog down his trouser leg. 'Stupid girl! He *owns* the police! The amount of drugs and guns he deals in, he couldn't do it *without* the cooperation of the police. Everyone knows that! Even the fucking school kids know that, Tuesday.'

'Yeah, well. I guess he owns you too, blood.'

Constantine smiles, blowing a plume of white smoke towards the girl. 'Nobody owns me, Tuesday. Or maybe everybody does. I'm just a gun for hire. Tell me, though. I'm interested. What did this man do to you to make all this happen? To fuck you up so royally? Oh, I know your baby died, and she died on a Tuesday. That's why you took the name, yes? Like a respect thing.'

'You've got no idea.'

'No, I get it. I really do. Your baby dies, and so by calling yourself Tuesday you keep her alive.' He taps his head gently. 'In here.'

276

'My baby didn't just die, Mister I'm a gun-for-hire, too-hard-for-cancer.' Tuesday spits on the floor. Her spit is flecked with red. 'My baby was stolen, and then broken down.' Constantine moves his head to one side, waiting. 'For parts,' she almost whispers.

For a while there's no noise in the station. Just the sense of noise; sub noise, coming up from the tunnels below. Tuesday is finding it hard to breathe. There is an ever-growing pool of blood beneath her thigh. After a time, she continues. 'The Refuge. The whole place was a scam. Not the nurses and shit, but the set-up. They'd take in runaway girls who were pregnant. Half of them were rape pregnancies from the gang-bangers in your mate's little outfit.'

'I told you, he's not my friend.' Constantine stubs the cigarette out under his suede desert boot.

Tuesday spits more blood onto the tiled floor. 'Whatever. Anyway it had police protection, all the way up. Nobody found us. Nobody bothered with us. We just waited there and had our babies, thinking the state might actually have a good side.' Tuesday laughs without humour. 'What a fucking joke. The whole place was a cutting shop. They'd deliver the babies, then kill the babies, then break them down. Kidneys. Hearts. Everything had a price. They'd harvest the babies, then your boss would sell them on. What do you think of that?'

Constantine contemplates her words for a moment or two, clicking his teeth together repeatedly. The sound makes a sinister echo around the hall.

'Poor girl. Sad little never-mother. That must have broken your mind, yes? Did you have to watch?' His eyes are alive with dark merriment.

Tuesday is crying, but she is quite clearly bleeding away too. Constantine sits down cross-legged in front of her, placing the tablet on the concourse floor. Tuesday swallows hard, fixing him with her gaze.

'But not everyone was in on it. There was this doctor, Suzanne, who sussed it all out. She told me her dad was in the police. The proper police. Not those fuckers in the tunnel. She told me that she was going to go to him, make it all end. But he never showed. They made *her* end, instead. They made everything stop.' She pauses, either because she has no breath left since she has two holes in her body through which her life is bleeding out, or because the memories playing on the screen in her head make a horror film. 'After they'd killed my baby and stolen her body I went blind, just white-ed out. They thought I was nothing, a street girl who was fucked up, but I grabbed a scalpel and followed him out. I was too late to save Suzanne, but I stopped his clock.'

'Yes. I saw the stills. Really, very nice work.' Constantine smiles at her, as if he's watching a clever animal in the circus, and then he stops smiling. 'I'm going to put you to sleep now, Tuesday, and when you wake up you'll be in hell, and I'll have been paid and will be long gone. What do you think of that?'

Tuesday gazes at him, empty. Head empty, heart empty, womb empty.

'I win, little girl,' Constantine, grins. 'You lose.'

Tuesday continues to stare at him a moment longer. Her pupils are pinpricks as the last of her adrenalin flies round her body, trying to keep it functioning.

'Honeytrap,' she whispers.

'What?'

'Just fucking shoot him, will you?' Tuesday looks up at the ceiling.

'What?' Constantine is confused. 'What did you say?'

'You heard what he did? What he does? I'm too tired for fucking about. Just put a bullet in him so we can all go to sleep.' Tuesday closes her eyes, and Constantine spins around, gun extended as the bullet enters his shoulder.

'You, my friend, are fucking under arrest,' says DI Loss, his gun rock-steady in his hand, pointing at Constantine's heart.

98

Mister Ice-Cold-Dickhead is so busy rubbing himself up on having shot me that he didn't see them by the ticket office.

Whoops.

My body feels like it's crashing every time my heart beats. The pain is so bad I want to shut down and throw up at the same time, but I have to keep the man's attention on me so that the detectives can get in a position to save my pretty self. I tell him about the Refuge, about how his people, the people he hangs with, would cut up little babies, and sell them off for scrap. It's absolutely no surprise to me that he is unmoved, but I can see that Loss and Stone are devastated. Of course they are. They're real people, one of them with a real dead daughter. I'm talking about Suzanne as well, trying to tell him what she meant to me. Trying to convey it to DI Loss, in case Fuck-head here goes all country and decides to shoot me dead anyway.

And all the time I can feel the tide turning. The waves of pain that crash in my body are having less impact. It's lucky the lights are back on, because my senses are only working part-time.

I'm shutting down now.

Eventually, when I think that Assassin Boy has dug a big enough hole, I tell them to shut him up.

He looks confused. He thinks he's so clever, bringing down a girl like me. What a shame he's not.

Win, lose, who cares. I'll leave it to them.

I lean my head back against the wall and close my eyes.

'For fuck's sake, just shoot him.'

I barely hear the sound of the gun.

99

DI Loss and DS Stone walk towards Tuesday and Constantine. Loss has his gun straight-armed out in front of him, and Stone is scanning the ticket office for signs of anyone else; anybody who might harm them. As far as she can hear, all the action seems to be coming from down on the platforms, but she's not taking any chances. Loss continues to point his gun at Constantine, stepping over the bodies at the top of the escalator.

'Well look who it is, Laurel and Hardy,' Constantine is speaking through clenched teeth. There is a small wound in his shoulder where DI Loss's bullet grazed it, but he does not appear to be too badly hurt.

Unlike Tuesday. Even if she isn't wearing ghost-white make-up, she looks more dead than alive. Her breathing is irregular and her eyes are closed.

'About bloody time,' she whispers. Her voice is like a breeze, barely disturbing the silence of the station.

'Tuesday,' says Loss, never taking his eyes off Constantine. 'I'm so sorry about your daughter.' Constantine just smiles at him, as though he's waiting for the detective to tell him a joke.

'Same,' says Tuesday, a worrying rattle in the back of her throat, eyes closed, her voice barely audible.

'Well here's another fine mess you've got yourself into, Mr Policeman,' quips Constantine, scratching the top of his head with his right hand, in an imitation of Stan Laurel. 'Why don't you go and get some handcuffs off your friends outside?' Constantine nods towards the steps leading to the street above them, and then widens his eyes in mock shock, and brings his hand down in front of his mouth. 'Oh, that's right; they're *not* your friends, are they? They're *my* friends. You and your partner are just in a little bit over your heads here. I tell you what. Why don't you let me take our teeny murder-girl here back to my employer, and I promise not to ruin your lives forever?' Constantine drops his hand to his side and grins at them.

DS Stone is still looking around. She can hear some noises coming from the levels below her. Maybe nearer than they were a few minutes ago. Maybe a lot nearer.

'Sir? I think the bad guys are on their way up. Whatever we're going to do, we'd better do it quickly.'

Loss shifts his attention from Tuesday, with her eyes closed, lines of pain mapping her face, to Constantine with his feral grin. He continues to point the gun at him. 'I tell you what, Sunshine: my life was ruined forever when your boss decided to kill my daughter. How about I stop your clock and we call it a night?'

Constantine stops grinning and licks his lips.

'Oh for fuck's sake,' croaks the girl on the floor. 'How about you knock him unconscious so I don't have to suffer the pain of listening to his brain trying to work, and I'll tell you the plan?'

'There's a plan?' Stone looks at the girl practically dead in front of her.

Tuesday opens her eyes long enough to return her look.

"Course there's a plan. I've spent three years doing this. There's nothing *but* a plan.'

'And this is part of it?' Loss nods at the small river of blood leaving Tuesday's body. Tuesday lowers her head slightly. Loss can't tell if it's in acknowledgment of what he said, or if she's about to lose consciousness.

'All right, Smart-arse. Plans, plural. Not plan A, I admit. More plan X.'

There is a weighty crunch and Constantine slumps prone to the floor. Behind him, Stone, holding a 20 centimetre length of a metal Tannoy microphone, looks extremely pleased with herself.

'Wanker,' she says, staring down at Constantine's unconscious body.

'There you are with the swearing, again,' says Loss, kneeling down next to Tuesday and examining her wounds. He does not like what he sees.

'Right, we've got to get you to a hospital. Immediately.'

'You think?' says Tuesday, managing to convey sarcasm whilst coughing. Her eyes are still closed. She takes a deep breath and then says: 'All right, here's how it is. You've got police and thieves coming up from the platforms below, hardwired to shoot anything that moves. You've got laughing boy here who, when he wakes up, will slit your throat just to clear his head. You've got corrupt coppers at every exit, no doubt with orders to make sure we never make it into custody, and you've got a half dead, but very good-looking, hard-as-nails girl who needs urgent medical attention. So how about you sack the double act and get me to hospital.'

Loss blinks as he takes in the information. The fact that there are enemy officers outside the tube station. That there are armed police officers working with underworld front-liners coming for them from the tunnels below.

If he believes her.

284

He looks at her. Dying in small ticks of time in front of him. He believes her.

'What are you, our agent?' says DS Stone, putting down the microphone.

'How well did you study the map of this tube station, detectives?' Tuesday asks.

In the silence that follows, Loss watches Tuesday. She has opened her eyes. Although they are fractured by pain, they are clear. He thinks about his daughter, and he thinks about *her* daughter, and the years she has lived on the street and underground, with nothing to do except grieve, and plan. And then plan again.

'Not as well as you, I'm sure.'

And Tuesday manages a lop-sided smile.

'Too fucking right,' she whispers.

100

The police from the street, and the police/gang coalition from the tunnels, arrive in the ticket concourse at the same time. From the way they all seem to be working together this is not an accident. All the lights are on and they find Constantine just coming to. Despite searching they turn up no trace of DI Loss, DS Stone, or the girl known as Tuesday. What they do find, however, is that the TV feed is working in the reception foyer, and that it is showing earlier CCTV footage from the tunnels. It is showing the police and criminals next to each other, shouting and waving their weapons about. Although there is no audio, the news channel has helpfully ticker-taped some of the dialogue across the bottom of the screen, courtesy of a lip-reading expert; it reads 'Kill the girl on sight, no f*****g witnesses'.

The screen then cuts to Constantine and his murder crew creeping down the escalator, armed to the teeth. Underneath, the scroll-line is now informing the audience of 'breaking news'. The policemen stare at the screen in dismay.

101

DS Stone and DI Loss close the metal access panel quietly, shutting out the noise of the policemen storming down into the ticket hall, and half carry, half drag Tuesday along the maintenance corridor to the basement of the White Bear pub, twenty metres from the Charing Cross Road entrance to Leicester Square tube station.

When they walk out of its side entrance and look back across the road at where they have come from it is a disaster movie. There are media vans blocking the road. Blocking the already police-blocked road. There are helicopters fracturing the sky, speaker-distorted voices telling the crowd to disperse. There are police unsure whether to arrest the reporters or other officers. There are cordons stopping people going in, cordons stopping people going out. Nobody seems to be in charge. The two detectives and Tuesday limp themselves into the back of a black LTI taxi, and leave the chaos.

DI Loss instructs the driver to take them to Charing Cross Hospital. Light rain is falling, and the sound of the wipers are breaking his thinking into moments with no order or meaning. Even in the dim light of rainy London he can tell that Tuesday is not doing well. She is propped against DS

Stone's shoulder. Loss cannot believe how fragile she looks. All her bones look as though they want to live on the outside. As if they want to escape into a better body.

'How the hell did they all get here so fast?' wonders Stone aloud, staring through the ribbons of rain at the media carnage outside.

'Well that was down to the blue-eyed boy who shot me, then stole my tablet,' says Tuesday, her voice wearied beyond weeping. 'Once he started pressing keys without the correct code it automatically sent the images I'd downloaded from the station CCTV to the *World Service*.'

DI Loss looks at her with consternation. 'But that's a radio station!'

'I know. I just thought it would be nice if they had it first. I knew they'd have to pass it on immediately. Are we nearly there?'

'I can see the gates,' says Stone, staring through the rain.

'Good, cos I can't. I can't see a thing.'

And then Tuesday falls unconscious in the arms of DI Loss.

The taxi pulls up outside A&E, and the detectives carry Tuesday in, held up between their arms, wave their badges around, and shout for a doctor. It is not lost on Stone, as various medical staff run towards them, that this is where her boss's daughter worked, and where Tuesday's daughter was born.

102

Constantine is not just hacked off, he's incandescent with rage. Hate courses through his body in lightning bursts of white-hot fury. In all the confusion he escaped out of the station, and is now in a taxi on his way to Number One, Hyde Park. The fact that he is not alone in his failure, that everybody else also failed to stop Tuesday, is not a consolation to him. He knows that it will be no consolation to his employer, either. His employer is not a man known for his understanding and acceptance of other people's failures.

Still, all is not completely hopeless. Clutched in Constantine's hand is the tablet previously belonging to the girl known as Tuesday. Constantine has been examining its contents. The girl has listed all her actions, and all the observations and data she has uncovered on his employer. On it are all the codes and path-bringers that allowed her access to the tube system, and the security systems of the department stores she broke into. Without it she will be useless.

Constantine smiles a smile that barely even touches his mouth, let alone his eyes.

'You may have won this time, little girl,' he says, staring

at the scarred and battered device. 'But without this you're nothing.'

Ahead of him, the glass and steel structure of One Hyde Park comes into view. Constantine breathes slowly, humming tunelessly under his breath.

103

'Constantine escaped, and the police are all over the place. Nobody knows what the hell's going on.' DS Stone shuts off her mobile and looks at the girl lying in the hospital bed. She looks better that she did two days ago, when she was brought in amid the shouting and badge-waving, but she still looks like shit. There are black circles under her eyes. Her shoulder is tightly wrapped in bandages, and there is a needle attached to a drip in her dagger-thin arm. From the time when they carried her into the hospital to now, the detectives' lives have been up for auction. They have been suspended from active duty pending an investigation by the DPS. They are not alone in this. Their commander is also under investigation, following the recovery of the dead and injured from Leicester Square tube station.

'Who's Constantine?' asks Tuesday, her voice butterflying with pain.

'Wow. Something you don't actually know!' Stone says in fake amazement. 'He's the man who shot you. He was identified by the blood he helpfully left on the bit of metal I hit him with. He's some sort of gun for hire, and wanted in more territories than exist in the world, apparently. Anyhow, he escaped, and presumably has your tablet with your entire life, such as it is, on it. '

Tuesday looks as though she's about to cry. After all that she has done, all she has been through, it seems almost comical that something like this should bring her to tears.

'It had the only picture I have of my daughter on it,' she says quietly. 'Apart from the one I left for you.'

Now DI Loss feels he's going to weep too. Out of his pocket he takes the picture he removed from the tube station. 'I made a copy of it. I hope you don't mind.' He hands the original over to Tuesday, who gently takes it in her hands. The room is silent while Tuesday looks at the picture of her daughter. Of his daughter. Tears slip slowly down her cheek, in no hurry to be anywhere.

'Tuesday, I'm so sorry. What was done to your baby, to all the babies. Well it's beyond unforgivable. I'm sure that when the story comes out you'll, well you'll . . .' He runs out of words. He has no more words. Not for Tuesday. Not to describe this.

'I'll what? Get off? Live happily ever after?' Tuesday snorts, her nostrils flaring. 'Fuck off, DI Loss. You're just an old man who couldn't even help his own daughter. Or Lily-Rose, for that matter. Don't try to adopt me.'

He doesn't look away. He knows Tuesday is just lashing out. Trying to spread her hurt. He watches as she takes her sleeping pill, washing it down with the glass of warm Coke on the bedside table.

'Speaking of Lily-Rose, I don't suppose you know where she is, do you? Only, she seems to have disappeared without a trace.'

Tuesday stares at him awhile, and then looks away.

'I'll see you in the morning, Tuesday.'

Loss and DS Stone quietly get up and head for the door. Before he leaves, Loss turns back and looks at Tuesday.

292

'It's because of the curves,' he says. Tuesday looks puzzled. Even this action looks as if it causes her pain.

'What?'

'You were talking in your sleep', he explains, 'about the tiles in the underground.' He waits for Tuesday to say something, but she is silent. 'The reason they're so small is because of the curve of the wall. The tiles are flat, you see. If they made them any bigger they'd crack.'

On the way out, he passes the policeman stationed outside the door.

104

I squirrel the sleeping pill under my tongue, right at the back where the little hollow is, and drink my Coke from a straw. I learnt that trick by watching the drug-dealing robot kids. That's where they hide their thrill pills, in case of street searches, before they sell them.

DI Loss watches me as I pretend to swallow it, and then he leaves. Sorry, detective, but I don't want you feeling pity for me. I can't have that. I might just fall apart if that happens, and I've still got things to do. Who'd've thought it about the tiles, though? Tiny so they don't break. So they can function.

Like me.

Once I'm sure he isn't coming back, I take the pill out and crush it between my empty glass and the table, put the granules into the glass, and add the powder from the other three pills I've smuggled away over the past two days. I lean forward, get another glass from the tray on my table and fill both glasses with Coca-Cola. It's one of the few luxuries I've been allowed, and me and my guard have developed a bit of a routine. Each time before I fall into my pretend drug-induced la-la sleep, we share a glass of Coke, and he tells me what's happening in London. It's like I'm the adult and he's the kid. Nothing this exciting has happened to him, ever. I do a lazy shout-out to him and he comes in. As usual, he's as animated as a puppy. Maybe it's the hours of standing outside my room with nothing to do except stare at a wall.

'You'll never guess, Tuesday, but they've just sacked my boss. My boss! He was a right bastard, anyway, but bloody hell, eh?' He sits down in the chair at the end of the bed and starts drinking his Coke, telling me about how it's like Operation Yew Tree, Alder Hey, and *Die Hard*, all rolled into one. I don't really care what he talks about, as long as he finishes his drink, so I nod and try to look suitably impressed that his life is so exciting.

Like what? Compared to mine?

Twenty minutes later he's snoring like a wino and spark out on the floor. I ease myself out of bed, and wince. The bullet in my thigh didn't break any bones but it hurts like fuck. All my clothes have been thrown away, so if I want to leave the hospital by any of the street exits I'm going to have to steal a nurse's uniform.

How fucking likely is that? Me, in a nurse's uniform?

Lucky I'm *not* going to leave the hospital by any of the street exits, isn't it?

105

Constantine and Slater are once again surveying London from the balcony of the apartment in One, Hyde Park. Some harsh words have been spoken and Constantine has a savage gash down the side of his face from the edge of a broken bottle. He considers he has got off lightly. Both Slater and Constantine are smoking; something Slater has not done for many years.

'So basically, she won't be able to do anything without it?' says Slater, turning over Tuesday's tablet in his hands. It is battered but little lights are still flashing on it.

'Nothing. She's as good as dead without it. It contains her whole life.'

'And you can open it, decode it or whatever?' pursues Slater, setting the tablet down and turning back to the London night sky.

'Sure. Give me the right equipment and it'll be as if it was always yours.'

Slater's face is white and shiny, with the hint of blue veins just below the surface. It looks as though his skin has been sprayed on but they ran out of paint. He flicks his cigar out and into the air, watching the embers firework off into the night.

'OK. Here's what I want you to do. I want you to go down to that hospital and kill Tuesday. No messing about. Just kill her, photograph her body, and then post it on fucking Facebook. Next, I want you to help me sort out anybody who's moved in on my business. That girl may have crippled me, but I kid you not, there will be a fucking miracle. Not only will I walk again, but I'll kick the shit out of anybody who thinks they can push me about.'

'What about the baby thing? There's no way the business can continue in this climate. Questions have been asked in Parliament.'

Slater thinks of his high-ranking police monkey, at this moment being questioned internally about his role in the Leicester Square fiasco, among other things. 'No, that's been fucked sideways, thanks to her.' The veins on the man's neck and head are very prominent, as if his skin has shrunk. 'There will definitely have to be a reckoning.' His clockwork mind is already winding, working out the new connections it will require to put his various businesses back together again, including the body-shopping one.

The two men stand in silence side by side. Then Slater takes a slip of paper out of his pocket containing a name and address, and hands it to Constantine.

106

Lily-Rose sits down on the beach. Small pebbles dig into her bony frame. The sun has died in the sky, and is bleeding into the sea. The red glow of the twilight sits like an oil slick on the little waves, and the sound they make as they stroke the beach echoes in her head.

Every night since Lily-Rose and her mother arrived in Brighton she has been coming to the beach to sit under the pier and gaze out to sea. Although not a great distance out of London, it is a world away from The Sparrow Estate. Sometimes there are people around her, and sometimes not. It doesn't matter. Lily-Rose never sees them. All she sees is the shimmer in the water, and all she hears is the sound of the waves as they drag the pebbles up and down the beach.

Lily-Rose and her mother have rented a flat overlooking the promenade, paid for with money transferred from the bitcoin wallet. The only person who knows where they are is Tuesday.

Lily-Rose can't stop thinking about her. She looks out across the sea and thinks about what Tuesday has done. What she is doing. Even in Brighton, she is all over the news.

Her exposure of the drug culture.

The rape culture.

The powerlessness and abuse of the runaways.

The one-stop body-shop brutalism of the London gang-scape.

Her murders.

Her never justifying or explaining.

And finally, her disappearance.

Where is she?

Who is she?

Lily-Rose is not asking these questions, as she sits, wrapped in an old army parka she bought in The Shambles, the collection of antique and second-hand shops near the seafront. She knows what Tuesday has done for her and for all the other people fucked over by the torture-boys who ruled her world for the last three years. She lived in a world where sexual, mental, and physical violence was just a way of marking time.

When she and her mother left London, she knew, deep down, that she could never go back. The bad people knew she had a connection to Tuesday. Knew she could be a lever.

The only questions Lily-Rose is asking, right at the back of her head where only her heart can see, are: Will she call? Will she reach out to me again?

Lily-Rose takes out her pay-as-you-go smartphone. It has no apps on it. All it has is the ability to make calls, send texts, and connect to the Interzone. A half-smart phone. She bought it off a girl outside a pub for twice as much as it is worth. It is not registered to her and so cannot be traced back to her. Each night she logs into the Pro-Anna Forum where she first met Tuesday, leaving a message for her.

Sending out her love.

Not expecting a reply.

Lily-Rose stares out to sea, a thin layer of fat on her ghost-body, hoping.

107

Detectives Loss and Stone are drinking lemonade outside of the Marquis of Granby. It is the first time they have seen each other in civilian clothes. Nearby, a man sits reading a newspaper while a busker serenades the pub customers.

Detective Loss sips a little of the fizzy drink through his straw and then places the glass on the table. He inspects his colleague. 'Really?' he says, looking at what Stone is wearing. 'That's how you want to present yourself to the world? Don't you want us to get any clients? You look like a hippy who accidentally wandered into a noir film.' The detective is wearing a dark paisley skirt with Mary Poppins boots, a black shirt and waistcoat, many silver bangles, and a leather beret, worn Rasta-style at the back of her head.

'That may be true,' says Stone, biting into and swallowing her lemon slice. 'But I look like a *cool* hippy who accidentally wandered into a noir film. You, on the other hand, look like you've been beaten up by your own suit. If that is a suit, and not some form of punishment.'

They continue to drink in companionable silence. It is a hot, sunny London day and the light is coming down into the narrow alley between the two buildings as though it has been sifted there. The violinist is back, playing a version of a tune that Loss recognizes, but cannot place.

'So, what did you find out?'

'Well, you wouldn't believe the crap that erupted after one of London's finest was found tanked to the eyeballs at the foot of Tuesday's hospital bed, while the girl herself spirited right off the face of the earth.'

Loss smiles. 'Actually, I probably would. Where do you think she is now?'

'God knows. Underground? Home, wherever that is. Seeing what happened to her daughter, I just don't know.'

They look down at the pavement, where only a few short weeks earlier, the chalk drawing of *Tuesday Falling* had been. Before London went into meltdown. Before everything was undone. Loss thinks of all the pain that Tuesday must have felt. First, because of whatever it was that had driven her to the streets, back when she had a home, parents, whatever. Second, because the daughter to whom she had only just given birth was murdered, and then because of the knowledge that her daughter's organs were going to be harvested. For parts, like some old appliance being recycled. Loss cannot even comprehend what she must have gone through. Is going through.

Finally, Loss asks, 'What about the organ-selling?'

Stone dips a finger in her lemonade, then draws an elaborate 'T' on the metal table, marshalling her thoughts. 'The police were definitely involved. Border control as well. It probably wasn't many, but they were hand-picked, and the trail goes high up. In fact, our precious leader seems to be in some very hot water indeed. So hot, in fact, that it's evaporated, leaving him completely fucked. Heads will be rolling for quite some time, and the dent in the sheriff badge is probably unfixable. The government has set up a special division; they're liaising with Interpol *and* some top secret unit in Latvia.'

'And Slater?' says Loss. Even saying his name seems to suck the warmth out of the day.

'Mr Scary Hyde Park?' says Stone, reaching over and taking Loss's lemon from his drink. 'Put out a bounty on Tuesday's head that you could raise an army with. The assassin who tried to snuff Tuesday was arrested at Charing Cross Hospital trying to break into her room, and is being assessed in a high-security, i.e. never-fucking-coming-out, detention centre. Half the schoolgirls on Sparrow Estate are in rape centres. It looks as though Mr Slater's business ventures will be quite low-key for a while.'

'Not in jail, though?' Loss is watching the violinist. Behind the busker is the man with his back to them, reading a newspaper. He still can't quite place the tune.

'No bloody chance. He's squeaky-clean, apparently earns all his money in stock market milli-deals, and has nasty friends in high places. Even higher than our boss. Ex-boss.'

There is a pause as the two detectives listen to the music. Loss definitely recognizes the tune.

'Lily-Rose?'

'A ghost. Like Tuesday.'

'I still can't believe it was going on . . . the baby shops.'

'A city this big? It's probably got *everything* going on. At least Suzanne was onto it. Tried to do something about it. You should be proud of her.'

'I hate myself for not being there. Not saving her.'

'With all respect, Detective, don't talk such utter bollocks. She was a grown woman, not some little princess. She lived a good life and died a brave death. Stop being so fucking selfish and get over yourself, yeah?' Stone finishes her drink, and places the empty glass firmly on the table.

Loss stares at his partner. 'You know, there are various techniques you can learn. To control your verbal tics.'

'What are you talking about?'

'What about your boyfriend? What does he think about your swearing?'

Stone grins widely at him, and Loss notices she has beautifully crooked teeth. He wonders idly why it is that he has not noticed this before.

'Wrong pronoun, Poirot.'

It takes a while for Loss to understand what his partner has just told him.

They share a smile.

'What about Five? What do you think her role is?'

'Fuck knows. She seems to have her own agenda. The hospital where we last saw her has been cleaned-out, again. Deserted. The company who employed her have no idea where she is. According to her passport, she left Britain on the Eurostar the same day she told us where Tuesday's hideaway was.'

'Well that's something.'

'Yes. Except the train she was on left two hours before she spoke to us.'

Loss thinks about this. 'So she's got a partner then.'

Stone grins. 'Don't we all? You know, I'm not even convinced she's Muslim. If it was her who drew the picture of Tuesday on the pavement,'

They both involuntarily glance down again at the area of ground where *Tuesday Falling* had been portrayed in chalk and rain. 'Well, she definitely wasn't wearing a hijab then, was she?'

Loss takes a sip of his drink.

Stone persists. 'And another thing, apropos to fuck all. You know that thing on the door, with the solar system?'

For a second or two, Loss doesn't know what she is referring to, then remembers. 'On Five's door at the abandoned hospital, yes. What about it?'

'Well you were right, there was something odd: Mars was

missing.' Stone looks at him expectantly. When he doesn't say anything she sighs loudly. 'Knows all there is to know about the mail, but sod all about classical mythology. Mars is the Roman god of war, right? Their equivalent to Ares, the Greek God of vengeance.'

'So what?'

'Both are associated with Tiw, the Norse god of War.'

'Fascinating. Does it have any relevance to anything at all?'

'Little bit. The word "Tuesday" literally means "Tiw's day", also "the day of Mars".'

Loss digests what she is telling him, and then growls, 'We're just being fucked with, aren't we?'

She grins cheerily at him and nods. 'Like little art pawns, yeah. I'm looking forward to meeting Five again. There is definitely a discussion to be had about the appropriate use of modern art.'

'Is there one?'

They drink in silence for a while.

'Will you miss the force?' she asks.

'Well, as the entire Metropolitan Police are in a state of civil war, I think it was best to leave before I was pushed.'

'Possibly off a cliff,' she agrees.

'What about you? What about your no-doubt magnificent career, all left in the gutter? You know, you didn't have to leave as well. You could have stuck it out.'

Stone reaches over, picks up the glass containing the last of his drink, looks at it, and then downs it.

'I don't think they would've allowed me to keep swearing. What do you think of the sign?'

They both turn and admire the shiny new brass plate beneath the one advertising the antique shop on the top floor.

LOSS AND STONE

DETECTIVE AGENCY

'Well, it's brief. I'll give you that,' says Detective Loss.

Detective Stone smiles straight into his eyes. 'Fuck off, partner. At least I put your name first.' They get up and walk into their office.

A few moments later the man reading the newspaper folds it away, throws some coins into the ragged busker's hat, stands up, and leaves. The busker finishes his rendition of 'London Calling', and packs away his violin.

108

What sort of ending do you want?

I'm sitting on the ground with my back against the head-stone of Suzanne Loss. She hasn't got a real grave. Like most of the people in London she was cremated. Only the mega-rich get to be buried in London these days. Who'd've thought being eaten by worms would become such a privilege. The graveyard is on a hill, and all of London is below me, like some glittering beetle.

I'm so tired I can barely keep my heart open, but I lean back and remember the doctor who looked after me. Who never judged me and tried to save my baby.

Slater has got my tablet, so at least that worked out.

That's his name.

Slater.

Constantine. He thought I was the honeytrap. He thought I'd set myself up to bring him and his goons in. To trap them underground and expose them and fuck them up.

Always so cock-sure and stupid.

I wasn't the honeytrap; the tablet was.

I look at the ghost-tablet on my lap. It's a mirror of my other one; the one in Slater's fortress of a flat. It's got a clone section in the hard drive that acts as a virtual copy of the one he's got. At the moment it's downloading all the data off his computer.

That's how I know his name. Not just the name he uses, but his real name. And Caleb's. And Constantine's. All of them.

Really, these people are so fucking stupid. Do they really think I'd spend three years of my life planning something and then make a mistake like losing my tablet? Of course they do. That's how arrogant they are. How mind-numbingly easy to read.

So now I know his business. I've got his contacts in Eastern Europe. I know where he stores all his drugs. I know the name of everybody who has ever sat down and done deals with him. I know who in the government he has bribed. Who he owns. With all of this I can not only stop his clock, but smash it into a million pieces.

But what to do now? I'm so tired. I thought I knew. I had it all worked out on the street. Night after night of being empty, filling myself up with hate. Find him. Fuck him up. Kill him. Slap him alive then kill him again. But now I don't know.

I'm seventeen-years-old and I feel a thousand.

I could turn myself in. A pretty girl; pretty fucked up. I've only killed rapists and monsters masquerading as people. They'd probably just put me in a loony bin. Or *Celebrity Big Brother*.

Frankly, I'd rather kill myself.

I could go after Slater. I see from my tablet that the Hyde Park complex has a tunnel leading to a top London restaurant.

Oh dear. That's got my name written all over it.

Or I could send all the stuff I've got to Loss and Stone; let them do the vengeance. After all, his daughter was murdered too. I could go back underground. Just tick. Just exist. Hope just living will make me not feel so numb.

But I just don't know if I can be bothered.

I've been thinking about Lily-Rose. Those chats we had in the Interzone. There was so much pain, but underneath there was so much hope.

I don't know, maybe I could do something with her?

Then again, two broken girls don't make a mended one.

Too tired.

Too tired to choose.

I lean back against Suzanne's grave and look at the city. I swipe at the screen in front of me.

I'm all over the ether.

Terrorist. Victim. Fucked-up girl school murder-bomb. They can't decide.

Still, nothing about me from before. Now I'm out in the open it's bound to happen, sooner or later. The line between then and now. Between her and me.

I scout and scan, but there's nothing there. Nobody home.

Close down.

Sit still.

Tune out.

I'm so tired I can't choose.

I lean back and close my eyes.

You.

I'm going to leave it to you.

I'm not in control anymore.

You choose.

Printed in Australia by Griffin Press
an Accredited ISO AS/NZS 14001:2004
Environmental Management System printer.